THE NIGHT SHE MISSED THE TRAIN

A Psychological Thriller

C.G. TWILES

MURACAL
PUBLISHING

Prologue

*A*ll she could think about were the leaves under her feet and her shaking hand. The leaves were making low crunching noises that went off like bombs in the dead-silent forest.

It was so dark that a part of her insisted something had happened to her eyes—the stress and terror had overloaded a neural circuit in her brain and she'd gone blind.

But then everything lightened almost imperceptibly. Her eyes began to adjust as the enamel-white moon glanced out impassively from behind remnants of rain clouds. There was no controlling her hyperventilation. Her quick, panting breaths boomeranged through the innumerable, endless trees, the air slathered with their thick, sweet pine smell.

Her vision started to tease out shadow from shadow, black from black, until a form took shape against the deep abyss of night. A solid silhouette on the ground, jerking back and forth. For a moment, she imagined it was an animal of some kind, rooting in the dirt, foraging for berries, or digging up a decaying body with its knife-sharp claws.

It was an animal, all right—the most dangerous kind.

When the black shape moved again, her heart accelerated to a pace she thought impossible to maintain, and her hand shook so violently that she clamped her trembling wrist with her other hand.

She raised the gun and said, "Where's Jules?"

Chapter One

*T*he night Jules went missing in the Hudson Valley, the train was only seven minutes away.

"I have to use the loo," she said.

"Babe, the train will be here any second," Bryn said.

"Minutes," Jules corrected, pointing at the digital timetable. She hiked her red saddle leather bag onto her shoulder, giving off leaving energy. "Seven minutes to be precise."

"Just use the loo on the train."

Jules came home from her senior year abroad rather pretentiously using the British slang term for bathroom. Bryn, wanting to sound just like her, had adopted it, and they'd both been using it in the twelve years since.

"Ugh, no." Jules crinkled her nose. "They're always so nasty and reek. I can't stick my face into that."

"Your *face?*"

"Babe, I can't talk anymore. Just stay right here. I'll be right back. I swear I'll make the train." She popped off the wooden bench and briskly headed down the platform.

"The next one isn't for an hour!" Bryn called at her retreating back.

Jules waved one hand behind her, shimmied around a cluster of people, and vanished into the doors of the station.

Unbelievable.

What did she mean by she couldn't stick her *face* into the toilet? This hinted she wasn't feeling well, but she'd shown no sign of illness during the long day.

They'd leaf-peeped through a thousand-acre state park, taking obligatory photos of the spectacular fall foliage, resplendent with blazing crimsons and shining golds. They'd ambled in and out of Main Street's hip galleries and artisan boutiques. Neither had bought anything. Bryn, because she had no money to spare. Jules because—who knew why. Maybe because she had everything.

The day had been unseasonably warm. As the temperature climbed, Jules had tied her black cardigan around her trim waist, leaving her in a fitted tee and tan flared corduroys with exposed front pockets. Paired with the vintage Hermès silk scarf Bryn had given her, she looked refined and chic despite the outfit being very simple. It was her superpower.

Bryn couldn't remember a time when her cousin— and best friend—wasn't the most put together, most stylish, most *whatever* person in the room. And with her iridescent blue-green eyes and tousled buttery blonde hair, she was usually the most attractive person in the room, too.   Her eyelashes were invisible and, from certain angles, her overbite was apparent. But these little imperfections enhanced the whole, gave her a face that was unique and captivating, rather than just pretty.

Bryn's foot began to jiggle as the time table showed the train was four minutes away. She fixed on the station's double doors, willing her cousin to walk back through them. The people on the platform were breeding, the atmosphere's energy intensifying.

Bryn stood, eyes plastered on the doors, picturing Jules sailing through them, urgent but not panicked. It was nothing Bryn would attempt, squeaking through a sliver of time to catch a train, but it wouldn't faze Jules. She had that air of expecting things to work out for her. And they did.

One damn minute. One! Unconsciously contorting her fingers, Bryn watched as more last-minute types scrambled through the doors—and none of them were Jules. A small moan escaped her lips as the twenty-ton, red-and-blue steel tube appeared like a leviathan in the distance, gliding rapidly down the tracks, accompanied by its shrill *whaaaa* whistle.

Jules was nowhere to be seen.

* * *

Bryn pulled the handle to what appeared to be a restroom, but the door didn't budge.

"Baaabe?!" she called, rapping on the wood. She

tried not to sound aggravated should Jules be inside puking. "The train left. I didn't want to get on if you're sick."

Bryn was not happy about having to catch the next train, a local. It would stop at every blip of a town on the Hudson line all the way back to Grand Central. Add in the knotty weekend subway ride to Brooklyn (a car service would be beyond her budget), and she wouldn't get into bed until around eleven, and be lucky to fall asleep around midnight.

"Are you okay?" she called into the door, then pressed her ear as close as she could get to the wood without touching it.

No sound.

Bryn exhumed a mini bottle of sanitizer from her backpack, shook the clear gel into her palm, and rubbed it into where her skin had touched the door with the little generic person shape on it. She doubted this bathroom was any cleaner than the one on the train.

A weary-looking older man in Army-green overalls came along pushing a mop bucket of mud-colored water.

"Excuse me," Bryn said. "This is the bathroom, right?"

"Yep, but it closes at six."

Typical New York. If a public bathroom wasn't gruesome enough to send you screaming into the night, then it was shackled up like bullion was stored inside.

"But it's five to six," Bryn said, checking her phone.

He passed her a *What do you want from me?* look and continued on his way. No further explanation. No offer to open the door or to find someone who *could* open the door. If Jules had questioned him, the man would have provided a satisfactory answer. Also likely produced a key and unlocked the door.

You need to use the lavatory, pretty lady? No problem, I got the key right here. Anything else I can do for you?

Bryn knocked again. "Jules, you in there? Can you hear me?"

She dialed her cousin even though she knew Jules' phone was dead, her battery drained from uploading pictures of foliage to her social media. Because her cousin had lost access to the credit card stored inside, Bryn had paid for the meal they'd had at a winsome cafe before heading to the train station.

"Babe, where are you?" she said into Jules' voice-mail, struggling to curb her tone, in case her cousin was ill. "If you find a place to charge your phone, call me, okay? We've missed the train. I really have to catch the next one, but I want to know you're alright."

Bryn wandered through the rapidly darkening, nearly-empty station. A few stragglers were reading the digital timetable, but most people had grabbed the express. She descended the glass-walled stairwell and stared out into the parking lot. Because it was Sunday, the lot was only about a quarter full.

Perhaps Jules had ducked in between vehicles for privacy so she could throw up. It would be like her to not admit she was sick—that would denote weakness in her mind. Could she have caught E. coli from something on the charcuterie board they'd shared—the salami, the olives, the *cheese*? Was Bryn next?

"Juuuuules!" she hollered, directing her phone's flashlight into the shadowy gaps between vehicles. She was about to turn off her phone's light when a small, dark mound on the pavement caught her eye.

She slowly approached the heap, shining her light on top of it. She crouched to the pavement and picked it up.

Jules' scarf.

It was Hermès, black raw silk dotted with little white stars. A couple of years ago, Bryn had gifted the accessory on Jules' publish day, along with a card that read, "To my cousin, best friend, and future publishing star."

She hadn't really imagined Jules would be a future publishing star. Bryn had been a reporter for seven years and had known several journalists who'd netted book deals. All of the books had disappeared without a trace.

But the sales of Jules' debut novel, *The Suburban Aristocrats*, had increased little by little until it hit the top of *The New York Times* bestseller list. There wasn't much that Jules didn't pursue that she didn't obtain with shockingly small effort.

Bryn cast around the parking lot with renewed intensity. "Jules!" she called, near-panic lacing her tone. Clutching the scarf, she paced around a row of vehicles. Jules must have dropped the scarf on her way *out* of the parking lot, not into it, because Bryn was almost certain she'd seen it wrapped around Jules' neck as they sat waiting for the train. For sure, she'd had it on all day, so she wouldn't have dropped it when they came out of the station in the morning.

Bryn was reluctant to commit to heading back into

the center of town, knowing this would mean missing the next train. If she caught it, she still had a chance of a semi-decent night's rest. Unlike Jules, who thrived on five hours of sleep, if she didn't get a full eight, preferably nine, the next day was a drowsy slog.

What drove Bryn up the steep, curving hill to Main Street, huffing in exasperation, was one simple, inconvenient thought. Her cousin would have done the same. Jules could be oblivious, but she wasn't a bitch. She'd always looked out for Bryn, in her own way. If Jules thought her younger cousin was wandering around a dark, unfamiliar town seeking a phone charger and a place to be sick, she'd come find her.

But with Jules' scarf stuffed inside her backpack, Bryn was now fully agitated. Her hectic newsroom job was *go go go* all day long. Jules, on the other hand, had quit working for designer Thom King last year to concentrate on writing her sophomore book. She could do whatever she wanted tomorrow.

It occurred to Bryn that her cousin had probably headed back to the cafe, where she could use the bathroom and find a charger. When the male server had first approached the pair as they sat outside at a small table in the back garden, Bryn had taken note of the man's country-fed, twenty-something good looks. With her chaotic auburn curls, freckled nose, wispy eyebrows that disappeared into her skin unless she filled them in, and thick, big-breasted body, Bryn was catnip to select men. But they were very select, and mostly kept to where Bryn couldn't find them. Nevertheless, she nursed a hope that the man would notice her back.

But his attention had zoomed over Bryn and fastened onto Jules. He'd returned to their table half-a-dozen times in the 45 minutes they'd been there, asking them (asking *Jules*) if they needed anything else, not seeing or willfully ignoring Jules' wedding band.

In a fit of pique, Bryn had left him a five-percent tip, which she now deeply regretted, not having anticipated having to face him ever again. Inside the cafe, Bryn spotted him at the serving station at the end of the long bar.

"Hi again," she practically shouted over the high decibel of the cafe. The cafe was small with only a dozen tables, but the retro decor—all shiny steel and chrome—wreaked havoc with the acoustics. "I was here a little while ago with my friend. We were in the garden."

Recognition slowly trickled into the waiter's blandly handsome face. He must remember Jules. Then his eyes hardened. He must remember the low tip.

"I'm sorry to bother you," she plowed on as if she couldn't see that he was glowering at her. "But my friend didn't feel well and left the train station. I was wondering if—"

"I remember," he said, pushing past her with a tray of drinks. "She was just here."

Bryn chased after him as he ferried the tray to a table of four. The cafe was narrow and she shuffled around to keep from blocking the aisle. The waiter spoke to the group at the table but Bryn couldn't tell what he was saying. The surrounding noise bounced around like balls in an air lottery machine.

"She was here?" Bryn tried to clarify. "Her phone isn't working and I really need to find her. When exactly did she come in?"

"Ten or fifteen minutes ago," he said, blasting past her. Bryn scurried after him. She was *really* regretting the five-percent tip. It hadn't occurred to her that she might later on need the server for vital information. At the digital register, he began pounding the keys.

"So she left?" Bryn shouted at him.

"Yeah, she didn't stay long. Just a few minutes."

Bryn was so relieved that her cousin was okay that she exhaled audibly. "Did she seem sick at all?" Bryn queried as he ignored her. "Did she say where she was going?"

The waiter turned. "Look," he said, tersely. "She was trying to get away from someone."

"Who?" she asked, somewhat absurdly.

"I don't know. You?"

"*Me*?" she gasped, as if she'd been accused of something offensive.

He shrugged. "You *were* the one with her. She said someone was bothering her. I asked if I could help her at all but she said no, she only wanted to charge her phone and make a call." He gestured at a charging station near several pitchers of water. Didn't look very safe. "So that's what she did. Then she left. I doubt she got much juice."

Bryn stood confounded, unable to make sense of these nuggets of information. Then she glanced at her phone again. No text, no call.

"I can assure you it wasn't *me* bothering her," she

said defensively, sounding more certain than she felt about it. Had a man on the street started harassing Jules as she made her way back to the cafe? "Did you see her make the call?"

"I think so," he said, staring toward the windows, lit by a warm, hazy glow from the outdoor sconces. "I'm pretty sure she stood outside for a minute, but it was getting dark."

He looked a little sheepish, having unwittingly confessed that, even after Jules had left the premises, he'd watched her.

"You're positive this was the same girl I was with earlier?" Bryn asked, suddenly wondering whether they were even discussing the same person. His account of their supposed interaction wasn't lining up in a clean, orderly way. "She's a tall, pretty blonde and carrying a red bag."

"Yes, of course," he sighed. "I don't forget people's faces." He paused, staring her down. "Or their tips."

Chapter Two

Outside, Bryn squeezed her arms and did a little warm-up dance. The temperature felt as if it had dropped thirty degrees in a couple of hours. Dressed in thick leggings and a gray acrylic long-sleeved shirt, she'd earlier been steamy, but now she needed another layer to ward off the cold breeze from the river.

She peered up and down darkened Main Street. The silent, swallowing emptiness of Hudson Hollow was unsettling. It would be so easy for someone to grab you and shove you in a windowless van. Unlike in her perpetually buzzing Brooklyn neighborhood, where a hundred people would see it happen. Whether they'd bother to help you was another matter.

She gave her phone another glance. Sometimes messages took a while to come through. Then she texted.

Babe, where are you? The waiter
claimed you returned to the cafe and
said someone was bothering you? Get in
touch because I'm getting worried.

She sent the text before thinking to replace "worried" with some other, less panicky, word. Jules liked to call her *worry wart* when Bryn got anxious about something. She had picked up that term from their grandmother, who'd once called a friend of hers a *worry wart* for some reason neither one of them could remember.

If Jules had charged her phone, why hadn't she gotten in touch? Did she decide to stay longer and not alert Bryn to her change of plans? Uncharacteristic. Jules would at least send a text advising Bryn to go on back to the city without her. Also, why would she stay longer if she wasn't feeling well? Or had Bryn completely misunderstood her comment about putting her face into a toilet?

And who was bothering her? A random harasser? Or was the waiter's supposition correct and Jules *had* been wanting to get away from *Bryn*? Chilly apprehension crackled within her. No. If Jules was angry, she wouldn't have come upstate with Bryn and acted perfectly normal, perfectly *the usual*, for eight hours.

Hiking through the park, they'd giggled like schoolgirls as Bryn delineated the comically egregious dates she'd been on. They'd gasped recounting scenes from the unhinged crime docuseries they'd both seen. They'd oohed over the park's kaleidoscope of autumn colors and tried to keep from squealing as a mother doe and her three lithe, wobbly fawns appeared in their grassy path.

They'd waxed on about moving upstate, renovating a barndominium together, raising impalas—knowing they'd never do any of it. Growing up in Seaside, Connecticut had been enough country for the both of them. The important thing is that they were bonding again.

We still have it, Bryn had reassured herself. *We still have that zing.*

But now that she thought about it, because the park trails were narrow, Jules had usually been in front or behind her. Even in the shops, Bryn would be in one aisle, Jules in the other. Inside the historical museum, they hadn't interacted much as Jules had left to go buy a bottle of water.

Bryn had spent much of the day not seeing her cousin's face, her expression. And right before Jules had jumped up to leave the platform, hadn't she looked a little… *off?* It was hard to parse out the reality of Jules from Bryn's paranoia which, admittedly, had tapered off but was still powerfully strong.

Bryn went into her phone contacts, a little more eagerly than she would acknowledge. But last week, she deleted his number—as if that would solve anything. She clicked around until she found an area where old voicemails were stored, then pressed his number. It rang until she got his outgoing message.

"It's me. You're the one who called, so I shouldn't need to identify myself, should I? Leave a message." Pause. "If you must."

Bryn had an aggravated look on the entire time she listened. What kind of message was that for a man who (supposedly) had a finance business?

Oh, it's a French thing, Jules would evade if Bryn fished for specifics about how her husband made a living. *They think it's so uncouth to talk money.*

"It's Bryn," she said into the phone. "I only need to know if Jules has called you. I'm still upstate and can't reach her. I don't know whether to leave or not." She pushed her mouth against the screen. "Is there anything going on that I should know? I'm really done with this shit, so please call me, Delon."

That last part had a bossy edge, more order than request. Because if he thought it was a request, he wouldn't call.

Bryn stood outside of the police station. It was a white Classical Revival building with Corinthian columns. Nothing like the squat, prison-gray precincts with barred windows in the city. It looked more like a bank or post office, but this is where her map app had led her.

She'd go inside and tell them her cousin was missing. And that her cousin had told a waiter she was trying to get away from someone. And they'd probably instruct Bryn to come back if Jules didn't reappear in 24 hours.

She knew this not only from watching the occasional police television show but because, years ago, she'd attempted to report a person missing. A college room-mate who'd gone on a bender. The local authorities couldn't have been less interested, telling Bryn to call again if the roommate didn't show up in 24 hours. But the roommate had stumbled back into the dorm the next afternoon, worse for the wear but quite alive.

The rules might be less stringent in Hudson Hollow. Or perhaps the police were bored and wanted some-thing to occupy themselves. She wondered what cops even did in this sleepy town. Round up truants? Corral cats out of trees?

A beautiful bestselling author who'd gone missing might capture their attention—even if she'd only gone missing an hour or so ago. Bryn was halfway down the paved brick walkway that led to the station when her phone jangled.

"Yes!" she almost shouted into the receiver, retreating to the sidewalk.

"Hello, Bryn. What's the big problem?"

Delon Pascal Callais had been born in Paris, went to boarding school in Zurich, attended university in London, and had lived in New York City for a decade, so his slight accent was all over the place. His bored delivery indicated that he assumed Bryn was calling him simply to make contact.

"Did you listen to my message?" she asked.

"Mmm… some of it."

"Did Jules call you?"

"She did not."

He often eschewed contractions. *She. Did. Not.* As if

17

the lack of a contraction made whatever he was saying unassailable.

"Are you sure? Have you even looked at your messages?"

Another thing that made her certain Delon didn't have any kind of real job was that he would go days barely glancing at his phone. In fact, more than once she had seen him leave it behind at his brownstone and not be concerned at all. Who can do that but a farmer?

"She did not call me," he stated in his contraction-free, how-could-you-possibly-question-me way. "Is there a reason she would?"

He sounded smug and a bit toying, as if Bryn was overreacting simply to re-establish a connection. This was *absolutely not* what she was doing. She had to set him straight.

"We're still in Hudson Hollow. Jules missed the train, which made me miss the train. She left the station to find a bathroom. But I can't reach her because her phone died. And I haven't spoken to her since."

"Then how could she have called me?"

"Because she charged it."

"Then why can't you reach each other?"

"Listen to me." Her gaze roamed along the dark-ened, empty street. "I'm starting to wonder if someone followed us here." This amorphous theory had only begun to coalesce as it was coming out of her mouth. "Like maybe that weirdo who keeps showing up at her readings."

"Who?"

"He's an older guy who comes to her readings and stands in the back and stares at her."

"People stare at her."

"Listen." She lowered her voice and pushed her mouth closer to the phone, as if the man himself might be nearby listening. "I went back to the cafe where we'd eaten and the waiter said she came in and told him someone was bothering her. He thought it was me." She indignantly blew air out of her mouth. "Then she made a call. But she didn't call you. And she didn't call me."

"Jules makes calls. She's always on the phone."

"Delon!" she exploded. The correct French pronunciation of his name was Del-*ah*. But like everyone, except Jules, Bryn called him Del-*on*. He even called himself Del-*on*. "What if that guy came up here? And he's the one who was bothering her? And now she's nowhere."

"What the hell are you talking about?" He sighed, as if out of patience. "It sounds like you both are just missing each other. I'm sure she got on the train. Why don't you get on the next one? By the time you're back, she'll be here."

"I'm walking into the police station."

She turned and stared at it. There was a light in one window, with half a dozen squad cars parked in a small lot to the side. But there were no signs of life inside. Is it possible that even a police precinct would shut down early in this snug little village?

"Police station?" Delon laughed edgily. "Don't be crazy, Bryn."

"Men aren't allowed to call women crazy anymore. Your wife is missing."

Her eyes widened. A thin, shadowy figure was threading down the sidewalk. But as the figure approached, Bryn saw it was an older woman who looked nothing like Jules. Nothing at all. The street was so damn dark. Could this town not afford streetlights?

"Oh, come on," Delon implored. "Missing? This is how you get. Remember that time you called hospitals when I was a little late?"

"It was two hours. You could have texted." Why remind her of that at a time like this? Was he trying to start them squabbling?

"I am sure she's on her way home," he said. "As soon as we hang up, I'll call her. Do not go to the police. Don't start trouble, Bryn."

* * *

AT THE RIVERSIDE INN, Bryn set up her nearly-drained phone on the bed and plugged it into the nearest outlet. The inn had a charger that it loaned to guests who didn't have their own.

The historic inn was dark wood-paneled, high-ceilinged, and far, far more expensive than she could afford, but it was the only place she could find on such short notice that was within walking distance of where Jules had been last seen. She couldn't go back to Brooklyn tonight, not without knowing what was going on.

Could the waiter be right and someone had been bothering Jules? Could it be that bloated older guy in the gray suit who came to her readings? Bryn and Jules had started calling him "El Creepo." He never purchased *The Suburban Aristocrats* or lined up with the women who wanted her signature. He never tried to speak with her. He would listen to the reading and her question-and-answer session, linger near the back until the event was almost over, then depart.

Had Jules really made a call while standing outside the cafe? If so, who did she call since it wasn't Bryn or Delon? If she'd dialed 911 to report being stalked, she would have charged her phone more in the police precinct and sent a message to Bryn. Or called her husband. She hadn't done either, so where was she?

In the bathroom, Bryn washed her face using the inn-supplied mini-container of body wash left by the sink. She'd have to email her editor that she couldn't come to work tomorrow, and he wouldn't be happy about that. For weeks, she'd been assigned to the "police commissioner beat" despite her already overtaxed work-load. She and two other reporters were tasked with looking over the tips regarding NYPD Commissioner Tony Melani, who'd recently been indicted for accepting bribes from foreign officials.

Her newspaper got all kinds of tips about him. The vast majority were from people making outlandishly wild claims. It wasn't unusual for someone to insist the police commissioner was spying on them, or had broken into their home and stolen their pet, or was currently blocking their driveway with his car.

Bryn knew the police commissioner was bad news but it was unlikely he was doing any of that. (Except for possibly that last one. Bryn checked it out and indeed the police had placards that allowed them to block people's driveways.) Bryn had to call the tippers who sounded even remotely non-insane, then write up their rants, and give them to her editor with a judgment call about how credible each ranter was.

She couldn't tell her editor she was upstate searching for her cousin, who may be missing but probably wasn't, and that Bryn was likely panicking because she had a tendency to do that. No, she had to claim illness, so that's what she did. Her editor, Evan Riptoe, was a germaphobe who had a mini-bottle of sanitizer hooked to his belt, so that would hold him.

If Jules didn't make contact with either her or Delon by tomorrow morning, she'd feel justified in going to the police. And she'd do it over Delon's objections.

But he had to be right. Jules was *somewhere*. People don't go missing in twee Hudson Valley towns. There was a mix-up of some kind happening, one where, when the explanation is revealed, you go, Oh! Of course! Bryn had to admit there were endless examples of her overreacting—like the time one of her neighbors had dropped something on the floor. The *pop pop* had, in Bryn's imagination, sounded like gunshots. She'd called the police, and honestly, wanted to forget the rest of that embarrassing story.

Jules may have charged her phone only enough to make one call before it went dead again. Then she'd caught the local back to the city. She and Bryn had managed to miss each other on the dark streets. But how did Jules access her train ticket, which was also in her phone? There were no chargers on the train seats. Didn't she usually carry a bit of cash for emergencies? Or, being Jules, some random man checking her out had noted her ticketless distress and offered to pay for the beautiful blonde to get back home.

Bryn and her cousin would have a story for the rest of their lives: That time Jules caused a ruckus by disappearing for a few hours in Hudson Hollow. Bryn could hear her: *I can't believe you wanted to report me missing because my phone died. Jeez, Bryn, you really are a serious worry wart!*

Chapter Three

*S*he awoke with the sun a barely-detectable smear on the horizon, the light in her windows hardly even light. She turned over and snatched up her phone from the bedside desk. Her text icon had the number "5" in it. She'd missed five texts!

What had made her miss them was her phone being auto-scheduled for "Do Not Disturb" mode at 11 p.m. She hadn't remembered to turn it off. She'd also popped an antihistamine before bed. Her sinuses were raw and runny from being assaulted with state park pollen all day. The pill had sent her into a deep slumber. Bleary-eyed and cotton-mouthed, she thumbed open the icon and read the messages.

I can't reach her either.

It's midnight. She's still not here. Where are you?

Okay, this is getting serious. Why aren't
you picking up? Are you with her?

What's going on? Did you find her
or not?

Bryn! Get back to me!

All from Delon. The latest at 2:37 in the morning.
Her stomach churned sickeningly as she read the texts.
The hand holding the phone started to tremble. Bryn
had genuinely thought this misunderstanding would be
cleared up by morning. Jules would call and say she was
home safe in her brownstone and she'd marvel that Bryn
had been so worried about her.

*You crack me up, worry wart! It's sweet you were so worried
about me though. But seriously, babe, have you thought about
medication? Just to take the edge off, you know.*

She pressed Delon's number and was sent to his
voicemail. She gritted her teeth through his ridiculous
outgoing message.

"It's me," she said, hoarse from her overly-deep
sleep. "My phone was on silent mode so I missed you. I
still haven't heard from her. Are you with her now? I'm
at an inn on Main Street. I forget the name. There's
only one. If she's not with you, I'm going to the police.
I'm not kidding."

* * *

At seven a.m., Bryn stood outside squinting into the gem-laced morning. Everything was so indelibly clear, as if the world lay under a giant magnifying glass.

The leaves on the trees lining the street were golden-fired and poker-red. They littered the sidewalk, smelling plain and earthy, smelling *moral*, like there could be nothing terrible going on in this pretty little town. She swept her gaze along the street, which looked like a movie set.

The stores were still closed but she spotted several people herding zombie-like toward a storefront a couple of blocks away. Must be a coffee shop, the only thing that would be open at this unseemly hour. Rubbing her arms, she made it to the crosswalk when a man came up behind her and said, "Bryn."

Unexpectedly hearing the sound of her name sent a jolt through her. She whirled around and took in the man in front of her. Tall, wearing a long, dark woolen coat. Black hair with thick waves that called out to be grabbed. Dark eyes you could spend a lifetime examining and still have little idea what was going on behind them.

"Delon!" she got out of her mouth before he wrapped his steely fingers around her arm.

"Why didn't you answer me?" he practically growled.

"I did! I just called you. Like five minutes ago."

He jammed his other hand into his pocket and brought out his phone, staring at it. Then he said, "Oh," and dropped his iron grip. "Didn't hear it. Have to keep the sound up."

Well, yeah, moron, she wanted to say. But given that she'd left her phone on Do Not Disturb mode all night, she was in no position to rebuke him.

"Where is she?" he said, staring over Bryn's shoulder as if his wife was following.

"I was hoping she was with you."

"You *still* haven't found her?"

"No! It would be helpful if you listen to what I'm saying. How did you know where I was?"

"Are you kidding? This town is one street." He cast a glance up and down the quaint storefronts. "I can't believe this," he muttered. "Is this some kind of game she's playing?"

He suddenly looked at Bryn like she was in on the game.

"I don't know. And I need coffee or I can't think."

"Me too. I fell asleep in the car."

He jutted his chin toward a row of cars where his small, red Peugeot was parked. Bryn noted the indentation on the upper portion of his stubbled cheek, where he must have fallen asleep with his hand crushing into it. She had the strong impulse to reach out and rub the little dent until his skin regained its elasticity.

But she didn't.

THE PAIR SQUEEZED into the only free table in the back of the busy coffee shop. Most of the customers would grab their coffees and pastries, then hustle down to the train station for the commute into the city. Bryn had a go-to latte and a croissant that she was picking apart on top of its white bag.

"Start from the beginning," he said.

Bryn recounted how Jules said she needed to use the bathroom and hurried off the platform, promising to be back in time for the train. How her scarf had been lying in the parking lot. How the waiter had said Jules came in and charged her phone. How Jules had (supposedly) told the waiter that someone was bothering her. And that she might have made a phone call while standing on the sidewalk.

"Listen," Bryn said as quietly as she could. The small, packed shop was no place to have a sensitive conversation. There were full tables on either side of them, a foot away, tops. "I think we really might have to go to the police."

Delon tapped his lower lip with one finger and glanced from side to side, hushing Bryn.

He waved at her and they weaved their way outside. They walked down Main Street, past its still-closed row of boutiques. When they got about a block away, they saw a small park with a statue of a man on horseback in the middle of it. Some kind of American Revolution thing. They crossed the street and sat on a bench.

"I think she's probably off somewhere thinking," he said.

"*Thinking*?" she asked, incredulously.

Delon turned and stared at her. The clear, bright day glimmered in his dark brown eyes. She'd never seen this particular look on him before. He looked so concerned. None of his usual aloofness. Why would he look like that if he only thought Jules was off somewhere thinking? Which made no sense anyway. One can think perfectly fine on a train.

"Thinking about *what?*" Bryn snapped. "Did she say something to you? Did you—"

"Just hear me out," he interrupted, putting up a hand. "Was she acting normally the entire time?"

"Yes. Until the moment she took off." Bryn furrowed her brows and sipped her latte. Its heat was warming her insides but there was no doubt she would have to buy a sweater. "Wait!" She stared at the man on the horseback statue, unable to read the dark plaque's print, reaching for a memory. "We went to a museum, a historical museum. While we were there, she decided she wanted to get a bottle of water at the pharmacy we'd passed. I said I'd go with her but she was insistent I stay in the museum, since we'd both paid ten bucks to get in. I thought it was odd. We could have gone after we left. I had water she could drink. But she wanted her own bottle, and she walked out."

"Hmm," he nodded, deep in thought. "That makes sense."

"Why? What's going on? You didn't—"

"You said before that she may not have been feeling well?"

"She wasn't explicit about it. But she mentioned not wanting to stick her face in the train toilet. Why else does anyone put their face in a toilet unless they want to puke?"

He pushed one long leg out. She noticed he wouldn't look directly at her. "The morning she left to meet you…" He began to fidget and pinched a piece of a wayward leaf off his coat. "She told me that she hadn't gotten her period overnight. She was expecting it."

Bryn's gaze shot from Delon's face to the ground. She stared at a pile of leaves that gusted round and round in a mini cyclone of wind.

"Oh my god. She's pregnant."

"Well, I don't know for sure," he said.

"That's why she wanted to go to the pharmacy. Alone. She waited until we were in the museum and had already paid. She wanted to buy a pregnancy test."

"I think so."

"At the station she wanted to take the test in the bathroom. Or she was getting sick. Morning sickness. But in the afternoon."

"Possibly."

Now they looked at each other. She sighed, more like a moan, a sound that contained too many emotions in it.

"Now you understand why we may want to keep the police out of it," he said.

* * *

THEY WALKED up the quaint street toward the hotel. Bryn's mind was a scrambled mess.

Jules. Pregnant.

Exactly what she'd wanted since she was a teen. Jules always claimed she wanted to have four children: two girls and two boys. She'd hoped the first child would be a girl and told Bryn various names she'd picked out. The only name Bryn could remember was Autumn.

Bryn had made a couple of jokes: *What if the baby is born in winter? You're not going to give birth to all four seasons, are you?*

Passing a boutique that had opened, Bryn veered inside without telling Delon what she was doing. If he wandered off and returned to the city, she wouldn't mind. Then she could shop, have lunch, and pretend none of this was happening.

She found the overpriced hoodies on a hanger, picked out a white one that said, predictably, "Hudson Hollow," and brought it to the register. Delon, who hadn't done her the favor of wandering off so she could pretend none of this was happening, stood silently behind her as the cashier rang up her purchase. The cashier put the item in a paper bag with the store's logo on it. Bryn absently removed the hoodie and left with the bag still on the counter.

Outside, she clutched the hoodie, staring off across the movie set street. Why had she bought this thing? She hated it. And it had cost her eighty dollars. When she saw Jules again, she'd say, "Babe, that disappearing stunt you pulled cost me a shitload. At least pay me back for that ugly hoodie."

"We have to go to the police," Bryn said.

Delon waved her away from the store and they kept walking.

"Sure, Bryn," he replied in a low, simmering voice. "So we report her missing and the next thing you know, they're inside my phone records."

"N-no," she stammered. "They'll go look for her. Drive around."

"Drive around? They're not parents. They'll start a full investigation."

"They don't need to know anything," she whispered urgently.

Delon made a back and forth gesture several times from himself to her. "As soon as they figure this out, they'll stick us in jail. They won't look for her. They'll put us in cells and call it a day."

"There's nothing to figure out," she insisted. "I haven't seen you in a while."

"A week?" he scoffed.

Had it been only a week?

It felt much longer.

* * *

Inside her room, she sat on the bed while Delon stood at the window staring down to the postcard street.

"Where did you go after the museum?" he asked.

Bryn couldn't stop twisting her hands as she examined the silver and blue wallpaper's entwined lilies. Then she saw no more of the room. Everything faded into her memories of Jules and their last minutes together.

"To the station… no, wait, sorry, to the cafe. I just remembered, I suggested to her that we get a drink at a wine bar we'd passed. But she said, no, she wanted to eat. I was surprised she would turn down a drink. But it was because of the pregnancy."

"I don't know she's pregnant."

"And she was feeling sick. Oh, my god. It's true." She clutched the hard glob of turquoise on her drop chain. "Why didn't she tell me what she suspected? Maybe she needed to use the bathroom to take the test. Why not take it on the train?"

Jules had been correct. Bathrooms on the train were often grotesquely dirty. Perhaps she couldn't stomach the idea of learning that her first child was a reality while trying to stay balanced in a toilet-paper littered, stinky mess. Bryn looked imploringly up at the beautiful medallion on the ceiling, refusing to consider any other reason why Jules might not want to share pregnancy news with her.

Delon shook off his long woolen coat and flung it to the room's only chair. Despite Bryn's world being consumed with Jules, his movement pulled her gaze to him. Out of habit, her eyes traveled over his body. He was wearing jeans and a white, long-sleeved thermal. The shirt was a bit too tight and showed off his lean, muscled physique. Catching herself staring hungrily at him, she turned away, ashamed.

"Bryn, think," he said. "If she bought a test at the pharmacy, they'll probably have it on surveillance video. Then, you two go to a cafe and there might be a video of that, too. If she *is* pregnant, it will look like she told you about it."

"But she didn't!"

"That is not the point."

That. Is. Not. The. Point.

"No one will believe she didn't," he went on. "She tells you she's pregnant, then she vanishes."

Bryn's mouth dropped open. "And?"

"What do you mean 'and'? And you've been fucking her husband!"

Bryn balled her fists around her ears, like she was a child being scolded. She didn't want to hear that. There was a time when she would have relished hearing it, but that time no longer existed. Not with Jules missing.

"They're going to think you did something to her," Delon said. "If not you, then me. Or, more likely, both of us."

"But we didn't!"

"Who will believe that, Bryn? Who?"

He suddenly smacked his palm onto the thick two-hundred-year-old wall. *Thud.* The gesture startled her into their cold, hard reality.

He was right. Absolutely right.

She'd known that this terrible, twisted thing she was doing with Delon, this all-consuming thing that had burned up her brain cells, had tackled her common sense and moral compass, was bad. Very bad. But she'd convinced herself that since Jules had everything, and had *always* had everything, then Bryn could have one thing. Even if that one thing was Jules' husband.

Now that one thing meant they couldn't report Jules missing.

Chapter Four

*A*s Bryn and Delon walked down the sidewalk to the cafe, Bryn thought about all that had led her here. The whole sordid nonsense, and how long ago it had started.

Jules grew up in a twelve-room, white-columned brick Colonial with five fireplaces, a sunroom and an in-ground pool—the kind of place that realtors inevitably called "majestic." Behind the main house on three acres of prime Seaside, Connecticut property was a small guest house where Bryn lived with her mother. It only had one bedroom. Bryn's mother, Jess, had always slept on a daybed in the living room.

Jules' mother, Jacqueline, was the older sister. She got the model looks, the brains, and the ambition. She'd founded a successful real estate brokerage and married an equally ambitious young entertainment lawyer, Rich (yeah, that's his real name). Bryn's mother was the problem child. Never made it to college. Too busy boozing, drugging, and getting involved with losers.

Then, at seventeen…

"He took me to that drive-in," her mother had said.

Out of the blue. How old had Bryn been when her mother had told her? A teenager. That's all she remembered. Not even where they were or what they'd been saying to each other or how the topic had horribly made its appearance.

"Right before it shut down," her mother had said. "I don't remember the name of the movie but it was something about a dog who talked. We smoked pot. I was so high, I couldn't function. He pressed in on me. I didn't know how to open the door. He left town a couple of days later. I only remember his first name. John."

So he raped you, Mom.

This is not what Bryn had said or even thought at the time. It's what she'd think years later. It's what she'd never say to her mother for many, many reasons. It's what she held at the shadowy borders of her mind, far enough from the active center that she could tolerate it, as one can tolerate a solar eclipse, but only by glimpsing it through elaborate, protective filters.

Post-university (Jules: Top-tier school in Boston. Bryn: Cheapish local state school), Jules landed a coveted internship for a famous designer, Thom King, then was swiftly promoted to his full-time publicist. There was no doubt that Jules' astonishingly quick rise in the fashion world had as much to do with her patrician beauty and sociable, easygoing comportment as with her mystical way with clothes.

Jules could pull on department store jeans and a five-dollar white tank top, pair them with a vintage blazer and strappy stilettos, and look more stylish than any runway model. Bryn had accompanied her cousin to high-end events where Jules had worn nothing special. A black cocktail dress. Or a pencil skirt and a button-down white shirt with a turned-up collar. But women would line up and fawn at her, "I *love* what you're wearing, where did you get it? The entire look. I want the list."

Thom King was no dummy and knew whatever he put on Jules would look fantastic, a walking advertisement for his brand. How can one explain that kind of alchemy with textiles? Very few had it. Jacqueline Onassis. Coco Chanel. Babe Paley. Princess Diana.

Jules Allegra Aston-Callais.

That was another perk of a French husband, besides that he had an estate in Burgundy. Jules got to add an elegant French name to her string of already-cool names. Meanwhile, Bryn got her mother's last name. Bastid. Imagine having that name as a kid. And not having a father on top of it. If you'd written that in a novel, some editor would tell you it was too "on the nose." But she took a perverse pleasure in how occasionally someone would slip up and say "Bastard," then stammer out a red-faced apology.

A few months into her stay at Jules and Delon's stunningly gorgeous across-from-the-park brownstone, Bryn landed an entry-level reporter job. It paid just enough for a studio apartment over a Chinese takeout joint in a noisy, densely-littered neighborhood. Each night, workers sat on their e-bikes chattering loudly under her window as they took off on all-night deliveries. Then there was her mentally disturbed neighbor, who routinely erupted at his walls with a string of blazingly purple epithets. No silence, ever.

Without this almost comi-tragic, topsy-turvy imbalance in Jules' and Bryn's fortunes, would Bryn have been willing to do what she did? Would she have been able to justify everything to herself, to say, finally, it's *my* time? It's *my* turn?

As Delon took long, determined strides in front of her, she had an odd feeling of pride about how masculine and dashing he looked, with his stormy dark eyes, and his long, woolen coat flapping behind him.

She rushed forward, standing on tippy-toe to reach his ear. "He definitely remembers her," she said of the waiter. "He was flirting with her the whole time we were here."

Delon was not the jealous type. She'd learned that. But she wanted to see if she could inflame his jealousy, anyway. A little payback to the server for being so snappy with her, and suggesting that the person bothering Jules had been *Bryn*. Inside, a hostess rushed up to them, her cheeks glowing. Delon had the same effect on women that Jules had on men.

"Table?" she smiled, reaching for the holder pocket and slipping out only one menu. She hadn't even noticed Bryn.

"Thank you, no," Delon said. "I need to speak to the waiter."

"Oh," the hostess said, dialing down her puppy energy. "Hold on a moment, please, sir."

She went off and, a minute or so later, returned with

the waiter. The guy didn't have the arrogant look on him that he'd had when Bryn had shown up alone.

"Can I help you?" he asked Delon.

"I'm looking for my wife. Apparently, you're the last person to have seen her."

Bryn got a little thrill to see the waiter's eyes widen in surprise and intimidation.

"What?" the guy said, laughing uneasily.

"My friend?" Bryn said. "The blonde, remember? We still can't find her."

"Listen—" the waiter said, flustered. He held up his hands in an I-don't-want-any-trouble gesture. "I told you everything I knew."

"But you were kind of a dick about it."

Delon shot her a *be quiet* look. Then he refocused on the waiter. "Tell it to me then."

"She—she came in. It was really busy. She asked me if there was a charger she could use, so I plugged her phone into it." He wagged his thumb over his shoulder. "That was it."

"What about her saying someone was bothering her?" Bryn prodded.

"Oh. Yeah, uh, we were sort of standing there by the station and she said something about that she was trying to avoid someone or get away from someone, something like that."

He didn't sound as convinced as he had when he'd originally told Bryn this.

"Did she say who?" Delon asked.

"No. I asked if she needed any kind of help and she

said she only needed to make a call. As soon as her phone charged enough to turn on, she left."

The waiter glanced nervously from Delon to Bryn. Then, seeming to realize that the young hostess was watching the interaction, puffed up his chest slightly.

"Hey," he challenged. "Why don't you guys go to the cops? They're right up the street."

"We're trying to determine if we need to do that," Delon said, staring down the waiter as if he was the culprit.

"I told you everything I know. She plugged in her phone for a few minutes, said thank you, and was out the door. It was sort of like she was in a rush."

"And you saw her make a call?" Delon probed.

The server shrugged. "I don't know. She stood outside for a bit but it's not like I was watching her."

Yes, you were, Bryn nearly blurted but decided against it.

"That's it?" Delon said. "Anything else? Even if you think it's small, it could be something."

"No, man. Nothing."

Delon examined the ceiling, scrubbing the corners with his dark eyes. "You have cameras in here?" he asked.

"No, man."

"You sure?"

"I work here. I'm sure."

Delon flicked something out of his coat pocket and handed it to the waiter. Bryn saw it was one of those cards he carried around with him. They had his name and number on them, and under that they read, "Consultant and Advisor." Nice and vague.

"If you think of anything else," Delon said, "please call me."

Outside, he strode ahead of Bryn in the direction of the inn. She could hardly keep up with him.

"No cameras in there," he said. "That's good for you."

"How is it good for me? We could have confirmed what he said."

"Now you can claim she never told you about any pregnancy."

"She didn't!"

"Bryn," he said, irritably. "I'm not going over this again."

"I don't think that waiter is telling us everything," she tossed out, not certain why she'd said that. Probably to get Delon off the insinuation that if Jules had mentioned a pregnancy, the news would have sent Bryn into a jealous, murderous tailspin.

"Why would he lie?" Delon asked.

"I don't know! He definitely doesn't like me."

He turned long enough to scowl at her. "Why? Didn't you tip him?"

Christ, Delon knew her too well.

"Of course I tipped him," she protested. "I'm not an animal. But it was only five percent."

"Five?" Delon threw her a look of disdain, then picked up his pace again. "That's the kind of thing you do, Bryn. Why tip him at all? Why bother with five percent? I bet you acted like everything was fine and when the bill came you got your little revenge for whatever nonsense complaint you had that you never bothered to tell him about."

He was flirting with Jules and not me, she thought but would never voice aloud, not even under torture.

"Will you slow down?" she asked plaintively before stumbling over a tree root bulging under the uneven sidewalk. "What do we do now? Where are we going?"

"I'm getting a room at that inn. I'm staying here until I find her."

She came close to suggesting he might as well stay in her room to save money. It's not as if they hadn't slept together dozens of times—could it even be hundreds? Yes, it could be—and had viewed each other in every form of nakedness imaginable.

This is a sickness, she thought. *I have a kind of sickness. No one can tell me otherwise.*

Perhaps this is what evil was. Evil didn't know it was evil. Evil thought it was good. Or at least average. Evil justified itself as Bryn had justified all these lunatic months with Delon. How she'd told herself that if Jules truly cared about her husband, she would know what was going on. She'd *smell* it on him.

How was Bryn not heading straight to the police station? Yes, the police would find out she and Delon had been having an affair. They'd find out that things had ended only a week ago.

Bryn and Delon, or maybe only Bryn, would become the prime suspects in Jules' disappearance. Police would surmise the pair had bumped her off so they could continue their affair unencumbered. Or that

Bryn was solely responsible. Realizing that Delon would dump his mistress instead of his newly-pregnant wife, she'd done her own dumping—of her cousin and romantic rival into the Hudson River.

Given her cousin's newfound authorial fame and former job as an iconic designer's publicist, everything would be blasted all over the news in an unending loop. Bryn would make the cover of her own newspaper. What did the news love more than a missing blonde woman? A missing blonde *pregnant* woman! Add in that she was practically famous? The moon could explode and as lunar shards rained down, headlines everywhere would scream, "Pregnant Bestselling Author Missing as Police Question Husband and Cousin."

Bryn's aunt and uncle would despise her. The couple helped support Bryn's mother who still couldn't get her life together and, Bryn supposed, likely never would. Even now, Jess lived in the Aston guest house. She couldn't hold a job for more than a year and had something ill-defined wrong with her. Was it depression? Alcoholism? Sheer laziness? All of those things or none of them? Why did a sad cloud hang over her mother, one so potent it was practically visible?

What would Jacqueline and Rich do if they knew Bryn had not only been having an affair with their son-in-law but also had the perfect motive and opportunity to...

You know.

Would they demand that Bryn's mother leave the property? Would they say, "Jess, you've been a burden on us for years. And your daughter is an evil murderer.

Since you're the one who raised her, and therefore the one who made her evil, you need to leave."

Where would her mother go? To one of her terrible boyfriends? Bryn made an effort to know as little as possible about any of them, but the last one she was aware of had spent time in prison for selling drugs. But none of that mattered. They needed to find Jules. Going to the police offered them the best chance of that. Cops could put out an APB or whatever it's called.

But Bryn didn't voice this to Delon as she trailed him into the fusty, grand lobby of the Riverside Inn.

Chapter Five

*I*n her room, Bryn organized the items she'd purchased at a nearby general store. A toothbrush and toothpaste. Floss. A razor. Travel-size deodorant. Three pairs of socks. She hadn't bothered buying underwear, as she wasn't a big believer in it.

It was now clear she'd be here longer than a day. She'd have to tell her editor that she was still feeling ill. She hardly ever took days off, so he shouldn't have a problem with it. But considering the team was in the middle of the police commissioner scandal, he might feel inconvenienced.

Bryn dialed Amika, another reporter on the tip team, and also her best friend at the paper.

"Thought you were too sick to get out of bed," Amika scoffed, not bothering with hello.

"How's he taking it?" Bryn asked quietly, as if their editor, Evan Riptoe, was in the next room.

"He hasn't said anything. Just be glad he hasn't looked at your social media."

Bryn cringed, remembering that her profile was filled with photos from yesterday's excursion through the brazenly colorful fall foliage.

"Ugh, thanks for the reminder. I'll delete everything."

"Still upstate?"

"Yes, but it's not what you're thinking."

"That's too bad because what I'm thinking is you met a hot country guy and decided to make a long weekend of it."

"I wish. Is anyone around you?"

Amika paused, then said, "Let me go to the kitchen."

The open plan reporters' area was a nightmare in terms of offering no privacy. Anyone who wanted even a modicum of it went to the kitchen area and stood against the wall-to-wall windows.

"Okay, I'm alone. Pretty much," she said. "Spill."

"Remember my cousin?"

"Jules? Yeah, of course."

"We came up here to see the foliage and she kind of... went missing."

"Huh? What do you mean?"

"It's a long story but I can't find her. She never got on the train or went home. Her husband is here too and we're looking for her."

"Oh my god, Bryn, did you—"

"No, we haven't called the police. There's some other stuff going on. We don't want to get them involved right now."

"Okay." Amika sounded mystified but didn't pry further.

"We don't want this out there. I can't tell Evan the truth. He might gossip to someone. Or even try to assign it."

"I don't think he would."

"I can't risk it."

"I understand. Is there anything I can do?"

"Yes, you and Molly please keep up on those tips so Evan doesn't come gunning for me. I might need a couple more days up here at least."

The tips all came into one central account. Bryn, Amika, and the third team member, Molly, and their editor, were the only ones with access to it. Evan never went into the account as he had a million other things going on.

If you looked at it from the outside, the set up appeared to be rather sexist. Three young underpaid women had the thankless task of trawling through the tip hub and interviewing the crazies, while their much better-paid male editor cracked the whip on them.

That's because it *was* sexist.

"It's crazytown in there, as usual," Amika said. "One of those lulus kept me on the phone for two hours last night. Melani sneaks into her house and sleeps in her attic. The whole deal."

"Sounds fun."

Amika sighed. "Do you think she's okay? Your cousin, I mean, not the lulu lady from Long Island. She'll never be okay."

"Yes, yes. She's fine. It's just… mental health… you know."

"Oooohhh," Amika breathed. "I get it. I really do. I have my struggles, too."

Bryn almost laughed. Of course. Who didn't? Yet this didn't stop them from continually mocking those with the serious mental health struggles inside the tip account.

* * *

BRYN KNOCKED on Delon's room.

He'd ignored three text messages. Could he really be taking a nap? She supposed it was possible given he'd been up most of the night. Would be strange to bunk down for some afternoon shut-eye with his wife missing, but she wouldn't put it past him.

She had no idea what they were going to do next. They needed to eat—or at least *she* did—then go back outside… but to where?

Bryn had started to entertain the notion that Jules had taken a tumble, tripped over one of those tree roots bulging under the sidewalk as Bryn had done earlier, and hit her head on the sidewalk. She could be unconscious in a hospital. Or wandering around with retrograde amnesia.

Because of Bryn's conversation with the waiter, and his assertion that Jules had said she was trying to get away from someone, Bryn's mind had jumped to nefarious activity. Like maybe the older guy who'd show up at

Jules' readings had tracked her down here and taken her.

As for that guy, Bryn had basically forgotten about him. She didn't know his name and had no clue how to find him. Then the conversation with Delon had distracted her even further. That Jules might be pregnant. Was pregnant. Probably.

So her mind had never come around to the most obvious explanation for Jules' disappearance. That she'd injured herself and was in the hospital, unable to speak. Bryn would tell Delon they had to find out if this podunk town had a hospital. If not, they needed to locate the nearest one.

"Delon?" she called when he didn't answer her knocks.

Just what she needed, another missing person.

She heard something inside. His phone had jangled and she heard a muffled male voice. She knocked louder.

"Delon, what's going on? Let me in!"

When he finally opened the door and waved her inside, he looked unlike any Delon she had seen. He'd gone from concerned, perhaps a little frightened, to seeming as if he'd been crying. Delon crying. *Unfathomable*. He was normally infuriatingly reserved.

Except in bed.

"I had to make some calls," he murmured, wiping his nose with the back of his hand. "I know you think I don't do anything, but I do. I had to talk to a client."

He shuffled to his fluffy white bed and sank down, plopped his head in his hands, and stayed like that for almost a minute. Bryn stood watching him. Suggesting they get to a hospital seemed like it might break him.

"Where is she?" he moaned. "What's happened?"

Bryn walked over and gingerly sat next to him. She wanted to touch his arm but didn't dare lest it be taken in the wrong way. Any time she touched him, they ended up having sex.

"I don't know. But we'll find her."

"We did this."

"No. No, stop. What do you mean? We didn't do this."

She didn't know he was capable of this level of being distraught. She wasn't even sure how to take it. He clearly loved Jules more than he'd let on. Certainly, more than his behavior indicated. Why hadn't he ever told Bryn that he loved Jules, really loved her? Bryn would have found the strength to leave him alone if she'd known that. At least, that is what she preferred to tell herself at the moment.

"Delon," she practically whispered. "I thought you said... you said..."

He lifted his head from his hands and looked at her, anguish creased on his face.

"Well... didn't you say... that... you'd told me you weren't... ah... sleeping with her."

The distress in his eyes drained away, replaced by a flash of anger. "What has that got to do with anything?" he demanded.

"I'm only saying... I mean... if you were telling the truth..." She grasped a curl and nervously tightened it around her finger. "You weren't telling me the truth, were you?" she finished, quietly.

How had she thought he had been? What kind of absolute imbecile was she to have believed him? A man lying to his wife was a liar. And a liar lied. To *everyone*.

"Bryn," he said, jaw clenched. "Sometimes you did not want to know me."

She said nothing.

"You'd tell me it was over. Remember? So, of course, there were occasions…"

"Fine, but why tell me you weren't? I never asked you not to sleep with her."

"Because, I don't know… there were times that I wasn't and I thought you should know that I wasn't."

"I didn't need to know then or now. I don't know why I even asked."

"No, Bryn, you *do* need to know. You *do* need to hear it. Everything that's gone on. My god! There were days and days… weeks and weeks… I could think of nothing but you. Even with my wife. My body—it rebelled and rejected my own wife."

She looked away and released the curl from around her finger.

"Then you would tell me to go away. You'd say, never again. Never, ever again, that's what you'd say…"

She stuffed her hand over her mouth.

"So, I'd try, Bryn. She is my wife. I didn't understand what was happening between us. I've never had such a thing happen to me. For someone to irritate me the way you do… Yet, I'd want you more than I've wanted anyone or anything."

She pushed her hand onto her head, jutting one leg up and down against the carpeted floor.

"I'd go to your place and wait outside… One time, it was raining. I was soaked to the bone. I couldn't bring myself to leave. It was so absurd. Like a bad movie. I'd be frightened I was going to see you with another man."

She bit her lip and stared at the carpet. Beige, with a faded floral pattern of various reds and blues.

"Then you'd say you hated me. That I'm poisoning you. That my face makes you want to retch."

She shook her head though she clearly remembered saying all of that.

"You'd say that. You think I don't remember? I'd do all kinds of things to forget you. But I couldn't because of her. I'd see you everywhere. You'd come into my home. I couldn't get away from you. Then she'd ask me why… what was wrong with her… or me… why didn't I want her…"

"Please, just stop."

"So, yes, she and I would… here and there… sometimes. She's my wife. But I'd think of you. I'd try to rip you out of my mind. But I couldn't. It was terrible."

"It *is* terrible."

"I know it. It's terrible. *We're* terrible."

"I know. We are."

She felt that familiar, unstoppable pull between them, and then they were tearing at each other, biting each other, and the sex was fast, rough, and stupendously good.

Chapter Six

*S*he couldn't decide which was worse: the camera or the maid. She saw both as she came out of Delon's room. The camera was oblong shaped and fixed to the ceiling by the elevator. There was no way to avoid it.

Then there was the maid pushing a trolley of fluffy white towels and toiletries. No avoiding her either. Bryn tried to not make eye contact in hopes the maid wouldn't notice her. But the woman stared straight at her, nodded, and smiled, probably looking forward to the day she could pick Bryn out of a police lineup.

She couldn't tell police she'd gone to Delon's room so they could strategize their search. What they'd done would have been painfully obvious to the room's neighbors. It sounded nothing like strategizing, unless it was strategizing how to give each other mind-altering orgasms.

Sex was one hell of a powerful drug. Great sex? You

stood no chance against it. You were trying to outrun a cyclone. Not even the fear of prison had deterred her and Delon from having it. Her newspaper once published a story about a couple who'd killed someone and had sex right next to the dead body. At the time, it was the most repugnant thing Bryn had ever read.

But now she understood that couple.

God help her, she understood.

* * *

Bryn showered and pulled on her clothes. The only clothes she had, other than the new overpriced hoodie. And new socks. Using the scrunchie she'd bought, she pulled her shoulder-length curly brown hair into a half-ponytail, half-bun. It was a continual bother to tame or style. Easier to sweep it off her face. She'd always wished she had thinner, straighter hair, like Jules, whose long blonde tresses hung in sinuous, tousled waves. Jules had magic hair, the envy of every girl in high school, where she'd been voted "Most Beautiful of All Time."

And it wasn't just her hair. There wasn't anything that Jules had that Bryn didn't want for herself.

Right down to Jules' husband.

Though she hadn't wanted him. Not for many years. In fact, she wondered how Jules could want him. She'd thought he was arrogant, smug, vapid, not particularly intelligent, and that Jules could have done better. She did give him credit for being attractive, but even that was in a too urbane, too polished way that wasn't to her tastes.

She couldn't pinpoint when exactly their mutual coolness began to warm into mutual attraction. Maybe it was when Wyatt broke her heart.

Delon had been so unexpectedly compassionate about it. Jules had gotten very busy with book duties, so Bryn had talked more about the breakup to Delon than to Jules. He'd said, darkly, "*Il est un tas de merde.* Say it with me, *Il est un tas de merde.*"

She had repeated it over and over for him, eventually tossing it out with a convincing French accent.

But no, it had happened before that. Once, she'd found herself fantasizing about him sexually, and she was shocked. Revolted. As if she'd caught herself fantasizing about strangling a puppy.

Desire had crept up on her. Crept up slower than anything else in her life. Hour by hour and day by day and week by week and month by month.

Until eight years into his marriage to Jules, Bryn felt a current of electricity crackling between them. It was so bright and strong, she was convinced her cousin would see it, too.

She began lining up her justifications.

Something must be wrong in their marriage.

They never seemed that close, come to think about it.

Jules is more into her career than her marriage.

Delon has a dry sense of humor and Jules doesn't. She probably never laughs at a joke of his.

Delon seems bored when he goes to Jules' events.

They aren't very affectionate with each other.

One day in the park, she saw a man in a white t-shirt and black sweats running towards her on the pedestrian loop. A second before she recognized the man-shape, she thought, "I'd fuck that in a heartbeat."

When Delon spotted her on the loop, he turned and walked in the opposite direction with her, all the way to the other end of the park, where she lived. They kept up a steady, banal conversation, with that crackle zipping right underneath it.

Jules' career had taken off several months earlier with her debut novel, and they talked about how unexpected and bizarre its success was.

They talked about an article that Bryn was working on at the time. What it was, she couldn't remember. They talked about how scary-warm it was for January.

She brought up a guy she'd gone on a date with but Delon didn't respond to anything she said about him, so she dropped the topic. At some point, Bryn realized they were exchanging words not to communicate but to stay on the loop together.

Then they were walking into her worn-out building, neither commenting on what was happening, as if it was expected that he would hike up four flights of creaky, slightly-crooked stairs with her. As if it was expected that he would come to her place without Jules, which he'd never done before and had no reason to do now.

Outside of her door, they stood staring at each other for what seemed a long time but was probably only a few seconds.

Then she unlocked her door, took his hand, and led him inside.

* * *

The hospital is in a place called White
Bluffs, about fifteen minutes from here. I
couldn't get anywhere with the
switchboard so I'm headed over. I'll let
you know what I find. You may want to
go back to that cafe. It's the place we
lose her trail and there might be more
there worth knowing.

She read the text from him, then put her phone in her backpack. She'd told Delon her hospital theory as she was dressing after sex. As if, provided they kept talking about trying to find Jules, what had happened between them wouldn't count.

Before she left her room, she glanced in the mirror attached to the desk and noted a garish purple bruise, about the size of a half-dollar, on her neck. She took Jules' Hermès scarf out of her backpack and wrapped it around her throat, hiding the mark. What was this type of dark mark called again?

A hickey.

Outside, she walked down the sidewalk until she reached the cafe where Jules had last been seen. The lunch crowd had left and it wasn't busy. She didn't see the hunky waiter, but the young hostess was the same one as when she'd been here earlier with Delon. This time, the hostess recognized Bryn and dutifully smiled.

"Hi," Bryn said. "I'm still looking for my friend. This is the last place anyone saw her. I thought I'd come back to see if anyone remembered anything."

"I heard what was happening," the hostess said.

The young woman looked about twenty and had a freshly scrubbed face that gave off the impression it had never experienced an ounce of distress. In a few years, she'd marry her high school sweetheart, have four or five kids, and get a part-time job teaching kindergarten.

There was nothing wrong with that kind of life. It was one that Bryn could have lived if she hadn't been desperate to get out of stodgy, *nothing exciting ever happens here* Seaside, Connecticut. A bit of a boring life, but better than the one Bryn was currently living, scurrying around trying to figure out if her cousin was lost, hospitalized, kidnapped, or dead.

"You know what I was thinking?" the hostess said. "Have you tried the deli?"

"The deli?"

"Yeah." The girl indicated that Bryn should follow her and they walked down the short steps to the sidewalk. The hostess pointed in the direction of the train station and the river. "There's Joe's Deli on the corner of Main and Barn. It has a camera outside because it's been robbed a couple of times."

"Robbed? In this town?"

The girl shrugged and laughed. "Kids. It's still New York, I guess."

"Did you see my friend when she was here last night?"

"No. I wasn't working. I only work three times a week. The boss is cheap. But Derek told me about her."

"Who?"

"The guy you talked to earlier. He's in the kitchen."

"Oh."

"He told me he couldn't keep his eyes off her. He called her a 'ten' and he doesn't think anyone is a ten. He said he wanted to ask her out but she was too intimidating."

"She also happens to be married."

The hostess giggled self-consciously. "I'm not sure he knew that. Anyway, you might want to try the deli. Ask for Joe. Tell him Soren sent you."

"You're Soren?"

"Sure am." She smiled. Nice white teeth. Never missed a dental appointment.

"Thanks, I'll give it a shot."

At the deli, Joe, who looked as average as his name implied, was behind the cash register. Once Bryn confirmed his identity, she said, "I'm searching for a friend of mine. A girl named Soren said you might be willing to show me camera footage from around the time she was last seen."

She realized she was softening her language—not using loaded words like "missing" or "vanished"—so as to not alarm the man and spur him to call the police.

He looked at her like she was speaking another language. Then he rang up a teenager who plopped a bag of chips and a fluorescent green sports drink on the counter.

"You go to the cops?" he asked, a little gruffly, once the teen had left.

"Not yet. It hasn't been 24 hours. I'm not sure there's anything wrong. She could have gone off on her own to think. I don't want to make this into a big thing unless it seems like I should. But if I know which direction she went, it would be really helpful. Her phone died."

The man eyed her suspiciously. It was time to bring up Soren again.

"I only came because Soren suggested it. She said you'd help me."

Bryn reached for three trail mix bars from a display on the counter. Buying something might nudge him into doing his civic duty.

In a cramped back room filled with all manner of clutter—boxes and boxes of who knows what, half-filled paper cups of stale coffee, an ashtray mountainous with butts, some of them barely smoked, and several smaller boxes that were clearly rodent traps—Joe guided Bryn to two monitors.

On them were sepia tinted live images. One showed inside the store, and the other, the sidewalk and front street.

"When did you last see her?" he asked.

"She might have walked by here about 6:30 last night," Bryn said. "She's blonde, tall, and very pretty."

"Hmmm."

Joe seemed more interested. He began moving a mouse around in front of the two monitors. One of the images went blurry and began rewinding.

"Without knowing the exact time, you probably won't see much," he said.

"I understand. I only want to try. Thank you so much."

She put on her girly voice. It was an octave higher than her natural one and helped to get men to give her what she needed.

The guy stopped the video and pressed play. Then he took one of the longer butts out of the ashtray and lit it. He didn't ask her if she minded but he at least blew the smoke away from her direction. Bryn kept her eyes on the screen. No one walked by for thirty seconds or so. Then a small group of teens passed through the monitor. Maybe ten seconds later came a woman who clearly wasn't Jules. Then a couple.

How was it that so few people were outside? Bryn was habituated to the city's ceaseless crush of humanity.

Suddenly, a thin, blonde woman entered the frame and disappeared out of it. It happened so fast that Bryn actually gasped.

"Wait!" she cried. "I'm pretty sure that was her! Can you rewind?"

The man pulverized the still-smoking butt in the ashtray and leaned over the table with the monitors. He smelled disgusting. Bryn forced herself not to grimace. He clicked the mouse, rewinding the video.

She watched as the blonde figure fuzzily walked backwards into the frame. Joe pressed play and the blonde strode forward.

Joe pressed stop. The image was blurred slightly but it was undoubtedly Jules. It was already twilight but her bright blonde hair and fire engine-red designer tote made her unmistakable. Bryn had worn a beat-up backpack, prepared for hiking in the state park, but not Jules. She still had to look stylish.

"That's absolutely her," Bryn said, biting on her thumb knuckle. "Which direction is she walking?"

"Towards the river."

Bryn stared wide-eyed at Jules' frozen image. She didn't appear injured at all. Could she have amnesia? It wasn't as if amnesia could be seen on a video. Bryn squinted, trying to determine if her cousin looked confused at all, but she couldn't tell a thing about Jules' mental state. Could she have become injured after she walked out of frame?

"You have no idea where she is?" Joe asked.

"No. Can you, um, can you play it a bit more? I need to see if anyone is following her." Her voice was slightly hoarse and breathy, and felt thick, like phlegm she was having trouble pushing out of her lungs.

The image moved forward and Jules strolled out of camera range. Bryn kept her eyes on the screen, afraid that if she even blinked, she'd miss something important. But ten, then fifteen, then twenty seconds later... nothing. No one was behind her.

Bryn had fully expected to see someone. Possibly that older creep who kept appearing at her cousin's book readings. Maybe he'd be wearing the same ill-fitting gray suit. She was relieved she didn't see him but at least that would have helped solve the mystery about where Jules was and Bryn could confidently go to the police, and they would focus their attention on someone who wasn't her. Her eyes traveled up the screen to the street. The image showed cars driving past the camera, but she couldn't see as far as the opposite sidewalk.

"Can you rewind?" she asked, aware that she was taking up a lot of Joe's time. It didn't seem to matter what crazy thing was happening, her mind would tell her that she was being burdensome. Because that is what she'd always been—a burden.

"I want to see if anyone crosses the street," she said.

Joe languidly took a long drag off his cigarette, blowing the billow of smoke uncomfortably close to Bryn's head. She managed to not scowl at him and wave away the toxic cloud. Then he leaned over and hit the mouse.

Bryn watched as Jules walked by the camera again. She rabidly scrutinized her cousin's body language. Jules seemed to be walking faster than usual. Bryn remembered how the waiter had said that he thought Jules was in a rush when she left the cafe. Maybe she was hurrying to get back to the train station, hoping to catch the next train. Or perhaps she *was* trying to get away from someone, as the waiter had said. But who?

The monitor emptied of people. Bryn's eyes flicked up to the street again. Empty. Then one car went by.

Several seconds later a truck whizzed by. Still no people. Maybe thirty seconds later, another car drove past, speedily in and out of the frame.

"Can you—can you rewind?" she asked.

Joe leaned forward, the stale smell of smoke lingering on him, and played with the mouse. The car drove backward into the frame. Joe hit play and the car zoomed past the camera again.

Bryn stood paralyzed with shock, unblinking, lips open. Her heart was thudding spasmodically against her ribcage.

"Can… rewind?" she croaked.

"Rewind? Again?"

"Yeah, um, that, um…"

She touched her throat, brushing the smooth silk of Jules' scarf with her fingertips. She'd forgotten she had it on. She dug her nails behind the raw fabric, to the dark purple bruise on her neck.

There could be no going to the police now.

Even without the inn's hallway camera. Even without the maid seeing Bryn exit Delon's room. Even if no neighbors had heard them having sex. She couldn't go to them, not with a bruise on her neck, this undeniable evidence of a sexual relationship. Delon had sucked on her skin as if he'd tried to swallow her. Why did he do this? Even teenagers know not to give hickeys if they don't want to be found out.

"Can you—?" she said, gulping down the rest of the sentence.

"Ya know," the man drawled. "You probably wanna go to the cops."

He looked at her as if he'd offered her a choice piece of wisdom.

"Please," she said impatiently, gesturing at the monitor. "Just rewind."

Joe rewound the tape. Bryn watched the car drive back into view. The tape stopped. She stared at the slightly blurry image.

A red Peugeot.

Chapter Seven

*B*ryn moved down the sidewalk in a foggy mental haze. She'd asked Joe to rewind the tape several more times. When the image was stopped, its sharp edges would blur. She could not identify who was driving the red Peugeot. But she knew the car's model. She'd seen Delon's car enough to know what that model looked like.

He hadn't driven up to Hudson Hollow in the middle of the night once Jules didn't return home. He'd been here all along.

But no. There had to be more than one red Peugeot in the world.

In little Hudson Hollow?

The temperature had risen again. Tingly heat gushed all through her body. She gasped and unwound the scarf from her neck, feeling as hands were wrapped around her throat.

Yesterday morning, Jules had told Delon that she might be pregnant.

Then she left to meet Bryn at Grand Central.

Delon had sat around digesting this news, then got in his car and drove upstate.

If he'd called or texted Jules to find out where his wife was, he couldn't reach her because of her dead phone. So, he'd tooled around looking for her.

Why?

Why didn't he tell Bryn that he'd been here all along? Why had he sent her text messages acting like he wasn't already in town?

All those things he'd said to Bryn this afternoon. Things he'd never told her before. That he'd once stood outside her building in the rain. That he'd been scared he'd see her with another man.

She had broken up with him last week. For good. *Never again. Never, ever again.*

No point going into the details. Like Bryn's grandmother used to call over when she and Jules were playfighting on the vast lawn, smacking each other with plastic wands: "It's all fun and games until someone loses an eye."

That's what the affair had been. Fun and games until Bryn started to lose an eye.

Those times they'd get into fierce arguments over nothing important but were really arguing about their situation, unsure how to get out of it, and unable to stop it. Maybe if they had an argument big and nasty enough, they could stay away from each other.

Those times she would cry after he left her place, not because she missed him, but because she simply could not believe her behavior. Those times Bryn met with

Jules for brunch, or drinks, or a bike ride, and would be so close to confessing everything that she could feel the words forming on her tongue.

I'm fucking your husband. Can't you tell? Can't you see it on my face? In my eyes?

I can't stop, Jules. I've tried. I've become addicted to him.

This afternoon, she realized something... Delon felt the same way. She'd never thought she could do that to a man, addict him. And certainly not a man married to a woman like Jules.

Once, Delon had stood behind her in the full-length mirror in her studio, and drew his hand slowly down her naked body. She had heavy breasts and thick legs that a neighborhood boy had once called "stumpy," causing her not to not wear shorts for years. But Delon had said, "You're the sexiest woman I know."

Sexier than Jules? was her first thought but she didn't ask him that.

Then she'd tried to put what he said out of her mind. He said a lot of things after sex. They were cotton-candy words, thin and sugary, made of nothing. But for days, the words had lingered, giving her a buoyant, fuzzy feeling, a salve to her soul.

Bryn grimaced and again dug her fingers behind the scarf, resting them against the bruise. Had she inadvertently caused Jules' disappearance?

What would be the odds that another red Peugeot drove along the street mere minutes after her cousin had walked down the same one? As Bryn had been taught in journalism classes, the simplest explanation was ordinarily the correct one. But not always.

Certainly not always. She'd covered real life stories so tangled and outlandish that if they hadn't actually happened, you'd never believe them. It wasn't out of the realm of the impossible that a red Peugeot driven by a stranger had passed Jules right before she vanished.

Not out of the realm of the impossible.

Not exactly a ringing endorsement of her faith in Delon's innocence.

* * *

BRYN AND DELON took a table on the patio of the inn's restaurant. Because of the unseasonably mild weather, there were other people outside too but not many. Delon had pointed the hostess to a table on the outskirts.

"I don't think we should text anymore," he said when they sat down.

Bryn had asked by text message what was happening at the hospital but he'd only replied, "Talk later."

"Why not?"

"Bryn," he said, leaning in and keeping his voice in a low register, "everything we say can and will be used against us."

A waitress came over and handed them menus, asking if they wanted anything to drink. Both of them ordered a glass of wine.

Bryn felt alcohol was an imprudent idea but couldn't help herself.

"I gather she wasn't at the hospital," she said.

"No one matching her description came in last night or today. Did you find out anything?"

"Well, yes, actually."

He stared at her.

"She walked by a surveillance camera in front of a deli on Main Street."

"What?" He thrust forward across the table. "You're positive it was her?"

"Definitely. I know what she was wearing. And I recognized her tote bag."

"Why the hell didn't you tell me before?"

He quieted down as the waitress reappeared with their glasses of wine.

"Anything else?" the girl chirped.

Something about the waitress's upbeat servitude made Bryn ashamed to look at her. As soon as the girl was safely out of earshot, Bryn whisper-shouted, "You just told me we shouldn't text anymore so it's better I didn't!"

Despite keeping her voice as quiet as possible and still having it project her irritation, she felt as if everyone on the patio could pick up each word.

"Is she wandering around here?" Delon sounded baffled to his core and scanned the street as if Jules might appear in front of them.

Could he be this skilled an actor? Had he really not seen Jules walking down the street last night? It had been fairly dark at that point; he could have driven right past her without seeing her. Or had that not been his car, and it was a wild coincidence that someone with the same type of vehicle had passed Jules at the same time she vanished?

Suspicion had risen inside of Bryn like an icy wave but she kept shoving it back down. And it wasn't difficult to shove down as she took in Delon across the table from her, watched his edgy yet hopeful energy while his darting, dark eyes continually searched the sidewalk, as if Jules would pass by any moment.

Could he manage to look this convincingly distressed if he'd done something to her?

After her success at the deli, Bryn had walked to the pharmacy where she suspected Jules had gone after leaving Bryn to browse the small historical museum. Bryn wanted to see not only if Jules had come in but if she'd bought a pregnancy test.

She used the same approach on the teen behind the register as she'd used with Joe at the deli. But the girl, sullen and dead-eyed, had said she'd have to call the corporate office to ask if Bryn could view camera footage. Not wanting to draw that kind of attention, Bryn had thanked the girl and got out of there.

"I don't know that she's wandering around," Bryn said. "I only know that after she left the cafe, she headed in the direction of the station."

"This makes no sense," Delon said, bouncing a leg, his body vibrating. "Why is she doing this?"

"You don't know that she's doing anything. Something could have happened to her."

"You think someone grabbed her off the street? In this little town? Come on, Bryn. She's a fighter. She could have fended anyone off. I never told you this, she didn't want me to. But a year ago, a guy tried to push his way into the house. He was dressed like a deliveryman. She's so strong, she managed to keep him out."

"Jesus," Bryn gaped. "She never told me that either."

"She didn't want to worry people, especially you."

For the first time, Bryn realized that her chronic anxiety might be a burden not only on her, but on those who cared about her. That Jules felt she had to carefully consider and weigh what she shared with Bryn, so as not to disturb her fragile psyche. At this idea, shame spread within Bryn, coursing through her veins like an acidic chemical.

"What are the odds that someone could snatch her up?" Delon continued. "Stuff her in a van? Very unlikely."

Not if she knew the person, Bryn thought. *Not if she knew the person very well and it was someone she trusted. She'd simply get in the person's car. Go wherever the person took her. By the time she realized she was in danger, it would be too late.*

"That's a very man thing to say," Bryn countered. "Millions of women disappear every year precisely because it isn't easy for women to fend off men."

Before she could bury the thought, Bryn's mind went to her mother.

Got into the car of a man she trusted. Couldn't fend him off.

"What was she doing in the video?" Delon asked. "Just walking? No one was with her?"

"I didn't see anyone, no."

Bryn startled as the waitress asked if they were ready to order. She hadn't seen or heard the young woman approach. She'd been consumed with scrutinizing Delon's body language, trying to decide what side all that restless energy fell on: Anxiety or guilt.

Bryn knew she should eat. She hadn't consumed anything since this morning's croissant but she had no appetite. The idea of swallowing food made her queasy. Both she and Delon ordered and kept an eye on the waitress until she disappeared inside.

"I need to see the video," he said. "Take me to this deli."

"Delon, no. I've bothered the guy enough. I tried to make it seem like this wasn't a big deal so he wouldn't call the cops. You go storming in there demanding to see a video and he might."

"I'm supposed to take your word that you saw her?"

"Excuse me?"

"I'm supposed to believe whatever you say. You saw a video with Jules in it."

"Why would I make that up?"

"You tell me."

"I won't tell you because I have no idea what you're insinuating. Or maybe I do. What about me taking your word? You went to the hospital, huh? Where's my proof? This goes both ways, pal."

Bryn took another sip of wine. The alcohol was buffing her spiky nerves but she worried it would make her say too much or say it in the wrong way. And that was already happening. A self-preservation instinct insisted she couldn't confront Delon with her viewing of the red Peugeot. She had to tone it down.

They didn't speak again until the waitress returned

with the tray of food. The girl cheerily deposited Bryn's veggie burger and Delon's salmon steak.

"Can I get you anything else?" she inquired.

They sent her away, barely glancing at her, as if they didn't deserve to lay eyes on anyone so sweet and innocent.

"You know what?" Bryn said, using all her willpower to keep from shrieking at him. "We're in a mess, okay? A big pile of shit. But it's the kind of shit that gets you the electric chair."

"There's no electric chair in New York," he countered, peppering his fish with aggressive shakes.

"Looked that up, did you? Well, genius, did you know that the feds can charge you anyway and *they* can give you the chair or the needle or whatever the hell they use now?"

He said nothing and took a bite of his fish, chewing grimly.

"I've been seen going in and out of your room. There's a camera right by the elevator. A maid in the hallway stared straight at me."

"I didn't tell you to come into my room," he said.

"What are you talking about? Did I force my way in?" She wanted to punch him in his face. Punch that pompous, undeservedly handsome face. "Then you start going on and on… *standing in the rain*." She made a scoffing noise. "You said all that to get me into bed."

"Oh, please. It's such a challenge to get you into bed. One must resort to all kinds of machinations." His slightly hostile gaze focused on her neck. "Why are you wearing Jules' scarf? What do you think the police would say about that?"

"You left a hickey." She jabbed her finger in its direction. "It will take a week to fade. Or more. I don't know how long, because the last time anyone did this to me, I was twelve."

He started eating as if she wasn't there.

"You branded me so I can't go to the police."

Up until the moment this accusation sprung out of her mouth, she hadn't allowed her mind to bring this nebulous suspicion into sharp focus. But once it was voiced, it seemed undeniable.

"*Branded* you," he snorted. "You weren't going to them anyway."

"Because you told me not to!"

"You were with her when she disappeared and you're sleeping with her husband. She told you she was pregnant. You look worse than I do."

He wiped his lips with the cloth napkin and glared out over the street.

"She didn't tell me, asshole," Bryn said, clenching her hands on the table so she wouldn't hit him.

"Let's not talk about this," he sighed. "It's really spoiling my appetite."

"Sure, let's not talk about this. Hey, here's a thought. Why don't we pack up and go home? Maybe no one will realize she's missing. Maybe her parents won't notice she's not around. Or her million friends or readers. Or that fucking agent who gloms to her like a parasite."

Bryn covered her mouth as a sickening realization rushed up on her.

"Oh no. Jules has that big talk coming up Friday night at the Y. When she doesn't show up, Gilda is going to call the cops in a hot second."

Gilda was Jules' literary agent. Gilda Hortense. She was in her late fifties, very stern looking, and when she was with Jules, stood protectively by her client as if ready to drop-kick anyone who got too close. She was the co-founder, with her husband, Max, of the Hortense Literary Agency, one of the most prestigious in the country. The 92nd Street Y event was for the introduction of Jules' sophomore novel, *A Woman Stands Alone*.

Bryn had spent many weeks smirking internally at the title. What exactly would Jules know about standing alone? Whether it was her adoring parents, her cadre of loyal girlfriends, her weirdly possessive agent, or her husband of nine years—Jules was always standing with someone. Or, rather, someone was standing with Jules.

Even Bryn. *Especially* Bryn.

And yet—now Jules was out there somewhere. Alone.

"I'll tell her agent that Jules isn't feeling well and she can't make it," Delon said.

"Are you a certified idiot? This is a huge deal. It's sold out. Jules could be in a coma and she'd still go. Gilda knows that."

"I'll handle it." He cut off a chunk of salmon and shoved it into his mouth while glowering at nothing.

Bryn couldn't take a bite of her burger, the bun looked as if it would stick in her throat and choke her. So she picked at her droopy, overly-oiled salad. Her perception narrowed, the periphery of her vision darkening as the world closed in around her.

"You don't understand Gilda," she persisted. "She'll want to talk to Jules. Oh my god, we've got four days to find her."

"I said I'll handle it."

Bryn forced herself to take a bite of her burger. Predictably, she could hardly swallow. She gulped down the bread, feeling as if a chunk was left behind in her windpipe. With Delon thinking he could handle Gilda, they were even more doomed than they'd been a few minutes ago.

BACK IN HER ROOM, Bryn plopped on the bed, and called Amika. It was past nine o'clock and Bryn was absolutely exhausted, yet thrumming with adrenaline.

"Hey, girl," Amika answered. "How're you doing?"

"Not good. I don't suppose there's any way you can come up here? I really need someone to talk to and don't dare do it over the phone."

Amika paused. "Well, there's no way I can take the day off. Not if you're not coming back tomorrow. It's only me and Molly on those tips."

"What if you told Evan that someone wants to speak to you but will only do it in person?"

"That might work. How long does it take to get there?"

"I'm in Hudson Hollow. You can be here on the train from Grand Central in a little more than an hour."

"What's happening up there, Bryn?"

"I feel like I can't talk over the phone. Call me crazy, but…"

"Okay, I get it. Text me where to meet you and I'll hit up Evan in the morning. If he thinks a credible tip is involved, I imagine he'll go for it. I'll send one from a made-up account in case he checks. Then I'll tell him it didn't pan out."

After Bryn hung up, she peeled off her clothes and collapsed into bed. She was asleep before even pulling up the puffy white comforter.

Chapter Eight

She woke up early, showered, and slipped into the same clothes. Then she went down the hall and knocked on Delon's door, acutely aware of the camera that captured her walking in that direction.

He cracked the door a few inches, eyeing her suspiciously, as if she was a stranger trying to trick him into opening it.

"What are we supposed to do if we can't text?" she asked throatily, leaning into the door gap. "How are we supposed to communicate?"

"Just do what you're doing."

"Standing in the hallway talking about Jules?" She rolled her eyes. "Yeah, that's real bright."

"What do you want?"

"What's your plan for the day?"

"I'm going to the train station. There might be a camera there that picked her up."

"And you think someone will show you footage?"

"Why not? Someone showed *you* footage, didn't they?"

She paused, staring at him. *Unbelievable.*

He was the one who lied about when he came to Hudson Hollow. He was the one who drove by Jules on Main Street when she disappeared. If anyone was guilty, it was him. Yet he was acting as if Bryn was hiding something. Like murder.

"Listen," she said, leaning farther into the door gap. "If we turn on each other, we're toast."

"I'm not turning on you." He blinked a couple of times. He was turning on her. "Come to the station with me."

"I will but I have to meet my coworker."

"What?" he spat, jerking the door open wider but not enough for her to slip through.

"It's nothing about Jules. I have a job, Delon. She and I need to talk about work. Unlike you, I don't have income from some mysterious source."

"Why's she coming here? Don't you have a phone?"

"Don't worry about it. She's my best friend and isn't going to say anything to anyone."

"For fuck's sake, Bryn."

"I'll meet you at the station at noon. Okay?"

He glared daggers at her before shutting the door in her face.

* * *

She met Amika at a taco joint across from the train station. It was too early for tacos but there was no brunch spot this far down near the water. And she wanted to get away from Main Street, where Delon might see her.

Amika had taken the 8:35 a.m. train. At almost ten a.m., she approached the outdoor tables at the taco place, where Bryn was already seated.

Amika looked very concerned, not her usual breezy self. She had short, dark, spiky hair, and was tall and lean, like Jules, and wearing her work outfit of all-black loose clothing that made it slightly more bearable to sit staring into a screen for nine hours straight.

Although Bryn and Amika had worked at *City Daily* for years, they hardly socialized with anyone but each other. It was a depressing place. Most of the employees were miserable, and no one was inclined to make friends, too preoccupied with figuring out a way to move on to something better. Occasionally, Bryn hit on her job as a prime reason she'd become involved with Delon. The atmosphere at work was so oppressive and soul-sucking that she needed something dramatic and sero-tonin-boosting to help her survive it.

The pair looked over the menus and both ordered the only thing they could stomach to eat this early: scrambled egg burritos. Bryn ordered hers with cheese and Amika went for spicy with peppers.

"Thanks so much for coming," Bryn said. "What did Evan say?"

"He wasn't thrilled but since I said I could be back in the afternoon he was okay with it."

"He's such an ass. I told him I was still sick and he wrote back 'Righto.'"

Amika rolled her eyes, then turned to admire the view of the river. They constantly talked about what an ass Evan was. Somehow that hadn't stopped Amika from having sex with him last year after post-work drinks. Amika still chastised herself for the hook-up, feeling that it had emboldened Evan to not take her seriously. A few months ago, she'd been passed over for a promotion that was rightly hers.

"I barely remember anything about it," she'd told Bryn. "Fifteen completely unmemorable minutes cost me my career."

Bryn held off telling her friend anything about Jules until the food came, which was quickly. But she'd taken the time they sat waiting in the stunningly clear and mild morning to swear Amika to secrecy about everything she was about to learn.

"So, here's the deal," Bryn said, turning her gaze to her scrambled egg burrito, fat and oozing cheese. Ordinarily, it would have looked scrumptious but her appetite was still nonexistent.

"I came up here with Jules on Sunday. To see the foliage and have a little day trip. Right before the train arrived, she went off saying she had to use the bathroom. That was six o'clock the night before last and I haven't seen or heard from her since."

"That's so crazy," Amika said. "But I really think

you should call the police. Especially if she has mental health issues."

Bryn stared at her friend, confused. Then she remembered how she'd told Amika that Jules had likely disappeared because of her mental state. In reality, Bryn could think of no one who had more robust mental health than Jules.

"The problem is…" Bryn glanced around even though there were no other customers outside. Mexican food in the morning wasn't a popular choice. "If I did that, I'd become the prime suspect."

"Because you saw her last?"

"And I've been having an affair with her husband. For about a year."

Amika's mouth popped open and she stared wide-eyed, saying nothing. She sat like that for so long that Bryn thought she might never speak.

"Oh my god," Amika finally breathed. "*That's* the guy? The one you've been seeing on and off?"

Bryn had told Amika she was occasionally seeing "a dude" and brushed away all attempts to discuss him further, dismissing him as "nothing serious."

Bryn nodded and tried to force-swallow some egg burrito. Her throat muscles were tight as a bow.

"Oh noooo. Well, um, Bryn…" Hope rose in her tone. "They can't arrest you for that, you know? It's only circumstantial."

"You know as well as I do that plenty of people go to prison on nothing but circumstantial evidence. The first thing they want is a motive and I've got a doozy. And it gets worse."

Bryn stared off over the beautiful, tranquil view. The powerfully wide river was a dark navy blue with striations of lemon yellows and maroon reds rimming the bluffs extending through the undeveloped forest. If only she hadn't been having this lurid, demented conversation, what an exhilarating view this would have been, like looking back hundreds of years to when the original peoples of the land sustained themselves with clean water and plenty of fish and game.

"Since he and I have been here looking for her, we've had sex," she said, quietly.

When Amika remained silent, Bryn drew up the courage to turn to look at her friend. Amika was staring at her as if Bryn had said there was an alien growing inside her brain.

"Why the hell would you do that?" Amika gaped.

"It just happened. He was upset. I was upset. In some weird way, it's like we were comforting each other." Her voice was strident, trying to convince Amika of something she herself was not convinced of, nor understood.

Amika's Bryn-has-an-alien-in-her-brain look mutated into one of profound disappointment. "Bryn, I don't think that's going to hold up in a court of law."

Bryn shoved her hand over her mouth as bile rose in the back of her throat. "I know," she gulped. "And it was caught on camera. I'm so fucked."

"In more ways than one," Amika agreed.

When the waitress bounced over and perkily asked if they wanted anything else, they both numbly shook their heads. Finally, Amika reached over and squeezed Bryn's hand.

"I get it," she said. "That's kind of what happened with Evan. Like it wasn't me who did it. It was my hormones. And the booze, of course."

"That was *one* time, Amika. I've been screwing my cousin's husband for a year. A *year*. And did it again while we were up here looking for her while she's missing. Who does that? And it gets worse."

"How many times can you say that?" Amika asked, her mouth in a little oval.

"Jules might be pregnant. She told him that morning. It will look like she shared the news with me here. And since I knew he wouldn't leave her if she was pregnant, I got rid of her."

"Did you?"

"No! No. How can you ask that?"

Bryn yanked her hand from Amika's and shoved it up against her lips, smushing them into her nose. It was something she did when she was stressed and ordinarily she would have forced herself to stop, concerned about creating wrinkles. But this time she didn't care. Wrinkles were the least of her problems.

"Okay, then," Amika rapped out confidently. "You can't randomly kill someone. You'd need a weapon. You'd need a place with no witnesses. Where would you have put her body? How would you have gotten it anywhere? Where would you hide it? You can't drag a dead body—"

"Stop!" Bryn pushed her plate away. The smell of cheesy egg was nauseating.

"I'm only saying, they can't pin a murder on you if you didn't do it."

"We're investigating the police commissioner, alright?" Bryn hissed, surveying the sidewalk for passersby. "You think the cops will give a shit about guilt or innocence? If something did happen to her, they'll pin it on me. And the fucked-up thing is, maybe it's her husband who *did* something to her. I saw his car on surveillance video, right after Jules walked down the street."

"Are you serious?"

"Yes, but the cops will assume I was in on it with him. That I lured her here. I'm the one who convinced her to come up. There are texts of me talking her into it. I'd broken up with him last week and was hoping—I guess I was hoping to bond with her here, have a fresh start. I know it makes no sense." She shook her head and yanked down the scarf a little. "I slept with him. Yesterday. He gave me a hickey. This is the first thing the cops will see."

"Does Jules know about the two of you?"

"No. No way."

"How do you know?"

"I know, okay? She would have said something. She's not the type who would let that go unremarked upon."

"She might have run off to get back at you two."

"She wouldn't do that. She's got this huge Y talk in three days. Even an affair wouldn't make her miss that. Besides, have you seen her? Her picture?"

"Yeah, sure. You were both at her book event. With Thom King. We ran that photo."

The summer before last, Bryn had accompanied Jules to a sold-out reading at a chain bookstore in Union Square. Bryn had been shocked by how many people had shown up, mostly women.

Bryn hadn't been sleeping with Delon yet, but she had the stirrings of desire for him. She caught herself repeatedly looking around the room, hoping he'd show up despite him rarely coming to Jules' readings.

It was understood that he didn't appreciate being stared at and tittered about as the real life counterpart to the princely "Fabian" of Jules' novel. In the book, a privileged young exchange student from Connecticut named Claire is traveling across Europe when she meets Fabian, an absurdly handsome Frenchman with noble lineage. In Paris, the pair fall instantly in love and are married a year later.

Jules and Delon exactly. In fact, there wasn't much in the novel that wasn't obviously based on Jules' life. Though Bryn and her mother, Jess, were noticeably—and thankfully—absent from the melodramatic narrative. Bryn had not asked her cousin why there was no fictional equivalent of herself in the novel, as Jules would only admit to the barest of real life inspiration, and kept insisting the book's world was mostly purely made up. Bryn didn't mind that a cousin who lived out back in a leaky guest house with her alcoholic mother didn't make an appearance in the plot.

Gilda's husband, Max, had been at the Union Square reading, too. He was a shortish, stocky man in his fifties with a bald head. His bright blue eyes made him more attractive, as did his warm, sociable manner.

Bryn wondered how he'd ended up with Gilda, who remained taciturn the entire evening, glowering at anyone, including Bryn, who tried to share a minute of Jules' attention.

A photographer had captured Bryn, Jules, Thom King, and Gilda in a group photo. When the photographer called out "Smile!," Bryn was rewarded with a photo of herself in the news with a bit of cilantro glaringly stuck to a front tooth.

City Daily had printed the picture in the "Goings On" section with the caption, "One of our own, *CD* reporter Bryn Bastid, with her cousin, author and fashion publicist Jules Aston-Callais, designer Thom King, and literary agent Gilda Hortense, at a reading of *The Suburban Aristocrats*."

"Then you've seen her," Bryn said to Amika. "She'd never think that her husband… with me? It wouldn't occur to her. It wouldn't occur to *anyone*."

"Don't be ridiculous," Amika said. "You're hot, funny, and smart. Any married guy would be happy to cheat with you."

"Erm, thanks?"

"Bryn, you need to call a lawyer."

"I can't afford one."

"Put it on your credit card."

"Credit card? I'm almost at my limit. I won't even be able to stay here much longer."

Amika didn't bother to ask Bryn whether she could get her parents to shell out for a lawyer. Amika already knew about them, or knew enough not to ask about them. The nonexistent father and the childlike, penniless mother. Bryn had no parental safety net. She'd *never* had a parental safety net. What she wouldn't give for one now. A parent she could call and tell what was happening, one who'd say, "Of course you're innocent, sweetie. Don't worry, I'll remortgage the house and get you the best lawyer money can buy."

There were people out there who had that kind of thing. Jules had that kind of thing. How wonderful it must be to go through life knowing you had people who'd come to your rescue—to know you'd never end up hungry, homeless, or in prison for a murder you didn't commit.

She remembered one of the times she'd let Jules have it—yelled at her. Bryn had been upset about something she could no longer even recall when Jules had said, blithely, "Shit happens."

"Don't you *ever* say that to me again!" Bryn yelled, furiously. "When shit happens to *you*, your parents come save you. When it happens to *me*, I could die. Do you understand the fucking difference?!"

Bryn no longer recalled Jules' immediate reaction. But she remembered the text Jules sent to her a couple of hours later.

It said, "I'll save you."

* * *

AT THE STATION, Bryn and Amika stood on the platform. The disappointment and astonishment that had earlier been so blatant in Amika's eyes had muted into somber concern.

"Whatever you do, don't sleep with him again," she advised.

"No, that's the last thing that will happen."

"You're going to, aren't you?"

Bryn avoided her friend's reproachful look by staring off down the tracks. There was no point in repeating what she'd said, she didn't sound believable even to herself.

"He might have done it, you know," Amika went on. "Isn't it always the husband? Don't fuck a wife killer."

"Amika, please. I can't hear that. I'm still hoping she's okay."

"I'm only saying… on the very-distant, very-slim chance she's transitioned to another realm, statistically, he's your man."

Bryn didn't respond and clutched her forehead, squeezing the onset of a headache.

"The longer you don't go to the police, the worse it looks," Amika chided. "Don't go to Club Fed for dick. Even a big one. You wouldn't be in this much trouble for a small one, would you?"

Bryn couldn't help laughing, kind of a gasping, pained laugh. They edged toward the tracks as the train began its no-nonsense glide towards the station.

"Thanks for coming," Bryn said, hugging her friend. "I had to talk to someone or I'd go mad."

As the train whizzed to a stop, Amika turned. "Oh, I

forgot to mention. There was a tip in the account that was addressed to you."

"Me?"

Amika headed towards the train doors as Bryn followed at a rapid clip. The train waited for no one. "Yeah," Amika continued over her shoulder. "It said, 'What, Bryn, no thank you? Isn't that what you wanted?' Something like that."

"I don't understand."

"I don't either. When I get on the train, I'll forward it to you."

They quickly hugged again before Amika hurried through the doors. Then she turned, cupped her hand around her mouth, and with no concern who else might hear, called, "Don't fuck him!"

Chapter Nine

*B*ryn stood in the parking lot outside of the station. At five to noon, she spotted Delon's red Peugeot swerving into the lot. Seeing his car—visualizing the one that looked exactly like it on the deli surveillance footage—made her body stiffen.

She slowly walked over to him as he parked and got out, his long, dark coat flapping in a cool, cutting wind that had been charging around all day and was even stronger by the water.

"Show me the last place you were with her," he said in an authoritative tone, not bothering with a greeting. He looked as if he thought Jules might be hanging around the station, as if his wife was a child sullenly hiding a tree fort to evade chores.

Bryn ushered him inside and to the platform, pointing at the bench where she and Jules had sat waiting for the train. He stared hard at it, as if the weathered wood might tell him where Jules had gone. There happened to be a woman on the bench waiting for the next train. She flicked her eyes up at him, then stood, put her nose in her phone, and hurried away.

Bryn took him from the platform through the double doors and down the staircase to the lower level, past the digital timetable and the three ticket machines, then to the door with the little human shape on it.

"When I got here, it was locked," she said. She pushed the door and reluctantly peeked inside. The room was small with two stalls, a sink, and a mirror so coated with crud you could hardly see your face in it. It reeked and there was no soap in the dispenser.

"Disgusting," she pronounced.

Delon pushed in after her. He banged open each stall door.

"She's not going to be sitting there, Delon," Bryn said.

She watched as he went to the metal trash bin attached to the wall of the larger stall and began digging around inside of it, flinging wads of toilet paper to the tiled floor.

"I can't believe you're sticking your hand in that!"

"She might have come in here to take a pregnancy test," he said.

"I'm telling you, the door was locked. She wouldn't have been able to get in. Come on, let's go before someone comes."

Outside, she retrieved her mini bottle of hand sanitizer from her backpack and thrust it at him. Would a man plunge barehanded into bathroom garbage bins, pretending to search for clues, if he'd been the cause of his wife's disappearance? Especially someone as fastidious as Delon?

The times Bryn had informed him she had her period, he would elaborately lay a towel on her bed and rush off to wash himself after sex as if he'd stepped in a giant mud puddle. And here he was digging through trash that probably contained used feminine hygiene products?

In the corridor outside the bathroom, they scoured the ceilings looking for cameras but didn't see any.

"I thought maybe she went to the parking lot to find a private place to throw up," Bryn said as he handed her back the sanitizer and she shook some into her own palm. She indicated they should head down another stairwell. "That's where I found her scarf."

As they were pushing out the doors to the station, Delon pointed up. "Look there," he said.

One camera was positioned under the station's awning. It was directed at the parking lot.

Inside Delon's car, Bryn's focus darted from one thing to another—the dashboard, the glove compartment, the cell phone holder, the vinyl rim lining the window. Anything that might tell her if Jules had recently been in the car. She could barely admit to herself that she was looking for smears of blood.

"There's a substation at the next stop, Deacon," he

said, staring at his phone. "I'm guessing that's where they watch surveillance footage. We've got to ask if we can see it. She came right through this lot."

"We need a story," Bryn said. "We can't charge in there demanding to see camera footage for a missing woman. These are city employees. They'll have protocol and could insist on us going to the police first. Or even call themselves."

He looked at her. "It's good for you, though, right?" he asked. "It will catch her leaving the station without you."

The way he said it, it sounded as if he half-suspected the camera had caught the opposite and had seen Bryn leaving the station *with* Jules.

"Listen, asshole," she growled. "I'm sick of these insinuations. If you think I'd kill my cousin—who happens to be my best friend—for *you*, you are out of your mind."

He held up his hand. The cold, pale light coming through the front windshield glinted off his gold wedding band. "Please stop with the best friend routine, Bryn. It's a bit disingenuous."

"*I'm* disingenuous? Why don't you stop with the caring husband routine, you cheater! There's a reason I kicked you out a week ago. That's because I don't care about you. At all. The only reason I'm here with you now is because of Jules. So you can stop your little—"

"I'm not accusing you of anything. I'm sorry if it sounded that way. I'm only very worried about her."

"So worried you refuse to let us go to the police."

"Fine, we'll go. They'll realize that you and I are

having an affair and even slept together yesterday. They'll arrest us and the case is closed. Maybe, later on, they'll figure out it wasn't us. But days or weeks have gone by and they've put no effort into finding her. Clues have dried up. Surveillance videos have been erased and memories have faded."

Bryn tried to keep from squirming towards the door. She didn't like being in such close confines with him, which was an odd, unfamiliar feeling.

She normally relished being squeezed in the small car with him, breathing in the heady, masculine scent of his skin and the traces of his cologne. But now the residue of his cologne in the air was too spicy for her olfactory senses. Even looking at his handsome, chiseled features was making her a bit ill.

"I thought you didn't believe someone could have taken her," she said, mockingly. "Why don't you make up your mind?"

"I don't know what happened to her, Bryn. I only know if we're doing all we can to find her, that's more than the police will do after they decide you and I are the reason she's missing."

She still didn't bring up seeing what appeared to be his Peugeot on the surveillance camera, as she didn't dare do so here in the car, potentially putting herself in danger.

She sighed, twisting a nail stub and rocking from nerves and stress. "Delon, I can't afford to stay here much longer."

He said nothing, then turned and stared out the front windshield.

"I'm about to hit my credit limit. The inn is going to decline my card."

"Why do you have only one credit card?"

"What kind of question is that? Because I do. The nearest Airbnb's are miles away and they're just as expensive. If we're going to stay up here, I need a room and I have no money."

"I don't either," he said, so under his breath she thought she'd misheard him.

"What?"

He turned from the window. "I'm broke."

"Since when?"

"Since a long time. We both are. Jules and I."

Bryn laughed sharply, like a cackle. "She has a bestseller! And she must have got a big advance for her second book. You have an estate in France. What about that damn brownstone?"

"Bryn, there's having income and having expenses. If you have more expenses than income, then you're broke. Jules fights like a tiger to get royalties out of Gilda. Did you know the publisher sends them to the agent and not the author? Forget the second advance. It was negotiated before the last book took off. Between Gilda and the United States government, the remainder was nothing to impress anyone. The estate costs a fortune and I've been trying to unload it for years with no luck. The brownstone is mortgaged to the clouds."

"Can't you sell it? It must be worth $10 million."

"Five or six." He sighed. "Any time I've brought up the possibility with Jules, she wasn't willing."

"What about all your *clients*?" she scoffed, looking

forward to hearing him finally admit they were nonexistent.

"I have one. He's very private and he'll disappear in a heartbeat if I draw any negative publicity."

"Well, I'm sorry," she said, untruthfully. She didn't feel sorry for him—or Jules. If they'd spent themselves into a hole, that was their problem. They could have lived in a dingy studio apartment in a less affluent neighborhood like she did.

"Bryn, you're not getting it," he continued. "We're in big trouble. Financially. Have been for years. A few months ago…" He trailed off, raked his hand through his waves of hair, and then resumed, haltingly, "Jules thought it would be best if we did our wills because she was worried if anything happened to her, I'd never see a dime of royalties out of Gilda. So, we went to a lawyer." He turned to her. "Are you getting it?"

"No."

"My parents still live at that estate that sucks the life out of me. I had a trust but it's empty after years of supporting the estate. About five years ago, Jules and I took out life insurance policies on each other. Something like a million each."

He turned to look at her, and his eyes had darkened into black onyx.

"I'm having an affair with my wife's cousin. My wife tells me she's pregnant. I'm drowning in debt. I'm her sole beneficiary. Are you getting it *now*, Bryn?"

Chapter Ten

She could only stare at him, open mouthed.

Then her right hand began clawing at the door handle. He must have auto-locked it, because it wouldn't open. He reached over and clamped his hand over hers.

Got into the car of a man she trusted. Couldn't fend him off.

"Get away!" she screamed.

Then they were grappling in the tight confines of the car. Truly fighting. She pushed up against the door and kicked at him but it had little effect.

"What are you doing?" he shouted. "I didn't hurt her! I'm telling you all this because it looks terrible for me."

"Let me out!"

"Bryn, stop!" He pinned her hands to her sides. She pushed up against the door and bore down with her rabbit-kicking, getting him multiple times in the shin with her right foot. Her other leg, thigh smashed up against him, was handicapped.

"I didn't do anything to her!" he insisted, struggling to hold her still. "I'm trying to tell you why I don't want to go to the police!"

"Then let me out!"

"Fine!"

He abruptly let go of her. She got the door open and ran half way through the parking lot, then stopped and turned, breathing rapidly, adrenaline surging through every vein. She'd had a terrifying glimpse into what Jules might have felt the night she may have slid into her husband's car and disappeared.

And her mother.

Got into the car of a man she trusted. Couldn't fend him off. Couldn't fend him off.

Is that what had made Bryn detonate in fear and violent defense? A paroxysm of generational trauma? Had her reaction not been entirely because of what Delon had told her? What exactly *had* he told her?

Finances, life insurance, royalties. A brownstone and an estate in France, neither of which he can sell. That's all she could remember.

Delon exited the car and stood peering at her over its roof, then called, "Why would I tell you all that if I did something?"

She noticed he was artful enough to sling a question so generic that if anyone in the parking lot overheard it, it wouldn't matter.

"Because you're psycho!"

"Bryn, please!" he implored. "I'm only explaining how bad it looks for me."

It looks worse than you know.

She was about to shout at him that she'd seen his car on Main Street only a few minutes after Jules passed the deli's camera. But a stream of people were disgorged from the station doors behind her. A train had obviously arrived.

"I'm sorry," he said, walking towards her holding up his palms as if demonstrating that he was harmless. "I was only trying to explain why I didn't want to—" He glanced from side to side, then said under his breath, "go to them."

He stopped about three feet from her, palms still turned up. "I didn't do anything to her," he said quietly but firmly. "I couldn't and wouldn't. But it sure as hell looks like I did. I thought you, of all people, might understand that. Think—"

He swallowed his words as a few stragglers walked by in close proximity.

"Think for a minute," he resumed in a guarded tone. "It would make no sense for me to come all the way up here to hurt her when I could do it at home. Unless *you* were helping me. You lured her upstate and we did it together. It's not so easy to hide a body in the city, is it? Then we'll get her insurance payout and book money and live happily ever after. That's what everyone will think."

Bryn squeezed her eyes shut, shaking her head. She couldn't believe this was happening, that it had all fallen together in such a way that every single angle converged into a big arrow pointing at the two of them as murderers.

"We're so screwed," she murmured.

"Then let's keep trying to find her. Because once they've got us in an interrogation room, we can't. And you can be sure they won't. We'll go to the substation. You can walk there if you want. Or call a car service." He smiled wanly. "My treat."

But instead, trance-like, she followed him to the Peugeot and slumped into the passenger seat. He was no dummy. The parking lot camera had caught enough of them together that she was safe for the time being.

"You're not turned on right now, are you?" he asked.

"No, you sick freak."

"Neither am I." He started the car. "Just thought I'd ask."

* * *

THE SUBSTATION WAS A SMALL OFFICE, glaring with harsh, retina-stabbing fluorescent lights. A man sat behind the counter. He was dressed almost exactly like a police officer, but his short-sleeved black shirt had a yellow patch that showed he worked for the train company.

The fact that he looked so much like a cop sent Bryn's heart thumping. Nor did he look friendly. But he did appear bored—and that might work in her favor. There was no parking lot at the substation and Delon had driven up and down several streets but couldn't find a parking space.

Bryn managed to convince him that it would be

better if she went in alone, anyway. Chances are the security guard was male and therefore more likely to respond positively to Bryn than Delon. Additionally, one person asking for information, as opposed to two, would seem more casual and less like a police-requiring emergency.

Of course, Bryn knew she was not Jules. She'd watched her cousin work her magic on bartenders, bouncers, store staff, even police officers. Once, coming back from a club in Seaside while they were both in college, Jules got disoriented and drove in the wrong direction around a traffic circle.

She drove right into a police cruiser. Well, not into it. Jules and the cruiser had narrowly avoided a collision. But when the officer got out and began stalking towards the car, Bryn sat paralyzed with fear. She and Jules had both been drinking at the club. They were about to be arrested. *They would have an arrest record.*

But Jules had rolled down the window and waved her beauty wand. Smiling, laughing, flirting, flipping her blonde tresses. She told the officer they were lost. He didn't give her a field sobriety test. He didn't ask for her license. He told her to get behind the cruiser and he'd chaperoned Jules' car out of the traffic circle.

Bryn had always been thankful it was Jules driving that night, not her. Because if it had been Bryn behind the wheel, chances are excellent she would have been handcuffed. Still, there were occasional men who preferred her type over the Jules type. She really hoped the security guard behind the counter was one of them.

But as his jaded gaze met her face, she got the feeling he wasn't.

"Hi," she said, smiling.

When the security guard didn't return her greeting, she said, trying to strike a balance between friendly and concerned, "I was hoping you could help me."

He groaned a little as if the last thing he wanted was to be put to work.

"I came here the other night with my cousin. She left the Hudson Hollow station to look for a bathroom, and that's the last I've seen of her."

The man's eyes widened. Apparently, this conversation was going to be more interesting than he'd imagined.

"I went to the police but they told me since she's an adult, I can't report her missing for another 24 hours," she lied. "But I'm getting a bit worried. She hadn't been feeling well. I can't reach her because her phone died. I noticed there's a camera in the parking lot of the station, and she walked right past it. I know that because I found her scarf on the ground." She pointed to the scarf looped around her neck, hoping he wouldn't wonder why she was wearing a missing woman's scarf. "I was thinking the footage from the time she came through the parking lot would show which way she went."

Bryn tensed, expecting the man was about to start interrogating her. Or simply say no to her request. She'd dealt with many city employees in her day and "helpful" wasn't exactly a word that sprang to mind with them. So, she was shocked into speechlessness when the man said, "Sure, what time did she come through?"

"Ah, um," she stammered, momentarily too thrown off to answer him. "Uh, five-fifty or so. The express train had just left."

He gestured at her and she joined him behind the counter. On the desk underneath it was a computer monitor glowing with several images from different stations.

"Hudson Hollow, you said?" he asked.

"Yes."

He typed on the keyboard and the grid of images shifted around.

"Five-fifty? Last night?"

"Sunday. Probably a little before."

He pointed at a small image in the corner of the monitor, then hit the keyboard so it enlarged to full screen.

"What's she look like?" he asked.

"Long blonde hair, tall. Wearing a black scarf. Red purse."

The pair watched the monitor. As the express was due to arrive, several people were hurrying into the station. No one came out of it.

Finally, Jules emerged from the station doors. Bryn covered her mouth. "That's her," she gasped through her fingers.

The guard did something to the monitor that made the image slow.

"Five-forty-six," he said.

The light was fading but it wasn't yet fully dark. Jules, with her almost-white blonde hair, stood bright against the subdued bluish-gray twilight. She walked out of frame.

About fifteen seconds later, a man emerged from the station doors.

"Can—can you freeze that?" Bryn blurted, squinting at the monitor.

The guard stopped the image. It was much clearer than the fuzzy images that would appear on deli owner Joe's less-professional security system. The male figure freeze-framed in the parking lot looked familiar. Caucasian, paunchy, not much hair left. In his late fifties or early sixties. Cheeks and a nose bloated from genetics or years of drinking too much alcohol.

"Oh my god," she breathed.

The man didn't have his usual ill-fitting gray suit on, so it had taken several seconds for him to crystallize in Bryn's mind. This was the same man who'd come to Jules' readings. Instead of his usual sloppy gray suit, he was wearing a short, black sports coat, and dark slacks. But it was definitely him freeze-framed on the monitor.

He was the person Jules had told the waiter she was trying to get away from.

"We have to go to the cops," Bryn said the second she hit the passenger seat. "That stalker guy who comes to her readings followed her out of the station. I saw him on the tape."

"What stalker guy?"

"Delon! I've told you about him!"

"Jules never mentioned a stalker guy."

She didn't mention him or you didn't pay attention to her mentioning him? Bryn wanted to shout but didn't.

"He's an older guy who comes to her readings and watches her," she said, trying to keep her words at a minimum as they tumbled out of her. "He was the one I thought might have followed her up here. I should have gone to the police right away."

When Delon only continued to stare at her, she yelled, "Start the fucking car! We need to go!"

"Wait," he said, holding up one hand. "Is there any proof it's the same person who comes to her readings?"

"Delon! I recognize him!"

"I'm only asking you what the police are going to ask you. What's to say you didn't pick a random guy who followed her out of the station? Those readings don't have cameras, do they?"

"What is wrong with you? Who cares? That creepy ass guy followed her up here. She went to the cafe, told the waiter about him, then disappeared. He probably has her right now."

If he didn't start the car in the next five seconds, she would get out and run up the hill to the police station.

"I agree, Bryn," he said. "But we need to be smart about this. Because once police figure out about you and me, they're going to think we're trying to pin something on a stranger who happened to follow her out of the station. I'm not saying we can't go to them. We only need to think first."

"While you're thinking, that guy could be torturing

her! Start the car!" She furiously pointed at the steering wheel.

With a sigh, he turned and started the car, then backed out. She really was beginning to wonder if he had something to do with Jules' disappearance. Otherwise, why would he still be reluctant to go to the authorities? Why was he moving at a snail's pace?

As they drove out of the lot and onto the small two-lane street that led to the downtown strip, he said, "Is there anyone else who has seen this guy? Besides you and Jules?"

"I don't know. I—wait! Gilda! Gilda is at all her readings and must have seen him." She stared out the window at a passing Gothic church and a short row of mom-and-pop stores, wishing they could drive faster down this small-town street.

"He's not just some—fan?" Delon asked.

"She doesn't have many guy fans. At least straight guys. And he's ugly enough to be straight."

"Would Gilda be able to identify him from the video?"

"I think so. I don't know. I mean, I don't know her memory. Or how much she even paid attention to him."

A minute later, they pulled into a parking spot near the inn. He cut the engine and turned to her. "We've got to find someone else who can say this is the guy," he said. "Or mark my words, cops will think we're making it up."

"I don't care. I'm going to the police with or without you."

Her hand grasped the door handle as she suffered a brief moment of regret for saying this, still not feeling entirely safe with Delon despite the latest discovery. But he wouldn't try to kill her in the car parked on Main Street with people wandering past and a store camera or two pointed at them.

"I didn't say I wouldn't go," he said. "We should. I'm only saying we've got to prepare. Because they are very likely going to arrest us on the spot. And they'll separate us. Do you have a criminal attorney on your phone?"

"Of course I fucking don't."

She wouldn't be surprised if he did, though.

"All right," he sighed, glancing warily at the inn. "Let's go inside, get our stuff, charge our phones, and walk to the station. It's going to be a long night."

THE PAIR MET in the hallway on their floor. Bryn had everything in her backpack and, as Delon had suggested, had fully charged her phone.

She'd also taken a quick shower as she didn't have a clue when she'd be able to take another. She was too frazzled to plan what to tell her editor, knowing there was an excellent chance she wouldn't be at work tomorrow—or perhaps ever again. So, she didn't email him. If she got arrested, Evan would likely be editing the story, so he'd find out about everything soon enough.

All Bryn could think about was that an obsessed predator had kidnapped Jules, who was currently tied up in a windowless van, suffering god only knows what. Bryn continually chastised herself for allowing her desire for self-preservation to override her instinct to go to the police.

And Delon. She would never forgive him for convincing her not to go. They had lost almost 24 hours —plenty of time for that animal to ferry Jules across the country.

On the elevator, they said nothing to each other. Their entire lives were about to be upended. Even if the police believed that Jules had been taken by the puffy-faced stalker, they were still going to investigate the pair of them. A rookie cop could easily conclude they'd been having an affair. Hell, with this hickey on her neck, she might as well walk into the station with a sign that read, "I'm fucking the husband of a missing woman! Yeah, even now. Yesterday, in fact!"

Attention—both media and law enforcement—was swiftly and glaringly going to turn to them. They were going to have a hell of a time getting police to focus their resources on the puffy-faced stalker.

But it's what she and Delon had to do. Bryn saw no other way.

The elevator doors opened. They had both stepped out when a man walked confidently up to them. He was holding something in his hand, some kind of identification badge with a small shiny decal on it.

"Bryn Bastid and Delon Callais?" he asked. He pronounced it "Cal-ay-sss."

Neither one of them said anything. They were too stunned. Bryn recognized the man standing in front of them as the puffy-faced stranger who'd followed Jules out of the station.

"My name is Andy Kroll," he said. "I'm a private investigator."

Chapter Eleven

---

*I*n the inn's restaurant, the three sat in a back booth, tucked into the shadows. A waitress approached and the man ordered a scotch on the rocks. Delon held up a finger to indicate this is what he would have, too. Bryn had never seen Delon drink hard liquor. She was tempted to order one for herself but instead managed to say, "White wine. Any kind."

When the waitress retreated, the pair stared at Andy Kroll, who was sitting across from them. "I was hired by Gilda Hortense," he said. "You know her, I presume."

He had a no-nonsense, slightly-gruff delivery. Exactly what you'd expect a private investigator to sound like. The word "hard-boiled" raced through Bryn's mind, plucked out of a noir novel she must have read ages ago.

"Ahh, yes," Bryn said, uncertainly. "We know her."

"Feel free to call her and verify what I'm telling you. If you don't have her number, I can provide it."

"I have it," Bryn said. Gilda had once called Bryn

when she couldn't reach Jules, and Bryn had added her to her contacts list, just in case. Not wanting to involve Gilda in anything yet, she only said, "Why, uh, would she hire you?"

The waitress returned with their drinks and all three took sips before continuing their conversation. Bryn had never been so grateful for a nearby font of alcohol.

"Jules Aston-Callais has been receiving letters. They were being delivered to the Hortense Literary Agency. The suspect was smart and used regular old mail. Much harder to trace."

Andy Kroll slipped a hand into the lining of his jacket and pulled out a white business envelope. He opened it and gave the contents to Delon. Bryn tried to read over his shoulder but the restaurant was extremely dark.

"What the hell is this?" Delon asked.

"One of the letters Ms. Hortense had been receiving, addressed to her client. She retained me to not only try to find out who is sending them but to keep an eye on Mrs. Callais."

Delon took out his phone and shined its flashlight on the letter. "I can hardly read it," he said. "The type is too small."

"In short, it repeatedly calls your wife rather strongly worded insults, some rhyming with hitch and some with hunt, and urges her to leave town," Andy said. "Not very imaginative."

The detective stretched out his palm and Delon dazedly returned the letter to him. Andy tucked the letter back into his coat.

"It's not uncommon for a person in any kind of limelight to draw a nutter," he said. "Ninety-nine percent of them are full of hot air. But Ms. Hortense thought, better safe than sorry."

"Someone was threatening her?" Bryn asked.

"Jules never mentioned any letters to me," Delon said.

"No. I advised her to keep quiet." He looked pointedly from Delon to Bryn and back again. "Since we didn't know who was sending them."

"You think it's me?" Delon said, angrily.

"I didn't say that. I only advised Mrs. Callais to keep it under wraps. The less people who knew, the better."

"What do we do?" Bryn demanded. "We're sitting in a restaurant when someone who's been threatening Jules probably kidnapped her."

"I'm on it," Andy said.

"On it? How?"

"You'll have to trust me, Ms. Bastid," he said, sniffing his drink. "Detective work doesn't involve standing on the street and calling for a missing person like you'd call for a missing dog."

"Wasn't that you who followed Jules out of the station?" she asked.

A slow smile crept over his face. Something about his mischievous grin made him better looking.

"You go see Carl?"

"Who?"

"Carl. Security guy at the Deacon station."

Not wanting to out Carl, she didn't respond.

"That was me," Andy said.

He shifted around on the booth's bench, then took another sip of scotch. They were large sips, as if he was downing water. Bryn followed suit, and chugged some of her white wine. It was dry and bitter, causing the insides of her cheeks to clench.

"Mrs. Callais began resisting my presence," the detective went on. "When she left the station, I tailed her up the hill and she clocked me. 'I'm not a fucking child, asshole,' I believe were the words. If not the exact words, certainly the sentiment." He shrugged. "I decided to make sure she got back to the station. But she took a turn and I lost her."

"Yes, and she's still missing," Bryn said. "We need to report it. Especially with this—" She gestured toward where the letter had disappeared inside Andy's coat.

Andy leaned in. His gaze shifted between Bryn and Delon in such a way that she knew what he was going to say next.

"They're going to focus on the two of you. Given your... *relationship*."

Bryn turned to see if Delon had caught the detective's drift. He had. She could actually see that his forehead was glistening with sweat—and it wasn't hot in the restaurant.

"Does Jules know?" he asked. He spoke so low he could hardly be heard over the television mounted on the wall.

"I certainly didn't tell her," Andy said, nonchalantly, making Bryn almost believe him.

"Why exactly were you watching *us*?" Bryn asked.

"Needed to see if either one of you was responsible

for the letters. My colleague observed quite a few visits." He raised his unruly brows, then became absorbed in the television's basketball game.

Bryn was allowed to work remotely twice a week. That made it very easy for Delon to come over for an hour or so in the afternoon while Jules was busy writing. Usually, it was direct and unrestrained, one of his groping hands under her still-on bra. Perhaps that's what made him come over again and again—the lack of having to be tender or intricate. He would tell his wife he was going to the gym. When he returned home showered and fresh-smelling, it made perfect sense, given where he'd supposedly been.

At first, Bryn had been acutely paranoid that her cousin would bang on her door when Delon was there. But over the months, she began to relax and even became complacent. More than once, Delon had bragged how the spouses "trusted" each other enough not to keep tabs on one another. He would say this with no irony.

"And Gilda?" Bryn asked. "You bring that information to her?"

Andy shrugged again. It was his go-to move, made with his left shoulder only, mouth cynically pursed, the implication being, *What do you expect?*

Bryn glanced back at Delon, who was staring at Andy.

"You told her," he said. His eyes were glowing black fire. Bryn wouldn't have been surprised if he lunged across the table and tried to throttle the detective. Probably the only thing stopping him was the wooden table's broad berth. He was unlikely to reach the detective's throat.

"I mentioned there were numerous visits from you to Mrs. Callais' cousin," Andy said. "This naturally made my team focus on you—" He looked at Bryn. "—as a suspect."

"I didn't send any letters," Bryn growled.

Andy shifted his gaze back to the basketball game. "They've been analyzed. Your prints aren't on them. Besides, it wouldn't make much sense for you to get Mrs. Callais to leave town. She'd take her husband with her."

"How in the actual hell would you know what my prints look like?"

"Can't tell you that," he said.

After several moments of staring at him in stunned irritation, a memory surged forth. A year ago, Bryn's employer had asked everyone to go into a room and press their forefingers into a small black digital pad. This was for a new time-clock that would open the door and keep track of everyone's comings and goings. No one liked it but no one quit over it either. Her print must be stored somewhere that Andy got access to.

"Is that legal?" she demanded.

"I don't think you sent the letters," he drawled as if doing her a favor.

Bryn lolled her head around, her neck cracking. She needed to calm down or she might throw her wine in this guy's face. Though there was less than an inch of it left, so it wouldn't be worth it.

"Couldn't she have worn gloves?" Delon asked.

Bryn whipped her head around so fast to glare at him that her neck cracked again.

"If people were that clever, my job would be a lot more difficult," Andy said.

Delon gave Bryn a sheepish look and murmured, "Was just curious."

"How do you know the police won't help?" Bryn asked, trying to draw Andy's attention away from the television.

"Hudson Hollow cops?" He pursed his mouth derisively. "There's a two-person crime division. Sergeant and detective. We can go to them, but I'll be obliged to tell them everything."

He jerked his chin at Bryn and Delon. His meaning was clear: He'd inform the police about their affair.

"At that point, they'll turn all their manpower—man and woman power, actually, the detective is female—on you two," he said. "Then they'll order me to back off. I'll have to do it. I can tell you that I'm putting in all the resources they would and more so."

He turned fully away from the television, picked up his glass and swished its ice.

"I was NYPD for two decades. You got a full-time crime division right here."

Chapter Twelve

*B*ack in her room, Bryn's temples pulsed with an oncoming headache. She occasionally got them if she was under extreme stress or drank alcohol. This temples-throbber was thanks to both.

In the small modern bathroom, she opened the drawers next to the sink and was grateful to find an individual package of pain relievers. She ripped it open and gulped the tablets down with water from the sink's tap.

Plugging in her phone using the charger she'd bought that morning at a general store, she sat on the bed and emailed Evan. She needed to take the entire week off and blame her virus. She didn't care if he disapproved. Her mind was too crowded with too many other things for her to worry about her job.

Opening her personal email, she saw the one that Amika had forwarded from the tip account. The subject header was "Here ya go."

The email read:

Hello Bryn,
What no thank you? Isn't that what you wanted?
Your pal

The email's address was from yourpal12345 and the domain was anon.co. She did a search on the domain and saw that it was an untraceable, anonymous email provider. Just what she needed, some whacko who hated the police, wanted to rant, and had picked her out personally from the tip team for some reason. She had enough going on.

On a whim, and so she could feel like she hadn't completely abandoned her job, she created a new subject header and wrote back:

Hi, did you have any information for me? I'd like to hear what you have to say. It's completely anonymous.

Best,
Bryn Bastid
City Daily

Just as she hit send, there was a knock on the door. Assuming it was the maid who would hand her clean towels, she opened it. Delon stood there, looking anxious and forlorn, his bottomless dark eyes wider than usual, his thick hair straggled over his still-sweaty forehead.

He was normally so debonair and in control. To see him falling apart was a bit of a shock to Bryn's psyche. She felt as if she was looking at a twin of him, a man who appeared uncannily like Delon but was lacking key ingredients: his coolness, his air of smooth detachment.

Jules being missing had made him… human.

"What do you want?" she asked.

"Let me in, we need to talk."

"Why the hell would you ask that P.I. if I could have worn gloves? What is wrong with you? Besides the obvious."

"I'm sorry," he said. "I get so nervous, I say the wrong thing. Please let me in."

"That camera is picking everything up."

"Who cares! We're done anyway!"

He had a point there. She opened the door, then reeled over to the bed, and belly-flopped onto it. She heard him close the door.

"I don't know about this guy," he said. "Something isn't lining up. Jules would have told me about threatening letters."

She felt him perch on the edge of the bed. They were quiet for at least a minute before she finally rolled over to look at him. He was bent forward, his head buried in his hands.

"I think we have to accept that she might have known about us, and she didn't feel like confiding in either one of us," Bryn said.

He sighed raggedly, rubbing his face before turning back to glance at her.

"We need to talk to Gilda and see if she really hired him," he said. "She hates my guts, but she's the only one who can tell us who this guy is."

"Why would she hate your guts?"

"Because Jules was always on her about royalty checks. She was never getting them. I got angry, called and told her if my wife didn't start receiving what was due to her, I'd hire a lawyer."

Hmm. No wonder Delon had disappeared from Jules' readings.

Bryn sat up and grabbed her phone. Typing "Andy Kroll NYPD investigator" into a search engine, she quickly saw his name and photo on a website: Kroll Detective Agency. She flashed her phone at Delon.

"He's legit."

"*Dieu, dieu, on est foutus,*" he moaned. "He told Gilda everything. Gilda must have told Jules."

"But if she knew, why not confront us?"

"Why confront us when she can torture us?" he asked despairingly. "Now she's trying to set us up for something."

Bryn's lips popped open. "Oh, shit."

She grabbed her phone and opened her email, then scrolled to the message forwarded by Amika.

"I got this strange email from my coworker. Someone had sent it to my job's tip account. It says…" She began reading. "'Hello Bryn, What no thank you? Isn't that what you wanted? Your pal.'"

She looked up at Delon. His face was frozen.

"Does that sound like… like it could be… Jules?"

Delon put his palm out and she handed him the phone. He stared at it, reading.

"Hello, Bryn," he repeated. "What no thank you? Isn't that what you…" He trailed off, then said, very lowly, "wanted?"

He looked at her.

"She could have sent it to the tip account knowing I'd get it," Bryn said. "It wouldn't be obvious to anyone but me that it was from her. It just looks like a tip from another loony. I was always telling her about them. No one has ever addressed an email to a certain reporter before. Jules is basically saying, 'I'm gone, so you can have my husband.' Damn. You could be right. She learned about us from Gilda and took off to set us up for something."

"Then she's alive," he said, glancing around the room as if Jules might be in it. "Or do you think she… ?"

They both went silent. Finally, Bryn said in a hushed tone, "Would she have done something to herself?"

She shook her head. "No. Not Jules. In fact, I can't believe she wouldn't go to the Y talk. She's not going to hurt her career to teach us a lesson. If she disappeared to punish us, I bet she'll reappear for that."

"But if she is pregnant…" he murmured.

Yes.

If Jules is pregnant—something she'd wanted since she was a teenager—and she finally got what she'd always longed for, only to find out her husband was having an affair with her cousin, the discovery could have been an emotional shock cataclysmic enough to override her career ambition.

In her despair or rage or vengefulness, Jules took off somewhere. If she harmed herself on top of it, then she'd be setting Bryn and Delon up for murder. But if she was pregnant, would she hurt the baby? That was impossible. She'd waited most of her life for a child. She wouldn't harm it no matter what was happening with her cousin and husband.

"There's only one thing to do," Bryn said. "We have to ask Gilda if she told Jules about us. If she did, that goes a long way toward confirming that Jules is out there and trying to frame us or, at the very least, messing around with us."

Delon reached over, and unexpectedly and gently brushed a stray curl off her forehead. "You look sick," he said.

"Thanks a lot."

"I mean, you don't look well."

"Of course I don't," she snapped. "You don't either."

She squeezed her thumbs on either side of her temples, a trick she'd learned long ago to dull a headache.

"My head hurts," she said. "And my neck. My muscles are hard as rocks."

"Can I help?"

"How are you supposed to help? I already took pain meds."

"How about a massage? You've always said it's the best thing for a headache."

True, she'd said this. Delon would get headaches sometimes, as well. She'd urge a massage on him as a way of priming him for sex, not that he needed priming.

"I'm fine. Don't worry about me."

"Come. Lie down. Just a short one. You look like

you're about to collapse. I don't need you in the hospital on top of everything else."

She stretched her neck from side to side, hearing small cracks deep within her vertebrae. Then she heaved onto her stomach on the bed. She was too riddled with stress, anxiety, and fatigue to argue with him.

"Okay, but be quick about it," she relented. "And don't try anything."

His strong, familiar fingers began to knead the base of her neck, then moved down in between her shoulder blades, squeezing the stress out of her stone-hard tendons, causing a deep, sharp pain that mingled with warm, intense pleasure.

Then his hands moved down, down to her spine, his firm, lean fingers expertly draining the stiffness from her tensed muscles, drawing out delicious waves of bliss, the exquisite relaxation and pleasure almost too much to bear.

Within thirty seconds, she moaned, rolled over, and her mouth desperately sought out his.

Chapter Thirteen

DAY FOUR: WEDNESDAY

"*Y*ou fucked him."

Bryn stood at the one public phone she'd found. It was scrawled with graffiti and looked like someone had bashed it with a hammer, trying to steal its coins. But it still worked.

Bryn didn't want to call Amika from her cell phone and have a record of it. Amika, like Bryn, tended to pick up calls from unknown numbers because, as a reporter, strangers were often calling.

"How did you know?" Bryn asked, drooping her head in shame.

"Because I'm not stupid. I can tell by your voice."

"I don't know what to do," Bryn whimpered into the germ-ridden mouthpiece. "It always makes perfect sense as it happens. Then I wake up from a sex-fog and I'm behind bars staring at a large woman who's plotting to shank me because I snore."

She shivered and huddled deeper into her hoodie.

The morning was glass-clear, and there was a snappy undercurrent of oncoming winter in the air. She couldn't believe she was being so self-destructive. Or how, terribly and incomprehensibly, the adrenaline of the situation was making her crave sex with Delon more than ever.

It was as if her brain, suspecting she would ultimately end up in prison, was making last-ditch attempts to pass down her DNA. Fortunately, she had an IUD or she suspected her raving hormones would convince her to ditch her pills.

"Now he wants us to share a room because I can't afford my own any longer," she lamented.

"Of course he does," Amika said. "He's a wife-killing psychopath. A real horny one."

"I don't think he did anything to Jules," Bryn protested.

She'd called Amika hoping that her friend would keep her accountable, and magically enable her to resist Delon. But now that she was receiving a scolding, she had the urge to defend herself.

"I think she disappeared on purpose. It's possible she's trying to frame us for murder."

"Girl, you've watched too many crime documentaries. You saw his car drive by her the night she went missing, remember? Have you conveniently blocked that out?"

"It must have been a crazy coincidence. Some other person's car. If you could see the way he's acting, you'd understand. He's genuinely distraught."

Even to her own ears, her words sounded hollow

and forced. Amika loudly tapped the phone on her end, causing Bryn to jerk the earpiece away.

"Are you listening to yourself?" Amika chided. "He's so distraught that he keeps fucking you? You know what? I'm not going to visit you in the big house. You're pissing me off too much. Did you get that email I sent you?"

Bryn kept sweeping her gaze around, on high alert for Delon. The payphone was only a few blocks from the inn, across from a historic theater with its Art Deco 1930s marquee intact. She'd left the room while he was taking a shower. They'd spent the entire night together, the first time they'd ever done so.

The experience had been a surreal blend of ghastly and wonderful. Everything about him filled her senses in the most exquisite way: his touch, his skin, his smell, his voice. But the two of them in the same bed, entwined like they were a couple—and not any couple but a couple in love— could only be blamed on the pair of them being damaged, deranged, not human. All night long, she suffered crashing waves of guilt stronger than she'd ever experienced before.

If Jules wasn't faking her own disappearance, then there was a good chance that she was being held captive, possibly being subjected to horrors beyond imagination. And here was Bryn, not only making love to Jules' husband, but wrapping herself around him and spending the night luxuriating in every atom of him.

She didn't realize it consciously, but being with him quieted thirty years of the raw ache of inferiority. It soothed the unrelenting feeling of being in Jules' shadow.. Of Jules being the princess, and Bryn being the afterthought, the rejected one, the disposable one.

The one who got whatever scraps might be leftover after Jules was served the full meal on polished silver dinnerware.

Jules was not only beautiful and popular. She also had parents who loved and cared for her. She was valued. She was wanted. She was the product of love, not violence. The product of two adults who'd chosen each other, not the product of a teenage girl who couldn't fight off an older, stronger male.

These dark feelings roiled permanently inside of Bryn. Until she made love to Delon. Then she had relief from this unrelenting mental torture. Then *she* was the chosen one. She didn't acknowledge this inconveniently unfeminist feeling—and, if she had, she would have loathed it, and it squashed it back down into the dark depths of her psyche.

"Yes, I did get the email!" Bryn said, still irrationally hoping she could sway Amika into approving of her affair or at least not judging it. "That's the main reason I think Jules is alive. The email sounded like it could have been written by her."

"Then why would she send it to the tip account and not to you directly?"

"Because that would be too obvious."

"Hon, you're an addict trying to justify your fix. You want that loaded syringe, only it's a loaded penis. Listen to me, use my credit card. Stay in another room. In fact, stay in another state."

"I can't do that. I have no idea when I could pay you back."

"Girl," Amika said with the quiet despair of someone who knew she was tossing her words to the wind, "you're dooming yourself. For sex. Sex you won't remember in a few years. But prison? You'll remember that forever."

"I'll call you later. Always pick up from this number."

Bryn hung up, then retrieved the sanitizer from her backpack and slathered the clear gel over her hands. She tried to push aside Amika's harsh but clear-eyed reproach, but she knew that her friend was right.

Bryn was dooming herself. For a man. A man who, if she were honest with herself, she didn't know very well, despite knowing him for almost a decade.

A man who may have driven past Jules the night she went missing.

A man who stood to inherit money if Jules died. A man who could now sell the brownstone that Jules had been preventing him from selling.

A man who—

"No!" she blurted aloud.

An elderly man shuffling by on the sidewalk shot her a startled glance, then continued on his slow, unsteady way.

BACK IN THE room at the inn, Delon was in the bathroom, shaving, a white towel wrapped around his hips. Every fiber in Bryn's body prickled with giddy anticipation to see him again. But her gut was also twisted and nauseous and rotten with the idea of seeing him again.

Hearing her enter, he backed into the door frame, cast her a long glance, then returned to shaving. "Telling your friend all about me?" he asked.

"No," she said, unconvincingly.

"Look, Bryn," he called. "I understand that you need to talk to someone, but it's not wise to be gossiping about this situation with your girlfriend. Friends aren't always what you think. You should know that."

"Just be quiet," she said, slumping on the bed. "I'm going to drive into the city to see Gilda, so I need the car key."

She heard the tap running but he didn't answer her. "Are you listening?" she called.

Finally, he came out and sat next to her on the bed. Still only wearing a towel. She had zero ability to think rationally when he was this near to being naked.

Unexpectedly, he picked up her hand and held it. Other than after sex, he'd never held her hand before. It was sickening how elated this gesture made her. How his hand pressed to hers made her feel seen and valued, like she had a reason for being on this ridiculous planet.

"Bryn," he said, softly. "I don't know why this keeps happening, or why we feel the way we do. But it is what it is."

He kissed her hand, let go of it, stood up, and

dropped the towel as he ambled to his small pile of clothes on the chair. She could only lock eyes on that supremely-sculpted ass. Truly, it was like something you'd see in the Greek statue section of a museum.

"Are you sure you don't want me to come?" He turned and grinned. "I mean to see Gilda."

"No. You said she hates you. It will be better if I go alone. She doesn't like me very much but at least she doesn't hate me."

"I'm going down to the tracks and the river." He stepped into his black slacks, no underwear. "Jules might have left something behind. Like she did the scarf."

"The railroad tracks? I don't need you electrocuting yourself. Or getting hit by a train."

He pulled his shirt down over his still-wet hair. "Worried about me?" he asked.

"Just be careful, okay?"

He held out his arms. She sat staring at him, unmoving, not sure what he wanted her to do. "Come," he said, wiggling his fingers. Light glinted off his wedding ring.

As if in a trance, she stood and drifted into his arms. He wrapped them strongly around her and buried his mouth in her hair. She could do nothing but shrink into him, breathing in his natural scent.

For whatever reason, Delon's embrace brought her back to the humiliation of Danny.

At fifteen, he'd been Bryn's first "relationship," which consisted of makeout sessions in his Jeep while parked at the Dairy Queen. He was more popular than she was, played on the softball team, and had billows of reddish hair that she loved.

But one day while she was talking to him in the school hall, Jules, a senior and a grade ahead, had approached. Bryn was left with no choice but to introduce them, despite having a sickening premonition of what lay ahead.

One bright, toothy smile from Jules, and Danny had tossed aside his high school reputation, hovering like an unwelcome fungus on the fringes of Jules' gatherings. She never bad-mouthed him—she didn't need to, her friends did it for her—but she'd sometimes stare at him pityingly as he tried various lame ways to grab her attention.

The memory of how Danny had discarded Bryn's genuine affection in favor of the indifference of her cousin and the scorn of his classmates could still sting.

"We can't help it," Delon said, drawing her back to the present. "Or we would. None of this means we don't want to find her or that we don't love her."

"I don't think a jury will understand that." Bryn barely understood it herself.

He kissed the side of her face and held her by the shoulders, peering into her eyes.

"You be careful, too. With Gilda. If she knows her golden goose has gone missing, she's going to call the cops."

Chapter Fourteen

*B*ryn found underground parking on Fifth Avenue, then walked five crowded uptown blocks. She'd only been away from the city for three days but had almost forgotten how much the island was crawling with people, like ants stampeding over dropped meat.

In the lobby, she told a security guard her name and that she was here to see Gilda Hortense. The guard made a call, then handed her a badge that allowed her to move through a turnstile.

Bryn came out of the elevator, opened double glass doors, and approached a young woman sitting at a desk. The receptionist was so young and fresh-faced, she looked like she'd left her college graduation ceremony and walked directly to the literary agency.

Behind the girl were framed blown-up book covers. One belonged to *The Suburban Aristocrats*. Bryn quickly averted her eyes.

"I'm here to see Gilda," Bryn said, trying to sound

as if there was no way she could be denied entry. "I don't have an appointment but she knows who I am. Bryn Bastid. Jules Aston-Callais' cousin. It's important and won't take long."

"Hold on, please," the girl said before standing and disappearing into the sunlight-filled glass of the main office.

About three minutes later, the girl returned and indicated that Bryn should follow. Bryn and the girl walked through a loft-like open desk area. There were about a dozen young people at child-sized desks staring into monitors like drones, their ears plugged with ear buds.

Every single one of them made Bryn feel old and shabby. At this point, she'd been wearing the same clothes for three days and was certain they were starting to stink. Her sneakers had bits of brown autumn leaves trapped in the laces and a mysterious stain had appeared on her shirt.

The girl opened an office door. Gilda came around an imposing antique mahogany desk. She, like everyone in the office, was impeccably dressed. A beige turtleneck with white slacks and a white fitted blazer. She was wearing a thick gold drop necklace in the shape of a swan. Her grayish-black hair hung coiffed slightly above her spindly shoulders.

Despite her hand out for a shake, the agent still looked inconvenienced. Bryn supposed it was the natural hard set of her face. Too many years dealing with publishing types, all with their own sets of whims and demands.

On the wall behind the wide desk hung a large oil

painting of Gilda and her husband, Max. Gilda, wearing all black, was seated. Max stood behind her, one hand draped over his wife's shoulder. Both wore unsmiling expressions with thousand-yard stares. It was an odd sight. Who in this century commissions an oil painting of themselves? Gilda and Max Hortense, that's who.

"Bryn, how are you?" Gilda said. She sounded more pleasant than she did when Jules was around. "This is unexpected. Can I help you with something?"

Gilda's astute eyes, expertly layered with a spectrum of gray eyeshadow, flicked from Bryn's head to her feet. Bryn's attire was not making a good impression. She still wore Jules' scarf, which was out of place with the rest of the outfit. She hoped Gilda wouldn't recognize it. Gilda gestured at the white Chesterfield chair opposite her desk. Bryn perched on its edge.

"I'll keep this brief," she said. "I met Andy Kroll, a detective. He tells me you hired him to follow Jules."

"When did this happen?" Gilda asked, fluttering her lashes. It was the only sign that she was surprised. Years of hardball negotiating with publishers had given her an impressively unreadable poker face.

"Did you hire him or not?"

"Well, yes, Jules is fully aware that—"

"Fine," Bryn cut her off. "This guy told you something about myself and Delon Callais."

Gilda was silent. You could tell she was very good at being silent, that she could out-silent anyone because she knew it made people uncomfortable while she wasn't bothered by it in the slightest.

"He did," she finally confirmed.

"I need to know if you shared this information with Jules."

Gilda opened the desk drawer in front of her. She looked inside for a few moments, then closed it. Strange move. It threw Bryn off as she didn't know what Gilda was searching for.

Gilda made direct eye contact and said, "I didn't tell her."

Bryn was vastly relieved though she wasn't sure whether to believe it.

"Why do you think I did?" Gilda asked. "And why did Andy share this information with you?"

Bryn held up her hand. "A strange man was following me around and watching my apartment. I don't have to answer questions from *you*."

Gilda's face remained impassive but Bryn could sense she was slightly flustered. People didn't normally tell her off. Bryn relished the moment of feeling in control of a situation, something she hadn't felt since Jules had walked off that train platform.

"Why didn't you tell Jules about me and her husband?" she asked.

"Let's see, ever hear the expression 'don't kill the messenger?'" Gilda crossed her bony arms. "I didn't want to be the messenger. He talks his way out of it and then *I* pay the price. And while I was informed that Delon visits your apartment on a regular basis, how do I know what's going on inside? Perhaps the two of you were planning a surprise party."

The way Gilda said this made it clear she didn't think the pair were planning any surprise party.

"Bryn," Gilda continued, fingering her swan necklace. "I've learned not to get involved in my clients' private affairs. If I did that, I'd never have time for anything else."

"Do you hire a P.I. to follow all your clients?"

"No, but most of my clients aren't receiving threats. Jules didn't want the detective but I insisted."

"I don't appreciate this guy—or someone who works with him—keeping an eye on me instead."

Gilda sighed. "I don't know what's going on with you and Jules' husband," she said. "As soon as Andy told me, I put it out of my head."

Bryn realized she had been subtly vibrating with fear and the possibility that Gilda had told Jules everything. Until this moment, she didn't even know how invested she was in Jules never finding out, in keeping her cousin's friendship and goodwill.

"Okay, well, thanks, I guess," Bryn murmured.

"I said I didn't *tell* her. I didn't say she doesn't know."

Bryn's eyes stretched wide open. "What do you mean? Did the detective tell her?"

"Oh no. That's not his job."

"Then how would she know?"

"Have you read her new book? *A Woman Stands Alone*?"

"Of course not. It's not out yet."

"I mean, did you read any drafts as she was working on it?"

Bryn turned her mouth down and shook her head, almost distastefully. Her job required her to read and write all day long. The last thing she wanted to do in her spare time was read or write more. She'd never asked to see the drafts of Jules' book, and Jules had never asked her to read them. Besides, Bryn was walking a fine line of trying to be supportive while letting go of the fact that her cousin had elbowed into a domain that had previously belonged only to Bryn—writing. But as fiction was a different animal to journalism, and one that Bryn had no affinity for nor any desire to try, she was able to let that particular irritation go fairly quickly.

"We don't do that kind of thing," she said. "When we're together, we want to forget about writing."

Gilda stood up and walked to a closet with sliding doors. She bent down and rummaged through something, then turned. In her hands was a beautifully smooth, brightly-colored, crackling new hardcover book.

"Advanced copies," she said.

On the forest green front cover was an illustration of a woman who looked remarkably like Jules. The woman's eyes were dreamily closed and her blonde wavy tresses floated all around her face. Behind her stood the Eiffel Tower.

In a looping gold font was the title: *A Woman Stands Alone.*

"You may want to read the back cover," Gilda said, handing over the book.

Bryn peered at the back flap copy. It read:

In the hotly anticipated follow-up to the bestselling

novel *The Suburban Aristocrats*, Jules Aston-Callais subtly and brilliantly delves into what happens after the fairy-tale ends.

When American college student Claire Bonnet falls madly in love with Parisian Fabian de Rambouillet while traveling across Europe, things couldn't be more perfect.

Fabian is not only rich, tall, dark and handsome, but hails from French nobility (which has never truly gone away, the French Revolution be damned).

After a whirlwind courtship and marriage, they have their first child, Duke, then return to Claire's hometown of New York. But when kind-hearted Claire hires a family friend's troubled daughter as nanny to their toddler, her husband begins acting less princely.

Irritable, distant, and suffering a loss of sex drive, Fabian continually blames the stress from work and restoring their fixer-upper brownstone.

Claire believes his excuses until she stumbles upon evidence that turns her world to ashes. Her prince, the love of her life, and father of her child, is having an affair with the nanny.

Now Claire must decide whether to try to save her marriage or to be *A Woman Stands Alone.*

There was a very long pause as Bryn tried to absorb what she'd read, including the last garbled sentence. Someone needed to fire the proofreader, if there had actually been one. "Who!" she refrained from saying to Gilda. "*Who* stands alone!"

A small cluster of junior agents stood chattering

outside Gilda's office, their voices penetrating the glass walls. "It—it's fiction," she stammered.

"Fiction? Did you read the first book? How much fiction was that?"

Bryn had read most of Jules' debut, rabidly consuming the words, hoping for insight into her cousin's feelings—especially about herself. But once she realized that there was no fictional equivalent of herself in the novel, she began to lose interest and started skimming. Not to mention that an intimate viewing of the idealized version of Jules and Delon falling in love was nauseating.

"I read most of it," she said, knowing how unsupportive that sounded. "Okay, a lot of it was based on Jules and Delon. But it definitely wasn't all real. I wasn't even in it." She tapped the back flap. "This is hackneyed, cliched crap. Cheating with the nanny. Come on."

Gilda stalked briskly around the desk to her chair.

"I had many discussions with her about the plot," she said. "I told her that fans don't want to read about Fabian cheating. They want the happily-ever-after. But she insisted that this is the kind of thing that happens in marriages. She wanted to show Claire and Fabian struggling with real issues."

Gilda stared pointedly as if to say, *Do you not comprehend the artistry involved?*

"It remains to be seen if the public will accept it," she continued. "Our first clue will be at the Y reading Friday night."

The way Gilda confidently mentioned the Y event as

if Jules was still guaranteed to show up at it made Bryn certain that the agent didn't have a clue her client was missing.

Why wouldn't Andy have told her? He'd been hired to protect Jules. Shouldn't he have reported to Gilda that the woman he'd been charged with protecting had vanished? Was he worried he'd lose his job?

"It's her best work," Gilda continued. "I'm going to submit it for all the awards. She's graduated from chick lit to literary fiction."

Another surprise to Bryn. Not that Jules couldn't write and write well. One didn't get as far as Jules had in such a fickle industry without being able to write decently. But Bryn had no idea her cousin could write on the level that might reap prestigious awards.

"You think she based the plot on Delon and myself," Bryn said.

"I'm only pointing out there are similarities between you and Gwen that—"

"Gwen?!"

"That's the name of the character of the nanny."

Bryn couldn't utter a word. Gwen and Bryn sounded awfully alike.

"She has curly reddish-brown hair and hazel eyes," Gilda added.

"Mine are brown!"

"Gwen grew up with a single mother and never knew her father. From the little Jules told me about her childhood, I gathered that was your situation as well."

"And half the planet!"

"Bryn, please stop being so defensive. I'm only

suggesting that you may want to consider the possibility that I didn't need to tell Jules anything about you and her husband." She leaned back into her chair and fingered her swan. "Because she's known all along."

* * *

But when kind-hearted Claire hires a family friend's troubled daughter...

Bryn scowled. Just the kind of thing that Jules would think about the two of them. Jules, the loyal, protective, kind-hearted saint—and Bryn, the troubled, backstabbing husband-fucker. Though she couldn't deny that this is basically what she was these days. She was almost to the glass doors of the lobby when the young receptionist stepped in front of her.

"Is Jules okay?" the girl asked breathlessly. Her young, bland, baby-fatted face was effulgent with concern. "You're her cousin, right? I saw you in *City Daily* and at a few readings."

"Um, yeah, she's fine," Bryn muttered, plotting how to get around the girl without appearing too rude.

The girl wagged her fingers, indicating that Bryn should follow her. Reluctantly, Bryn did. The girl ducked into a bare, empty room with one long conference table in the center.

"I haven't seen her since what happened, and I'm hoping—"

"Since what happened?"

"With Gilda."

Bryn turned and shut the door to the meeting room. The girl reverently rubbed her blouse. It was silky black and patterned with an intricate hand stitching of bright flowers. Must have cost about a thousand dollars.

"This is Thom King," the girl said. "Jules gave it to me last year. There's no way I could afford anything like this myself. She's the only author who's nice to everyone."

"You mentioned something happened." Bryn bored into the young woman's big, worried eyes. "With Gilda."

"I thought that's why you were here. To get the author copies. Because I figured Jules wouldn't want to come herself."

"If something happened between her and Gilda, I'd really appreciate it if you'd tell me what."

The girl, realizing she'd made a mistake in revealing too much, began to look frightened.

"What's your name?" Bryn asked, using her most ingratiating tone. She had to quickly gain the girl's trust.

"Elizabeth. Just Elizabeth. No Beth or Liz or anything."

"Elizabeth, please." Bryn smiled gently, as if trying to lure a skittish baby fawn out of the brambles. "I'm Jules' best friend. She's been acting strangely and I'm concerned. I'd like to know what happened with Gilda so I can help."

"But I wouldn't want to—"

"This is between you and me. I swear on my life."

She crossed her fingers and placed them over her heart, hoping this was a recognizable gesticulation of a covenant. Elizabeth glanced back at the door, obviously petrified that Gilda would notice she was missing from her post.

"A couple weeks ago, I was dropping mail off in front of Gilda's office when Jules was in there," she said hurriedly. "I heard them arguing."

"About what?"

"I'm not sure exactly. I heard Jules say that she wouldn't be followed around anymore. She said something like, 'Call off your hound.' I also heard Gilda call her an ungrateful bitch."

Bryn's lips popped open. She'd never heard Gilda speak that way to Jules. She didn't even know the agent was capable of it, given how protective she was of her author.

"I put down the mail and got out of there," Elizabeth continued. "About ten minutes later, Jules went flying past my desk. She didn't even say goodbye, which is unlike her. She always stops to chat. The rest of the day, Gilda stayed in her office, which is also unlike her."

"You're positive you heard her call Jules an ungrateful bitch?"

"Oh, yeah." The girl turned her eyes down and said, softly, "People don't know what Gilda is really like."

Chapter Fifteen

"*S*he didn't tell Jules about us."

Bryn stood at the gas station on a busy corner in Park Slope, a few blocks from the park. She'd noticed a lone payphone here years ago and sometimes wondered if anyone ever used it. Now these ancient public phones—perhaps simply forgotten to be hauled away by phone companies—were coming in handy.

While she doubted there were any taps on her and Delon's cell phones, the prosecution—if it ever got to that point—might as well not have a record of calls between them during this time. Delon was using the phone in the hallway outside the inn's restaurant.

"You believe her?" he asked.

"She made a pretty good case for it."

Bryn thought about the copy of *A Woman Stands Alone* sitting on the passenger seat of Delon's car. She decided not to mention Gilda's theory that Jules not only already knew about their affair but had used it for literary inspiration.

"She doesn't seem to realize Jules is missing," Bryn projected as a delivery truck roared by her. "I have no idea why Andy wouldn't have told her. Maybe he's scared. Gilda is pretty intimidating."

"He doesn't seem like he'd be intimidated by anyone."

"I don't know, but Gilda seems to think that Jules will be at the Y event on Friday. If you don't call the police after she doesn't show, it's going to look very bad for you. And Gilda will call anyway."

"Yes, I realize all this," he sighed.

Now an ambulance came by. Bryn stuck one finger in her ear and waited until its squalling atonal wails mercifully faded.

"I thought you had some mysterious way of taking care of Gilda." She couldn't help her jab.

"Maybe I do," he said.

"Like what? Kill her?"

They both went silent. Apparently too soon for this sort of joke.

"Did you find anything down by the river?" she probed.

"No, but I saw another camera. It's on a residential street right off Main, not far from the cafe. Just a regular house and it's attached to their porch. Was thinking of asking the owners to have a look at their video."

"Why don't you wait until I get back and we can do that together?"

If there was more video out there with Jules on it, she didn't want Delon somehow messing up their one chance of examining it.

"When are you coming back?" he asked.

"Tomorrow. I really want to stay at my place tonight. I need to change clothes and check work emails and come up with something to tell my editor."

"I'll miss you."

She turned her back to the swarm of people on the broad sidewalk, pushing her mouth as close as she could stand to the grimy decades-old mouthpiece.

"Delon, don't say stuff like that," she said. "You don't need to charm me. And it's highly inappropriate with your wife missing."

"But having sex is fine."

"No, it's not fine! It's not fine at all. Apparently, we can't stop that. But let's not do something really crazy like start talking."

"What does that even mean?"

"I don't know. Goodbye!"

She hung up. It was satisfactory how the old handset made a clang as she whacked it into the holder.

Bryn used the spare key she had on her key ring to let herself into Jules' and Delon's brownstone. She had the eerie sensation that Jules would be sitting in one of its cavernous rooms with its elegant prewar detailing and crown molding, reading a book or typing on her computer. Jules would look up as Bryn entered, and flash that big, white, slightly-protuberant smile.

"Hey, worry wart," she'd say.

Jules would explain that she'd been home the entire

time. That she'd thought Bryn was busy working and Delon had gone out of town to see a client and...

She'd have an explanation. Some kind of explanation that, in retrospect, would seem so obvious. The cousins would spend the rest of their lives telling the story about the time that everyone thought Jules had gone missing. And how Bryn and Delon had spent three days upstate trying to find her. (Bryn would leave out the parts about them having sex.)

The vision was vivid enough that Bryn checked every single room. It wasn't normal that the rooms were this quiet, this empty of life. It was creepy how the stairs creaked and echoed in the hollow silence.

Jules would not leave her beloved brownstone behind. Bryn would have spiffed up the century-old place with fresh paint and called it a day. But Jules and Delon—mostly Jules—had done so much work on it. They'd spent many weekends driving to various farms in the northeast that were selling or giving away salvaged materials—and Bryn could see those thoughtful touches in the chunky hand-hewn beams on the ceilings and the peach crates that Jules stacked against the walls in lieu of bookshelves. No basic subway tile backsplash for her. She'd scoured the Internet until she found a Presbyterian church in rural Pennsylvania selling its old brick floors.

Bryn headed to the office on the top floor where she knew Jules did her writing. The walls were mossy green shiplap, the trim moldings crisp white, the flat-sanded pinewood floors shined in a classic herringbone pattern. The decor of the room—of the entire brownstone—was as simple and enduring as Jules' sartorial style. You could walk into this brownstone in fifty years and not want to change a thing.

The bay window had a perfectly framed view of the park, bursting with peak autumn colors. An antique secretary desk with a foldout writing space faced the captivating scene. On it was a laptop. Bryn sat and pressed the computer's space bar. It awakened, wanting a passcode.

Bryn typed in DAISY—this was the Golden Retriever that Jules had grown up with. Bryn was certain Jules had once told her that Daisy was her passcode on most of her accounts. Unfortunately, the code wanted two more characters. After trying several combinations of numbers, Bryn got locked out.

She slid open the side drawers. Inside were numerous hanging folders. Jules was meticulously organized, so the folders all had little tabs with printed labels. Bryn expected to see writing topics but instead they were all fashion related.

Thom

Chanel

Fall Collection

Jeans

Coats

Winter Collection

Bryn thumbed through some of the materials inside of the folders but it was mostly pages excised from various fashion magazines. Satisfied that there was nothing interesting here, she closed the drawer and opened the smaller drawer in the middle of the desk.

Right on top was a printout with A WOMAN STANDS ALONE typed on the title page. Bryn's heart began to thud, her skin prickled with anticipation. She flipped through the pages. They were neatly typed in New Times Roman, double spaced. Several pages in, she saw a scrawl in black pen. It was Jules' handwriting. Bryn knew it well. Jules' handwriting, like everything else about her, was enviably beautiful.

Jules had crossed out the name Nancy and written "Gwen." Underneath, in parenthesis, was, "No one under 30 is named Nancy." A little farther down on the same page, Jules had crossed out "with shining black hair of the type swooned over in romance novels" and scrawled "red-brown hair tufted with curls" and on the next page "eyes of a cerulean blue" was crossed out and she'd written "Hazel!"

On another page "her overprotective parents" was crossed out and Jules had written "Give her a single mom. No dad." Chapters went by with no more handwriting. Bryn was skimming, barely absorbing the words, but even she could put together that the heroine, Claire, was beginning to suspect that her husband, Fabian, was sleeping with the nanny, Nancy/Gwen.

Then, on page 78, Bryn saw more handwriting. This time, the words stopped her breath. Jules had crossed out a sentence and, in the margin, she'd written, "I wouldn't say that!" Bryn's fingers slowed on turning pages, her body tensed with a dawning realization. On page 125, she saw, "Haha!" next to a line of Claire's dialogue, and a few pages later, "Yes! Get her, Claire!"

Bryn's gut curled sickeningly, as if she'd eaten something rotten.

"She didn't write this thing," she murmured.

* * *

BRYN LEANED into the aerodynamic office chair, staring out the stunning bay window to the park's multicolored ring of trees. She was dumbfounded. Yet, at the same time, it all made sense. Here and there, Jules would mention she was writing a book, but Bryn had never really taken it seriously. Pretty much everyone she knew claimed they were writing a book.

When Jules managed to land a top literary agent, Bryn had wondered how her cousin suddenly knew how to write fiction well enough to do so—not to mention getting a deal and then having the book climb the bestseller charts. Sure, Jules was smart. And she'd majored in English literature. She'd graduated from a Boston university that wasn't easy to get into. But her father's money and alumni status probably helped there. And being smart and reading classics didn't necessarily mean you knew how to write a novel, otherwise every librarian and teacher would be an author.

The first book, *The Suburban Aristocrats*, was clearly based on Jules' life. Had she simply hired a ghostwriter? Bryn was seized with contempt toward Jules, to take that easy road to writing a book.

Bryn's mind kept working its way back to the words *ungrateful bitch*. What the receptionist claimed she'd overheard Gilda call her own author.

Ungrateful.

Bryn recalled the image of Gilda as she extolled the stellar quality of *A Woman Stands Alone*. Pride, there had been so much pride in her voice and her body language.

It's her best work. I'm going to submit it for all the awards.

Given how much *The Suburban Aristocrats* was clearly based on Jules' life, she must have written the novel. But it was likely not very good. Or, at best, average. Jules being Jules, she wouldn't have a clue about this. She'd assume the novel was ready to go. She'd always gotten nearly everything she wanted and why should a book deal be any different?

When Gilda looked at the manuscript's author, she must have seen that Jules was attractive, stylish, and had a connection to a famous designer. A book based on her privileged life in Connecticut might do well. Only, it had to be better written to entice a publisher.

"Gilda rewrote it," Bryn said aloud as she watched a Hasidic family entering the park.

When *The Suburban Aristocrats* unexpectedly became a bestseller, Gilda's ego inflated. She decided to write the follow-up herself. Jules was able to make suggestions—such as changing Nancy's name to Gwen—but otherwise, the sequel was Gilda's handiwork entirely.

If Bryn's theory was correct, it could mean that the novel's plot—a marriage hitting a rough patch due to infidelity—was simply a coincidence, and Jules didn't know about Bryn and Delon. However, Jules' switching of key attributes of the nanny to be more like Bryn strongly hinted that she did know.

Jules had never spoken of wanting to be an author. She'd always talked about the two things she truly desired: to be in fashion and to be a mother. She'd likely written *The Suburban Aristocrats* on a whim, something to do in her spare time when four babies failed to appear.

Bryn remembered feeling mildly irritated when Jules informed her she was writing a book. Bryn had one area —writing—that was hers alone. Now her cousin was muscling into it. Bryn's main solace had been that most people writing a book never finished it. But Jules had. And not only finished it, but managed to get an agent for it.

Gilda Hortense.

The agent had spent her life helping, and watching, others get writing success. That might not be a pleasant thing to witness if she secretly wanted to be a writer herself. But she needed someone who could be the face of her writing, who looked great at events and could attract some press.

The day that Elizabeth heard them arguing, Jules may have gone to Gilda's office to demand two things: One, that Andy Kroll ("your hound") stop following her (why?). Two, that Gilda should give money to Jules that had been withheld from her because the agent was the real author.

Ungrateful bitch.

Two weeks later, Jules disappeared.

Chapter Sixteen

*B*ryn stared into Jules' deep walk-in closet. Every inch was stuffed with clothes, shoes, and handbags. There was also a hyacinth basket reserved for knitted winter hats. Bryn couldn't wear hats as they made her curls frizz out with static electricity. But Jules could pull on the oddest hat and look charming.

The brownstone, built in an era when most people didn't have mountains of clothes, did not have a walk-in closet when Jules and Delon bought it. The small side room had originally been a nursery. The couple planned to return it to a nursery... someday.

As Bryn stared at the tightly organized rows of clothes, she remembered the frequent walks she'd make as a teenager across the long, sloping lawn from the guest house to the main house. The mansion had always caused her a mini-riot of conflicting emotions.

The house was stunning and being inside of such grandeur was exhilarating. But Bryn couldn't help comparing the house to where she and her mother lived, and feelings of inferiority would wash over her.

The guest house wasn't only small and cramped. It was also leaky, cold, and the electrical wiring hadn't been updated, so Bryn and her mother were always blowing fuses.

At the Colonial, Jules would bring Bryn upstairs to her light-filled bedroom overlooking the inground pool, a rose garden, and the thick woods behind the house. She had a walk-in closet then, too. And, like now, it had been brimming with clothes. Jules and her mother regularly shopped together. It was how they bonded.

Bryn and her mother didn't bond. Jess was either working a low wage job or off somewhere with her latest loser boyfriend. If she was home, she was often intoxicated.

Jess was a friendly drunk, but Bryn did not wish to be with a mother who wanted to "check out" around her, so Bryn would go elsewhere when her mother had that shiny, dazed look in her eyes. She could genuinely only remember being alone with her mother a handful of times during her entire childhood.

Which made it so much more necessary—and painful—that she could enter into Jules' ideal life at any time. It was only a quick walk away.

Jules would take great pleasure ushering Bryn into her walk-in closet, and holding up a blouse or pair of jeans and saying, "Babe, you try this on. It would look so good on you."

Bryn wasn't the only one that Jules called "Babe." At first, she thought she was. Then she heard Jules using it with some of her closest friends. Bryn felt less special. But, eventually, over the years, all the other "babes" dropped away.

As Bryn got older, it became more difficult to fit into her cousin's clothes. Bryn was naturally curvier. And because she'd taken on after-school jobs at fast food places, where she ate her dinners and spent time snacking, she'd put on a lot of weight.

Resentment of her cousin was always pulsing within her, but the teenage years was when the feeling accelerated. There were the teachers who smiled at Jules and frowned at Bryn. The fellow students who bumped into Bryn in their rush to talk to Jules. And the strangers on the sidewalk, who stopped to compliment Jules on random things like her shoes or her eyebrows, while not acknowledging Bryn.

Every single day, the world told Jules she was someone and told Bryn she was no one.

Now, examining the brownstone's walk-in closet, Bryn felt herself pulled inside as if by magnet. She took off her slightly musty clothes and bra, standing naked in front of Jules' hanging row of designer dresses.

She pulled out a flowing, knee-length blue and black wraparound dress. Its label was Thom King. Jules had been given plenty of free clothes by her former employer. She not only was a perfect walking advertisement, but a wardrobe was considered part of her salary.

Bryn was able to get the dress down over her body but the little side zipper wouldn't close. Nevertheless, she gazed admiringly at herself in the full-length mirror at the back of the closet. She sucked in her tummy and turned from side to side. Jules had flat abs and long legs, but Bryn had great boobs, and the dress accentuated them.

A shadow appeared in the mirror behind her. She screamed and whirled around.

"What on earth are you doing?"

Delon stood in front of her. His expression wasn't angry but mystified.

Bryn's heart slammed up against her ribcage. It was astonishing that Delon, who was supposed to be in Hudson Hollow, was standing in the closet with her. So astonishing that she could only stare at him, wide-eyed and open-mouthed.

Then she burst into tears. Horrid, loud wails. She clapped one hand over her mouth, wanting to staunch the mortifying sound, but she couldn't. Every single humiliation she'd ever suffered was at the forefront of her mind, and they all came gushing uncontrollably out of her.

"Bryn, Bryn…" Delon said.

He came over and folded her into his arms.

Downstairs in the kitchen, Delon served her a cup of tea. She had changed back into her clothes, leaving the Thom King dress heaped on the floor. She'd been too distraught to find its hanger.

Her head was bent low, she felt completely defeated. She stared at the mug that Delon had slipped in front of her face, inhaling the minty odor of the tea. He sat opposite her and they didn't speak for a while. Bryn's throat was swollen and slightly sore from all of her crying.

Finally, she said, hoarsely, "I don't know what I was doing."

"I thought you were going home," he said softly.

"I thought so too but… "

More tears gathered warningly behind her nose, so she said nothing until she got control of them. Delon handed her a white tea towel decorated with a string of lavender English bluebells. This too she remembered Jules buying, as she'd been with her in the obscenely overpriced artisanal home goods store. The type of place that sold $300 silver pepper mills.

She stuffed the towel against the threatening onslaught. "You don't understand," she choked. "You will never understand."

"Try me."

She took a deep, shuddery breath, then let it back out slowly. She took a tiny sip of the tea, but it was too scalding on her lips.

"How I grew up and how she grew up and what it did to me," she said.

This was the first time she'd ever voiced the terrible thing she'd lived with all these years. And to voice it to the man married to Jules was so pathetic and humiliating that she could hardly breathe.

"I think I have some idea," he said.

"No, you don't. You can't." She pressed the over-priced tea towel to her runny nose. "She got everything and I got nothing. She was the only good thing I had. But she caused me so much pain, just by existing. How would you like to grow up knowing no one wanted you and everyone wanted her?"

"Your mother wanted you."

"No! No, she didn't. She was a teenager. A kid." She looked up defiantly, bottom lip quivering. "Some guy… some guy raped her. Okay?"

Delon flinched.

"A guy she didn't even know. My mother's most traumatic moment was my conception. Meanwhile, I've got this cousin who has everything. Parents who loved and wanted her. A huge house. She's gorgeous and is the most popular girl in school. Next thing I know, she's in Europe and comes back with you—" She flailed one arm at him. "A French guy. Who's rich and hot and madly in love with her. I can't get anyone to text me back after the first date."

There was nothing worse than being ignored, sending your mind into a spiral of speculation about what could have caused it. Soon, the vagaries of dating had become too stressful for an anxious mind like Bryn's, so at the height of her powers of attraction, she'd stopped completely. For years. Until she met Wyatt at a party she hadn't wanted to go to, and he'd been unthreatening and attentive in a way that made her think maybe, with this particular man, she could risk rejection again.

"It's not her fault," she said. "None of it is her fault. Which makes it so awful that I feel this way."

She sank into silence. The outburst had sucked up

all her energy. She hung her head again and stared into the mug of tea.

Delon reached over and patted her hand. Then he wrapped his long fingers around hers and squeezed. The touch was more friendly than loverly. Something about its platonicness was comforting.

"She doesn't have the perfect life, Bryn," he said. "You should know that more than anyone. I know it's hard to believe she has problems, but she's human. All humans have problems. Look what her husband is doing behind her back. The glorious 'Fabian.' If only people knew."

As Bryn was still recovering from her crying jag, she didn't have the stamina to point out that the glorious Fabian turned out to be a turd in book two—art imitating life.

"I'm sorry you grew up feeling that way and still have a lot of those feelings," he said. "It would have been tough living in that little shack behind the Colonial."

She remembered Delon being so kind to her when Wyatt broke up with her. He could be a wonderful person sometimes. In this moment, it seemed impossible how strongly she'd begun to imagine he might have murdered Jules.

"I do understand," he said, slipping his hand away. "There are times when she… well, I feel inferior around her, too." He chuckled. "She beats me at every game we play. Board games, card games, word games. Anything."

"Oh god, me too," Bryn laughed-choked. "I stopped playing games with her ages ago."

"One time, we went white water rafting," he said. "She zoomed down this boiling river like she'd been doing it her entire life." He chuckled again, clearly picturing the scene. "There's probably nothing she can't do."

They fell silent. Bryn took a sip of tea, feeling more in control of her emotions. It was incredible to her that Delon might have some of the same feelings, some of the same sense of inferiority, that Bryn did with Jules.

Then she said, "I think there's one thing she can't do."

"I'd be curious to hear it."

"She can't write a good book. So, Gilda rewrote the first one. Then I suspect Gilda wrote the next one by herself."

He stared at her, blinking his dark eyes in surprise.

"Did you ever see Jules working on her second book?" she asked.

"No. She'd go into the office on the top floor. She knows I'm not much of a reader and we didn't really talk about it." A little bemused smile crept across his mouth. "At one point, she pulled me into some kind of dialogue improvement exercise. But that was all for me and Jules' writing."

"I think that's why Gilda didn't want to turn over royalty checks," Bryn said. "She was doing all the heavy lifting. I talked to a girl who works at the agency. She told me she heard Gilda call Jules an ungrateful bitch. Then Jules stormed out of the agency and hasn't been seen there since. I think she went there to ask for money."

Delon began pinching his lower lip, appearing deep in thought.

"What I'm wondering is—what if Jules threatened not to attend the Y event unless she got more money?" Bryn asked. "Or, even worse, she threatened to tell everyone who was really writing the books. That kind of thing would blow up both their careers."

Delon snapped his gaze up. "Do you think Gilda would have done something to her?"

Bryn gave her nose a final wipe and deposited the tea towel in her lap. She rubbed her fingers over the nubby wood of the rustic teak table. She remembered Jules seeing it in a farmhouse furniture catalog.

What about this one, babe? Reminds me of the sunroom table at the Colonial.

"Maybe. Think about it. Gilda would know where Jules was at all times because Andy Kroll was reporting back to her. He was hired to follow Jules because of threatening letters, but what if Gilda was writing them? That would give her a perfect excuse to have someone track Jules. And it would explain why Jules started to resent Andy's presence. She had a suspicion that the letters weren't real."

"If only I could get into her cell statements," Delon sighed. "We'd know who she called that night. But she keeps everything on her phone."

"If Gilda's the culprit that could mean Andy Kroll is in on it," Bryn said. "Or he isn't, but he inadvertently allowed the person who took Jules to know where she was."

They stopped talking as an ambulance wailed by the

window. The sound grated badly and seemed to go on for an agonizingly long time. Bryn had only spent three days upstate but had gotten used to its tranquility. She had always been sensitive to noise and had probably made a mistake moving to a city with so much of it. She never would have come here if it hadn't been for Jules with her big brownstone and its extra bedroom. What would her life have been without Jules? Impossible to tell.

"By the way, why did you come back?" she asked when the wailing faded.

He shrugged. "To do what I thought you were doing. Get more clothes. Stay in my own bed for the night. So I took the train back." He paused. "It was strange. I kept looking at all the faces, hoping to see her."

"Delon," she said, staring out of the window. "Do you think we're sleeping together because we both feel so ordinary compared to Jules?"

Unexpectedly, he stood up and leaned over her. Only a few inches from her face, he kept stubbornly staring at her until she took the hint and turned her face into his.

"I can only speak for myself," he said. "But I think we're sleeping together because we want to."

Chapter Seventeen

*T*he pair decided to drive back to Hudson Hollow that evening. They wanted to get an early start looking for Jules, and in particular, visiting the house with the surveillance camera on its patio.

They also knew what would happen between them that night and having it happen in Jules' circa 1800s spool bed was too twisted even for them.

As they approached the toll pass, Bryn heard Delon's phone chime. She automatically grabbed it from the holder on the dashboard, thinking Jules might be getting in touch. She couldn't help still thinking that way, and imagining the text she might see from Jules: *Yes, it's me. I know what's going on with the two of you. I had to get away from both of you for a while. You've both broken my heart.*

But all she saw on the cell screen was a message that said, "Thanks for using EZ Fare!" with the date and time.

"Just the toll syncing with my phone," Delon said.

When Bryn had driven through the toll several hours

earlier, she had not heard the chime, as she obviously didn't have Delon's phone. But she'd passed through the toll because of the EZ Fare placard hanging on his rearview mirror. Not wanting Delon to see her intently examining his screen, she returned the phone to the holder.

As she hadn't yet contacted her editor, she decided to stop stalling. She opened her email and sent him a message: "Sorry, Evan. Still sick. This virus is the worst! Will definitely be back on Monday."

Then she cast a glance over her emails. Her eye immediately went to the thread with the subject line "From City Daily" that she'd written to yourpal12345:

Hello Bryn,
What no thank you? Isn't that what you wanted?
A pal

Hi, did you have any information for me? I'd like to hear what you have to say. It's completely confidential and anonymous.

The person had written back:

Strange game you're playing, Bryn. I did you a huge favor, didn't I? I did it at my own risk. Why no thank you?
Your pal

"Delon," she said urgently. "I got another message from that anonymous account."

She read the latest one to him.

"What's that supposed to mean?" he muttered, side-eyeing her phone while trying to keep watch on the road.

"Did me a huge favor…" she breathed.

Her stomach dropped. Exactly the feeling you'd get on a Ferris wheel as it plunged from its high point.

She read it again. One line leaped out from the rest:

I did it at my own risk.

"Could this not be Jules but rather someone who—who hurt Jules for me?"

"*For* you? What are you talking about?"

"Someone who thought I might want Jules out of the way."

She tried to think what person might harm Jules because they thought Bryn wanted her harmed. Very few people knew about Bryn's affair with Jules' husband: Delon himself, Gilda, Andy Kroll, and, recently, Amika.

As for who might know of Bryn's deep feelings of inferiority when it came to Jules, she could think of only herself. And, as of an hour ago, Delon. Perhaps a few long-ago friends from school who'd heard her make various snipes.

Of course, Jules gets picked Homecoming Queen, did you ever think it could have been anyone else?

Jules is voted "Most Beautiful of All Time"? Really? More beautiful than Marilyn Monroe? I don't think so.

No, that isn't my house. I live out back. Jules lives in the castle. She's the princess, I'm the troll, haven't you heard?

But which of these old school friends would care

enough about Bryn's adolescent peevishness to wait more than a decade, then hunt Jules down and kill her?

None of them. Then she remembered.

Wyatt.

They'd broken up right after Thanksgiving Day. About a month before she started sleeping with Delon.

Their last argument. She and Wyatt had gone to dinner at Jules' and Delon's brownstone. Jules had catered the event from one of the best gourmet shops in Brooklyn. Some of her impeccably dressed fashion friends had been there, holiday orphans.

Bryn had drunk too much wine. She couldn't stop herself from stealing long glances at Delon, devastated by how handsome he looked and disappointed that he'd been seated on the opposite end of the table.

Nervous that Jules and Wyatt would pick up on her feelings, she drank to tamp down her paranoia. Instead, the booze had only redirected it. She became convinced that Wyatt was attracted to Jules. He probably was. What heterosexual man wasn't?

But it was nothing he was ever going to act on. So why had she lit into him when they got back to her studio, yelling at him as she'd been halfway through brushing her teeth, toothpaste drizzling onto her chin?

You were eye-fucking her all night. It was so obvious. And right in front of her husband!

It had been Bryn doing the eye-fucking that night but she could scarcely allow herself to admit that. Nor was it the first time Bryn had lashed out at the poor man with one insecurity or another. Growing up without a father had left her with a permanent disability in the heart. A disability she didn't fully understand or know how to fix.

Wyatt had finally had enough. He'd slept over that night (no makeup sex) but the next day broke up with her by text, then blocked her. They had been dating for six months and she'd started to think he was the one. Her "Fabian."

She'd also started to think, more and more, about having sex with Delon. So much so that having sex with Wyatt had started to feel... *not right*. Much easier to accuse her boyfriend of harboring an attraction to her cousin—a woman he'd never met before the previous night. Much easier to push him into initiating a breakup.

Nevertheless, the breakup had crushed her. Especially when she'd sobered up and realized how out of line she'd been. She'd pushed a good man away. Would she always push the good men away? It wasn't her fault. She didn't know how to be around a good man. She never had before.

Could Wyatt have decided to get rid of Jules in a perverse attempt to please Bryn, alleviate her insecurities? She snorted aloud at the absurdity of her imagination. Wyatt hadn't contacted her since their split. The odds of him trying to get into Bryn's good graces by committing murder were... less than zero.

"Wait a second!" Bryn gasped, seizing the door handle as if ready to leap onto the highway. "Could my mom have hurt Jules?"

Jess might resent her sister Jacqueline as much as Bryn resented Jules. It couldn't be easy living in the guest house while her older sister lives in the Colonial with her wealthy, devoted husband, has a successful real estate business, and gets a perfect daughter. Bryn's mom might have decided to take away the thing that Jacqueline treasured most: Jules.

"Your mother?" Delon took his eyes off the road for long enough that Bryn pointed at the windshield, wanting him to pay attention. "What the hell are you talking about?" he demanded.

Bryn slapped her forehead, as if these perverse, intrusive thoughts could be halted by physical force.

"Nothing," she said. "I don't know what I'm thinking. My mom can barely get through a day. There's no way she could manage to get upstate and kill someone. And then taunt me about it. Forget her being not that diabolical, she's just not that competent!"

"Try not to lose your mind, Bryn," Delon sighed. "We've got enough problems."

With a shaky hand, she typed back to yourpal1234:

I promise you I'm not playing a game. Can you please be more specific as to what you did for me? Because I'm lost.

Yours truly,

Bryn Bastid

Chapter Eighteen

*B*ryn noticed Andy Kroll right away. He was sitting at the bar. There were only two other people at it. This wasn't a partying town.

"Strange you're sitting here," she said, coming up behind Andy.

"Is it?" he asked nonchalantly, as if he had been expecting her. He kept his eye on another basketball game that played silently on the television above the bar.

"I thought you'd be looking for Jules."

He turned halfway and smirked a little. "How do you know I'm not?"

"I don't see her across the bar." Bryn returned his smile with a small, tight one of her own.

"Let me explain, Ms. Bastid," he said, with his slightly gruff and condescending delivery. "There are many ways to search for someone. There's your way, which I gather involves lots of alone time with Mr. Callais. And there's my way, which involves having a Chivas and watching the Knicks. Ooh!" he grunted, pulling a fist as something happened in the game that earned his approval.

When the excitement passed, he said, "Both of our ways might seem a little odd to the casual observer, but perhaps we have our reasons, right?"

He placed his glass to his lips. Bryn could smell its potent contents from where she stood.

By now, she had a good sense that although Andy Kroll did an excellent job at seeming as if he wasn't paying attention to anything, in reality, he was picking up every scent and sound within a twenty-mile radius.

"Why didn't you tell Gilda that Jules is missing?" she asked.

"Why didn't you?" he returned, raising a brow.

She said nothing and walked away, asking the hostess to give her a booth. Within a minute, Delon slid across from her. He'd brought their belongings up to his room, which they were going to share. He'd packed a few more days' worth of clothes, and Bryn had retrieved a pair of leggings and two turtlenecks out of Jules' drawers, and grabbed a coat. The leggings were stretchy enough that Bryn could fit into them. The coat was one that Jules never wore. Bryn couldn't bring herself to take any of her cousin's favorites.

The turtlenecks were so she could stop wearing the Hermès scarf to cover the hickey, though it had already faded to about half its purple garishness.

It certainly looked terrible that they were sharing a room, something the camera would record, and the inn staff could testify to. And her brain was almost on fire with the warring emotions she had about sharing a bed with Delon every night. But she saw no other way to afford to stay in town, and she wasn't up to the task of sleeping in his tiny car.

At this point, there was a certain amount of resignation accompanying her decisions. It felt inevitable that they would be arrested and, eventually, fighting for their lives in a courtroom. The only thing to do was to keep pushing forward, trying to find Jules, and clinging to the hope that her disappearance was all an elaborate *fuck you* on her part.

Bryn retrieved *A Woman Stands Alone* from her backpack and placed the novel between them on the table.

"Gilda gave it to me," she said.

"You're not really going to keep that out while we eat, are you?" he asked, looking as if the book might bare its teeth at him.

"From the description, Jules may have known about us. I feel like Gilda wrote the book but Jules suggested the plotline."

"Why are you saying she knew about us?"

"Because this is about Fabian cheating on Claire with the nanny. Jules made the nanny sound like me. Similar name. Grew up with a single mother and didn't know her father. That kind of thing."

Bryn flashed to what was inside of her phone—that app and whatever it could reveal. But she quickly swooped it from her thoughts, as she had trained herself to do over the past several months.

The waitress came over and took their orders.

"By the way," Bryn said once the waitress had departed. "Andy Kroll is at the bar."

Delon turned and glared in his direction. "Why doesn't he go look for Jules?" he said rather loudly, probably hoping Andy would hear him. If the detective did, he gave no hint of it, still transfixed by the basketball game.

"He claims he is," Bryn said. "I suspect what he's really doing is watching us."

For the rest of the meal, she didn't mention Andy Kroll, Jules, or anything that wasn't strictly small talk, certain the detective had eyes in the back of his head and those eyes could read lips.

* * *

LATER IN BED, she skimmed through *A Woman Stands Alone* trying to grasp the major plot points.

Claire Bonnet de Rambouillet had taken pity on a friend's 19-year-old daughter, Gwen, who couldn't get a job after a shoplifting arrest. Claire hires her as a summer nanny to her three-year-old son, Duke, while Claire goes to work for a famous designer, clearly based on Thom King.

Why Claire would hire a troubled young woman fresh off an arrest to care for a toddler was a bit of a mystery. To keep the plot going, Bryn supposed. Although she could see Jules doing the same thing. Because life had always been good to Jules, she tended to see the best in people.

Gwen is almost immediately enamored with Claire's husband. Fabian treats the young woman cavalierly, and

Claire—being a real dumbass sometimes—encourages her husband to spend more time with the nanny, to "get to know her." Claire, with her perfect looks and naive manner, doesn't peg scrappy Gwen as any kind of threat.

Almost against her will, Bryn found herself fully immersed in the storyline and invested in what was going to happen. And, despite feeling that Gwen was at least partially based on her, she sympathized with the heroine, and kept hoping that Claire would wake up and kick the nanny out of the brownstone.

Delon, who'd been lying silently and patiently beside her all this time, finally said, "Is it us?"

"Hard to tell," she said, stifling the urge to shush him. She was getting to a good scene. "There are parts of it that feel that way—but, in other ways, it's not us at all. The nanny, Gwen, is basically throwing herself at Fabian and I never did that. At least not that I'm aware of."

"I'm not aware of it either."

"And Claire takes every opportunity to remind Gwen how much she's helping her. Gwen was arrested, so she can't get a job. Every few pages, Claire says something to the effect of, 'You'd be nowhere without me.'" Bryn furrowed her brows. "I mean, that's not me. I've certainly never been arrested. At least not yet. I've always worked as much as Jules, even more. I might have stayed in your brownstone for a few months but it's not like she ever helped me financially or anything."

The character of Claire was starting to remind Bryn of her aunt, Jacqueline. Bryn had once overheard her aunt and mother in the guest house kitchen. Jacqueline had said to her younger sister, "I've done everything I can for you, haven't I? Tell me one thing I haven't done for you. I told you I'd take care of things but you—"

Bryn had heard her mother crying, so Bryn quietly about-faced and whisked out the front door without them realizing she'd entered.

"Anyway," she said, "like a lot of things, I guess it's a merging of fact and fiction."

Delon reached over, plucked the book out of her hands, and dropped it over his side of the bed.

"Merge with me, Gwen," he said, pulling her towards him.

Chapter Nineteen

*T*he next morning, they grabbed to-go coffee at the one coffee shop within walking distance, then headed to the house where Delon had noticed a camera attached to its porch awning.

The house was a stone's throw from the main drag, down an idyllic side street named Birch Lane. It was a small Craftsman with square white columns holding up a modest porch with brick detailing and beige trim. The kind of house that makes you go "Oooh!" in a little squeal. Bryn might have done this herself if she wasn't hunting for her missing cousin.

As the pair approached, Delon drew her attention to the long, white camera pointed down on its arched entry.

"It's close enough to Main Street that it could have caught her walking by," he said.

Joe's Deli was only a couple of blocks away. And the little house was on the same side of the street where

Jules had last been seen walking. It may have indeed captured her as she passed.

The camera may have also recorded the red car that sped by mere minutes later. Bryn wondered why Delon would be willing to risk asking about videotape that could have his car on it. Did this prove it wasn't him who'd driven past? Or did he assume that a camera positioned this far from the street could not have picked up his Peugeot? He'd been the one to mention the camera to Bryn. If he'd thought there was any chance his car was caught on its footage, why would he even bring it to her attention?

"Bryn?" he asked, pulling her out of her ruminations.

"Yes, let's go," she said.

* * *

At first, it seemed no one was going to answer the doorbell. Bryn had a sense of relief about that. If no one answered, she could pretend they'd seen the video and there was nothing noteworthy on it, nothing for them to report to the police.

And nothing that would further solidify her intermittent suspicions that it was none other than Delon who was responsible for his wife's disappearance.

But soon, a tiny woman's face appeared at the gap in the door. She looked at least eighty years old. That's all Bryn could determine because the woman kept the door practically shut. Behind her, a small dog emitted a loud stream of yapping.

"Excuse me!" Bryn low-shouted over the dog's noise. "So sorry to bother you! We need to ask you a question about your camera!"

The tiny lady blinked rapidly, then said, "*Qué deseas?*"

Bryn looked to Delon, hoping his being European might mean he understood Spanish. But she could tell he didn't.

"*Buenos dias,*" Bryn said, scrounging in her memory for her high school Spanish. "*Ayuda, por favor?*"

The woman stared at her expectedly, but Bryn realized she had no more of the language in her.

"*Hablas Inglés?*" Delon contributed.

The woman shook her head no. When the pair stood silently, hoping something about the situation would correct itself, the woman flicked her small, wrinkled hand at them, then shut the door. The dog yapped for a few more rounds before quieting.

"So much for that," Bryn said.

The pair walked back down the patio, sipping their coffees, heading back to Main Street.

"Hey!" someone called.

The pair stopped and turned. A teenage boy was in the yard of the home. He loped in their direction, a spade in one hand. He'd apparently been gardening.

"That's my grandmother," he said. "She doesn't speak English very well. You all selling something?"

He looked about fifteen and was of medium height, with overgrown dark-brown hair, and distinct eyebrows that curved so gracefully over his brow bone that Bryn unwittingly wondered if he shaped them.

"No," she said, pointing at the camera. "We're searching for a woman and hoped your grandmother could show us video from her porch camera. The woman would have walked very close to this house."

"Oh yeah?" The teen looked mildly intrigued. "The camera doesn't work though. It's fake. Just there to scare off porch pirates. Though it doesn't." He rubbed his nose with his flannel sleeve. "Who you looking for?"

"My wife," Delon said.

"Your wife?" The teen almost laughed, then, noting the serious expressions in front of him, grew appropriately somber. "I mean... so... You can't find her or something like that? Did you call her?"

"Of course we called her," Delon said brusquely.

Bryn put her hand on his arm in a warning gesture.

"Her phone died," Bryn explained. "The last I saw her was Sunday, early evening. She left that small cafe on Main. I'm still looking for her."

"Woah," the teen said. "That's wild."

"So you can see why I wanted to have a look at your grandmother's footage. I didn't realize the camera was fake."

The teen appeared in deep thought for a few moments, then offered, "It's not that bad blonde, is it?"

"Bad blonde?"

"Bad. *Fine. Hot.*"

"What?" Bryn yelped. "Yes! She's blonde and very bad. Carrying a red tote bag. Did you see her?"

The teen shrugged. "I think so. Don't see girls like

that around here too much. I walked out of Joe's and she went right by me. I was coming here, so I was behind her. Wasn't following her but, you know, noticed her." He glanced at Delon. "Bro, that's your wife?" He sounded a little awestruck.

"Did you notice anything about her?" Bryn asked. "Did she look nervous? Did she make a call? Anything."

The teen held the spade to his hip and stared off into the solid blue sky. "She stopped at the corner—" He pointed. "I remember because I had to walk right by her. Oh, and she asked me what time it was."

"She did?" Bryn blurted.

"Yeah, that's right, it was six-something. Six-twenty, I wanna say. So, I told her the time."

"She didn't ask to use your phone or anything?"

He shook his head. "Oh, wait!" His eyes grew bright with a retrieved memory. "I walked away but then kind of turned around 'cause, uh…" He peeped at Delon with a slightly guilty expression. "You know, just to make sure she was okay… Anyway, this car drove up—"

"Car?" Bryn almost shrieked.

"Yeah, uh, the car stopped. And she got in."

"She got in a car?!" In her excitement, Bryn rushed forward until she was only a couple of feet from the teenager. She twisted around to peer at Delon. He stood utterly still, as if he'd been hit on the head.

"Can you describe the car?" Bryn asked. She realized she'd lowered her voice, as if she and the teen were about to share private information.

"Mmmm… It was dark by then. No street lights here."

"Please. Think."

The kid rolled his eyes up to the cloudless blue sky, then brought his flannel sleeve to his nose again. "Nah, don't remember. Just a regular car, I guess."

"Color?" Bryn said under her breath.

"Like I said, it was night by then. Dark color, I guess. Black, maybe."

Bryn realized her heart rate had skyrocketed. And the moment the boy said, "Black, maybe," it slowed a little.

He had not said "red."

"Did she get in willingly?" Delon asked from behind Bryn.

"Willingly?" The teen looked puzzled.

"Of her own accord? Her own volition?"

The teen appeared even more perplexed.

"He means, did you see anyone force her into the car?" Bryn said.

"I don't think so." The teen seemed rattled by this new line of questioning. "I didn't want to seem like I was checking her out—'cause, like, I totally wasn't—so I didn't keep watching."

"Can you describe the person driving?" Delon asked.

"'Fraid not, bro. Too dark by then."

Delon stalked forward and thrust out one of his business cards. The teen took it warily.

"What's your name?" Delon asked.

"Javier."

"Javier, that's my contact. If you think of anything

else, will you please call me? No matter how small it is. Call me any time. Or text. But I prefer a call."

"No problem," the teen said.

The pair began to walk away. Bryn got the distinct feeling even if Javier did remember something later on, they would never hear from him. He was a teenager and it was out of sight, out of mind. Plus, he'd probably never made a phone call in his life.

"Hey!" the teen called.

They instantly stopped and turned.

"You think she's alright?" he asked.

"We think so!" Bryn called back. "We hope so, anyway."

"That's good." Javier smiled, then offered, more shyly, "She's really pretty."

He gave a thumbs up to Delon.

BRYN WAS in a state of shock. They now had a stunning piece of information, yet she wasn't sure whether to classify it as good or bad information. Delon, silently walking beside her, seemed equally as stupefied.

"It sounds like she got into a car service," she said. "The waiter said he thought she made a call. It must have been to a taxi company."

"Then where is she?"

The sidewalk narrowed as a broad tree took up most of one side. Bryn allowed Delon to go first and he sped ahead. She murmured, basically to herself, "I hope *I* never go missing. No one will remember seeing *me*."

Delon halted and turned, staring down at her. His nostrils were practically flaring.

"I don't have time to console you and soothe your ego, Bryn," he said. "My wife got into a car with someone and disappeared."

The way he possessively said *my wife*—as if he were the perfect, devoted husband—raked her last nerve.

"*Your* wife," she sneered. "Funny how you don't remember having a wife when you're busy fucking me!"

A woman happened to pass by at that exact moment and shot them a disapproving look, then continued on her way.

"Why don't you shout it to the world?" Delon said, striding ahead of her down the sidewalk. "Get a bull-horn, Bryn. Call all your friends. Hell, write a news story about it."

"I'm not asking you to console me," she said, trying to keep pace with him. "I'm only saying it's lucky that the world values the way she looks. People remember her, so that will help us find her. Even that teen who probably spends ninety-percent of his time staring into his phone remembered her. If she was any other color, or older, or unattractive, or heavy, or—"

He halted again. This time, he was in full-on glowering mode. "Yes, I know. Or if she were *you*. You know what? If I didn't know better, I'd think you *did* do something to her."

"Yeah, well, that goes for me too!" she countered as

he stalked away and eventually disappeared behind several people staring into a vintage store window.

Chapter Twenty

*B*ryn sat in the small park with the Revolutionary War statue, finishing her cold coffee. She was wrapped in one of Jules' coats, which she'd found in the walk-in closet. There had been about ten of them, none of which Bryn recognized, as Jules tended to stick with a couple of favorites.

This coat was black and knee-length with a classic silhouette, and slightly oversized, even on Bryn. It must have been gigantic on Jules. The kind of coat anyone else would have looked ridiculous in, but Jules would have made work perfectly.

The fact that a teenager reported seeing Jules get into a car of her own accord filled Bryn with conflicting emotions. On the one hand, it seemed to indicate that Jules was alive.

On the other hand, it didn't. It made no sense that she would get into a car and not call Delon or Bryn to let them know where she was. Which intensified the chances that she had gotten into a car with the wrong person.

But if Jules had entered the car willingly, it certainly narrowed the suspects. The driver was either a hired one or someone Jules knew. Bryn's mind inexorably turned to Delon and the red car that drove past Jules mere minutes after she walked by the deli. Sure, Javier thought the car Jules got into was a dark color and not red. But as he'd said, there are no street lights on his small side street. And how many people correctly remember the colors of cars they see for only an instant, anyway?

Then there was Gilda. Bryn had no idea the color of the agent's car, but Jules would have very likely gotten into it. The agent could have told Jules she'd seen pictures of Hudson Hollow on Jules' social media, and driven up to apologize for their fight. Gilda would want to make peace before the big Y event. And as Jules' phone had died, the agent could truthfully say she couldn't reach her client.

Gilda may not have even planned to harm Jules that day, but once Jules was in the car, they got into another argument, and…

And what? It was unlikely that the older woman could overpower Jules. But given that Gilda had the element of surprise, and perhaps a weapon…

Bryn cringed and tossed her coffee cup in a nearby garbage can. She couldn't let her mind go down that road. And yet it was preferable to imagine that Jules had died quickly and painlessly, with a bonk on the head from something heavy, than that she was currently somewhere being abused by a stranger.

Bryn ambled down the sidewalk, in the opposite direction that would take her to the inn. She wasn't ready to see Delon again, ashamed that her first reaction to hearing about Jules getting into a car was to once more express her jealousy. Though she wouldn't exactly classify her outburst as jealousy. It was more like aggravation with the unfairness of it all.

It wouldn't be long before Jules too was relegated to the land of the invisible, aged out of her beauty and fertility and, thus, so far as the patriarchy was concerned, not worth noticing if she got into a car or not.

Bryn's phone jangled. With a fumbling hand she retrieved it from her deep coat pocket, imagining that "Babe" would appear on her cell screen.

The anticipation made her heart spasm with a disturbing mixture of euphoria that this nightmare would be over, and dread that she'd revert to her former life—the one where she constantly felt inferior.

And a small fissure had opened onto an imaginary alternative world in which Delon wasn't married. She'd been staring into that fissure, visiting that glimpsed world, more than she wanted to admit. To have the sight of it shut to her was something she didn't want to think about.

Right then she knew. What had been stopping her. What had really been stopping her from going to the police.

They might find Jules.

No, no, no.

She firmly connected her fist with her forehead, attempting to physically push that shameless thought out of her mind.

On the phone, instead of "Babe," the screen displayed the name "Evan Riptoe."

Shit.

Passing an alleyway between two stores, she ducked into it, wanting to minimize street noise. Years of being conditioned to pick up when her editor called overrode the portion of her brain that suggested she call him back once she was in the quiet of her hotel room.

"Hel-loo?" she greeted, straining to sound unwell but recovering.

"Hey, Bastid."

Evan called everyone by their last names, thinking it made him sound movie-newsroom. He'd never slipped up and called her "Bastard."

"How're you feeling?" he asked.

"Better," she said, trying to sound semi-hoarse. "I'll definitely return on Monday."

She pushed into the outer wall of a store, hoping to further muffle any street noise. Luckily, the small town road was empty.

"That's what I'm calling about," he said. "We won't need you in on Monday."

Bryn's heart plummeted into her feet. Like an elevator that had suddenly lost power. He was about to fire her. He'd figured out she wasn't really sick and thought she was having an unapproved mini-vacation.

"Oh?" she croaked.

"There's no pleasant way to put this," he said. "This morning, our publisher received a death threat."

Bryn perked up. Did she really hear that? She wasn't about to get fired?

"Because of the Melani investigation," he continued. "For everyone's safety, those of us working on it have been asked to stay home until police give the clear."

Police? Bryn almost snorted. They were probably the ones who'd made the death threat to begin with.

"You can work from home when you're feeling better," he said.

"Um, thanks," she said, still straining to make her voice sound slightly feeble. "Are we in any danger?"

"I don't think so but they wanted to take a precaution. The higher ups wouldn't show me the threat. I was only told I had to stay home. And I had to tell you, Amika, and Molly to do the same."

He paused, then said, "Maybe you want to hole up in your apartment for a few days, Bastid."

* * *

"We get the rest of the week off," Amika said. "If we're lucky, next, too."

"Yeah, I guess so. I'm kind of glad I'm up here and not home."

Bryn was on the payphone. It was the first place she went after speaking to Evan. At this point, she kept quarters on her.

"Tell me about it," Amika said. "I'm in the middle of packing. Headed to my friends in the Bronx for a few. This shit is way above my pay grade. Any luck with your cousin?"

"Sort of. We found a teenager who thinks he saw her get into a car."

"Oh wow," Amika breathed. "Could it have been her husband's car? The guy I'm sure you're still fucking?"

"Actually, the kid said the car was black. Delon's is red."

"Oh," Amika said, sounding disappointed.

Bryn didn't fill her friend in on how the teen had waffled over the car's color and finally settled on black, *maybe*.

"Then you're in the clear," she pronounced. "He's a liar and a cheater but probably not a killer."

"Amika, do you know of a way to get into someone's phone if it's password protected?"

"I'm sure there's a million ways."

"I mean quickly and easily."

"Christ on a stick, you want to get into his phone. You really do think he did it."

"No. I want proof he didn't. The phone will give it to me."

"How?"

Bryn pulled the mouthpiece tight to her face and darted her gaze up and down the quaint movie-set street, keeping watch for Delon.

"Because his phone syncs with his EZ Fare placard. It records every time he goes through a toll. It should have a record if he came up here the night she disappeared."

"Holy shit, you're right," Amika said. "But couldn't he have taken back roads? Or put his phone on airplane mode through the toll?"

"He could have, but he probably didn't."

She thought of Andy Kroll's *If people were that clever, my job would be a lot more difficult.*

"When I see he didn't come here until after I'd told him about Jules being missing, you can stop calling him a killer."

"I just said he's *probably not,* didn't I?" Amika huffed.

"But I can't think how to get into his phone."

"Girl, that's so basic. Everyone sets their phone to lock after a certain amount of time of not being used. The earliest is immediately, but no one sets it for that unless they're super paranoid. So, it usually locks after ten or fifteen minutes. You get him to unlock his phone, then you've got that amount of time to open it provided you can get him away from it."

Amika lowered her voice conspiratorially.

"I'm not saying I've done this—okay, I've done it— but morning is best. People wake up and unlock the phone to check email or whatever. Then they go take a shower."

"You're so devious and I love it," Bryn said. But she also knew Delon. He wasn't constantly checking his phone. In fact, he rarely did. Something was going to have to make him check the phone so he'd unlock it. "Now I really need you to help me."

"Bryn, I'll help you when you help yourself. Stay away from the guy."

"Jamaica, Queens," Bryn said lowly, teeth gritted.

A few months ago, Amika had been assigned to a story way out in the far-off neighborhood of Jamaica, Queens. That day was cold and raining, and she was crippled with a hangover from a date the night before. She'd begged Bryn to take her place—to take two subways and one bus to the middle of nowhere to check out an RV illegally parked on a tiny square of land in a nice neighborhood.

According to neighbors, the rusty RV and equally rusty man living in it had been there for two years, and no one would do anything about it. Bryn had used one of her days off and took the two-hour trip out to Queens, did all the reporting, then emailed her notes to Amika, who got the byline.

Goddamn it, her friend owed her.

"Okay," Amika sighed. "What do you need me to do?"

Bryn was a block from the inn when a man fell in step beside her.

Andy Kroll. It was like he came out of nowhere.

"Beautiful morning, ain't it?" he asked.

"Yeah, sure," she mumbled.

She had no idea how he was so fast and feather-footed. He wasn't a small man by any means. She glanced at his footwear but they were plain brown Oxfords, giving no indication how he could move so stealthily.

She stopped and looked at him. The clear, bright morning wasn't kind to his features or the deep crevices underneath his eyes. But now she saw that his irises, buried in pinkish folds of flesh, were a pretty light brown color.

"How is it that you follow people without them knowing?" she asked. "It's quite a skill."

"Easy enough," he said, grinning. "People can't see what's right in front of their faces."

That answer made her go silent for a moment. It seemed so devastatingly obvious. Then she remembered Jules yelling at him to stop following her on the night she vanished.

"Then how did Jules notice you that night?"

"I wanted her to see me. Let her know I was looking out for her."

Bryn refrained from retorting that he'd looked out for Jules so well that her cousin went missing on his watch. Best to not make an enemy of him. Andy stopped walking and thrust his arm in her direction. His hand didn't touch her but his intent was obviously to have her stop walking as well.

"Don't be afraid, okay?" he said. "Just keep off that social media like you have been. Terrible invention. In my day, you weren't supposed to let people know you weren't home because someone might rob you. Now no one can leave the house without announcing it to a thousand strangers. You should be safe up here and I'll keep an eye on you."

Bryn's jaw dropped. "You heard that phone call? With Evan?"

"No, but anyone who's blue or former blue knows your publisher got a threat this morning over the investigation. Which you're also working on."

Bryn didn't know much about her ultimate boss, the man so far up the masthead that many employees had no idea he controlled the paper: Sol Jaffe, the billionaire owner of *City Daily*.

Perhaps twice a year, he'd visit the newsroom, which was only one of hundreds in his media conglomeration. There would be an intense flurry of movement, heads turning and editors trailing, as he stalked to his glass-walled office. A couple days later, he'd be gone.

Those on the lower rung of the masthead, like Bryn, had never made direct eye contact with him, let alone spoken to him.

"Do you know who made the threat?" Bryn asked. "Was it Melani himself?"

The detective pursed his lips, looking amused. "I'm not that plugged in, I'm afraid. All I know for sure is it wasn't me."

The pair began walking again. Bryn figured she'd ask him what was on her mind since there was no television nearby and she had his full attention.

"Just tell me if you think I have something to do with Jules' disappearance," she said.

"I've learned to keep an open mind about everything," he replied vaguely.

"Then keep an open mind about the person who hired you." Bryn stopped and turned to face him again. "Gilda got into an argument with Jules a couple of weeks ago. It was so heated that Jules hasn't been to her office since. Did Gilda bother to tell you that? Have you considered that it was her writing those letters?"

He shrugged in such a way that Bryn couldn't tell if he was saying yes or no. He was too cagey to reveal anything that he didn't want to reveal.

She decided not to alert Andy to the teenager who saw Jules get into a car. If it was Gilda who'd picked up Jules, Bryn didn't know what the detective might do. Perhaps he'd try to cover up for the woman paying his salary. Perhaps Andy was even capable of getting rid of the teenage witness, as well as the people to whom the teen had told what he'd seen—none other than herself and Delon.

"I know it looks bad that I'm sleeping with him," she said, unable to bring herself to say Delon's name. "I'm very aware of that. He is, too."

"It doesn't look great, I have to agree with you there," Andy said.

"But we didn't hurt Jules. In fact, we love her. I know no one will understand that."

Why did people assume if two people were having sex, they were in love? And if they were sexually betraying someone else, that person *wasn't* loved? Sex wasn't the be-all-end-all calibrator of love. Far from it.

"Not many would understand it, gotta agree with you there, too," he said, giving his one shoulder *oh-well-*

what-can-you-do shrug. "We're agreeing on a lot this morning."

"And you're watching us, aren't you? This is your way of finding Jules."

He glanced at the sidewalk and made a motion as if he might spit on it, then, seeming to remember he had company, stopped himself.

"I have lots of ways of doing lots of things," he said, in his usual elliptical fashion. "You ever think about becoming a detective? You might be pretty good at it. Most of it is just allowing people to only see what they want to see."

"I want to find my cousin," she said, ignoring his dig that duplicity came naturally to her. "I know people—I know *you*—won't believe me, but that's the truth. Maybe, with all your powers of detection, you can see the truth when it's in front of you."

She picked up her stride into the inn's lobby, hoping to get through the closing doors of the elevator before Andy Kroll's impressive light-footedness guaranteed he'd be taking the ride with her.

Chapter Twenty-One

*I*n the room, she saw Delon standing next to the bed, folding a black sweater and layering it inside of his travel bag.

"What are you doing?" she asked.

"I'm going to the police so I figured I might as well pack up my things."

"Wait, wait," she blurted, rushing forward. "*You* get to make this decision? This affects me too, you know."

"My wife got into a car and disappeared," he said dully.

"Yes, Delon, I heard that. And we wouldn't have found out that information if we'd been in jail."

He ignored her and kept packing.

"And you've spent all this time telling me we can't go to the police, so now you don't get to unilaterally decide when we do."

He glided into the bathroom, gathering his few items —toothbrush, tube of toothpaste, razor—and placing them in his small leather toiletry bag.

"Delon!" she rapped out, standing in the bathroom doorway. "Listen to me. I can't walk into a police station right now. My big boss got a death threat this morning —probably from someone inside the police force. Maybe even the police commissioner himself."

"What's that got to do with you?" he murmured.

"Because I'm working on the case that triggered the threat."

"Bryn," he said, brushing past her. "That's the NYPD. These are small town cops."

"Yes, and we live in the city. When these small town cops begin investigating us, they'll look into us down there. So, the NYPD will get involved."

As he continued to gather his things, she threw out, "For instance, they'll check if you came up here the night Jules disappeared. Like that toll that you have to go through. That's in the city limits and they'll check what time you went through it."

She watched as the movement of his hands inside his travel bag instantly stopped.

"I passed the toll when she didn't come home," he said.

"I know. But they're going to look into it. Even Andy said that you and I will become the main focus of the investigation. Even if we tell them about a teenager saying she got into a car, the first thing they'll want to find out is if it was you driving the car. It's always the husband, remember?"

"It certainly wasn't me driving," he said, staring into his bag as if he was deeply contemplating its sparse contents. Then he slowly withdrew his hands from the bag, walked to the window, and stared down to the street.

"Well, I wouldn't want to put you in danger," he said. "One missing woman is enough."

"Let's give it until Friday night. That's only tomorrow. If she doesn't show up at the Y event, we'll have to report her missing, anyway."

"Yes, I suppose you're right," he said.

"Meanwhile, we can hope that the car she got into was a car service and she's hiding out somewhere until she makes her big appearance at the event. This was all to send us a message. Not only to you and me, but to Gilda."

"It's quite a message," he said, not taking his eyes off the window.

* * *

SHE HAD to get into Delon's phone. Something about how he'd instantly stopped the movement of his hands when she mentioned the toll reignited her intermittent suspicions. But he couldn't be stupid enough to cross a toll on his way to murder his wife, could he? A toll that was recording him inside his phone?

If people were that clever, my job would be a lot more difficult.

What if he hadn't come up here to murder his wife, but to talk to her about the pregnancy news she'd surprised him with that morning? He'd tried to call her, but as her phone had died, he kept going straight to voicemail.

But why? Why would he want to speak with her so urgently that he drove here rather than wait until she returned home?

Could he have decided to surprise her—have a little baby celebration? Maybe he'd bought flowers or a piece of jewelry for her. Or simply decided to offer her—and presumably Bryn, too—a ride home rather than have her take the train in her new "delicate" condition.

Or maybe… he feared what Bryn would do or say if Jules shared her pregnancy news. So he'd driven up, passed through the toll, then got Bryn's call about Jules being missing. Given that the two of them had been having an affair, he became paranoid and decided to pretend he hadn't been here all along.

It was all pretty far-fetched. If Delon had been in Hudson Hollow at the time of Jules' disappearance, and he had nothing to do with that disappearance, he would have just thought there was some miscommunication between Jules and Bryn. The logical thing to do would have been to tell Bryn that he was already in town and explain why.

Bryn sat inside of the cafe where Jules had last been seen. That had been only four days ago but it already felt like forever. Tomorrow night was Jules' Y event. Would she appear at it, eyes glinting with satisfaction that she'd sent Bryn and Delon into hysteria? And what would Gilda do? If she had nothing to do with Jules' disappearance, she'd certainly call the police when Jules failed to show up. But what if she *did* have something to do with it, what would she do then?

Bryn glanced around the small cafe. She didn't see

the rude server nor the young hostess, Soren. But Bryn had the strong, irrational sense that if she walked into the back garden, she'd find Jules sitting at the same table where they'd eaten on Sunday.

Told ya, worry wart.

Her phone rang. When she looked at the screen, her breath stopped in her chest.

Jacqueline.

Her aunt almost never called her. In fact, her aunt was only a contact in Bryn's phone because they occasionally texted each other on birthdays or holidays. Bryn debated whether to pick up and decided that not picking up would cause Jacqueline to go into full panic mode.

Bryn had no story prepared and didn't know how she could placate Jules' mother. Jacqueline and Jules had a relationship unlike the one Bryn had with her own mother. The pair spoke frequently, sometimes daily. Jules did things like confer with "Mommy" over various life decisions. Bryn couldn't imagine calling up Jess and asking for life advice.

"Hi, Jackie," Bryn answered.

"Hello, Bryn." Jacqueline's voice was its usual combination of gooey sweetness with hostility lurking just under the surface. But like a dog who could detect a silent whistle, no one but Bryn could hear this ripple of hostility.

She'd once asked her cousin, "Does your mom not like me for some reason?"

Jules had looked at Bryn like she'd lost her mind.

Perhaps Jacqueline felt Bryn was the cause of her younger sister Jess' inability to get her life in order.

Bryn's existence was also why Jacqueline was saddled with having to take care of Jess.

"I'm sorry to bother you," Jacqueline said. "But I haven't been able to reach Jules. Her father and I—" She always said "her father" rather than using his name, Rich. It was very annoying. "—want to come for that book thing she has on Friday. But he's stressed about finding parking. I thought she might have some suggestions for us."

"I can have her send you some information," Bryn said, her heart thumping as she wondered from one second to the next what to say. "Sorry she didn't get back to you, she's been prepping for the event and is super busy."

"I didn't expect we would have a marathon phone session, only that she'd return my call. She's never not returned a call."

"I know, but she's so full of nerves right now," Bryn said, impressed with how fast her brain was working. "She didn't get back to me either, so I finally came to her place. She's working constantly preparing for the event."

"I realize, Bryn," Jacqueline said, sounding slightly irritated, as if Bryn was responsible for Jules going incommunicado. "But to not return my calls… that's not like her."

"Well, this is a very big event. Very big. Her whole career hinges on it."

"Would you please tell her to at least send me a text message? So that I don't report her missing?"

"Ha, sure I will," Bryn said, laughing.

Jacqueline did not laugh.

* * *

BRYN WAS SCREWED.

Not only was Jacqueline going to get suspicious when she didn't hear from Jules within the next few hours, but she would eventually tell police that Bryn had blatantly lied during the phone call, thus making Bryn appear even guiltier.

She stared at the food on her plate. A Florentine souffle omelet. She couldn't take one bite of it. She needed to get back to Delon and warn him that Jacqueline was likely going to call him as well, if she hadn't already.

Her aunt was fairly icy to Delon. Even with his elegant accent, boarding school education, and actual estate in Burgundy, Jacqueline probably thought he wasn't good enough for her daughter. No doubt she'd imagined Jules marrying a surgeon or CEO, not some French guy with dubious employment credentials.

To be fair, that's what Bryn had thought about him when she'd first met him, too. Jules had gushed about Delon so extravagantly that Bryn had been expecting the most handsome, most charming, most *everything* man in the world.

But she'd found him rather standoffish and pompous. He occasionally made snide comments about Americans. He was so cryptic about what he did for work that Bryn suspected he did nothing. Sure, he was handsome. But looks faded. You couldn't marry a man based on that.

Just look at your father, Jules, she'd been tempted to tell her cousin. Rich Aston had been undeniably good-looking in his youth, with long blonde curls, like a surfer. Now in his late fifties, he was basically bald, had a bowling-ball paunch from too many expensive meals, and a forehead bisected with crevices from too much glowering over legal documents. Of course, Bryn never said this to her cousin.

Then, some kind of alchemy began to happen in regards to Bryn's feelings about Delon. She noticed that he had a dry, sly sense of humor. And he wasn't aloof so much as absorbing a conversation and weighing whether to contribute to it. What Bryn had taken as standoffishness was, in fact, the rare man who didn't need to constantly interject his opinion.

She did wonder why Jules and Delon didn't have children yet. Sure, the couple had married somewhat young. Jules had been 23 and Delon 26. Perhaps they were waiting until they were older. But given that Jules had always said she wanted four kids, it seemed like they would have produced at least one of them while still in their twenties.

This isn't the kind of thing you ask someone about. Not even your best friend. However, once, when she and Jules were at a bar without him and had put back several glasses of wine between them, Bryn had barreled into the topic. This was long before she'd been having an affair with Delon. Long before the idea had occurred to her.

"When we gonna get some little Juleses and Delons running around?" she'd yelled over the solid wall of bar noise. "Those kids are gonna be hotties."

Jules' face, which moments before had been luminous with the wine, the good cheer, and the flattering lighting, had suddenly changed. Her smile had frozen and her pale-blue eyes glistened.

Bryn had felt terrible. She was still in her mid-twenties and had scant access to diplomacy when she was inebriated. It hadn't occurred to her that the couple might be having trouble conceiving. They were both so glowing with health and vitality. It seemed as if they could look at each other and spontaneously produce a fetus.

Bryn had been about to stammer an apology when Jules' expression rearranged itself. She became herself again. Smiling, happy. The golden girl.

"We haven't tried seriously yet," she'd said, playfully. "We're having too much fun. But you know what? I think we're going to try soon. Very soon."

"Maybe tonight," Bryn had said, clinking Jules' wine glass with her own.

A crew of alpha males had surrounded them and tried to impress with tales of deals closed and slopes skied. But when the men spoke to Bryn, she noticed the slight shift of their bodies as they subtly turned toward Jules, like plants rotating toward the sun.

* * *

BRYN WAS FILLING in her credit card slip and hoping that it wouldn't be declined when she heard, "Five percent?"

Startled, she looked toward the male voice. The handsome but rude waiter was standing next to her table. He was wearing jeans and a dark hoodie, a long laundry bag slung over his shoulder, as if he was coming in for his shift, carrying his server uniform.

For a few merciful seconds, his comment made no sense to her. Then she got it. Her nervous reaction was to laugh.

"Ha, um, no. Twenty."

"Good to know," he said.

He smiled. He had a nice smile. Bryn hadn't seen it directed at her before. It had been directed to Jules, but not to her. Without Jules around, people actually saw her.

"Any luck with your friend?" he asked.

"Um, no. But we think she's okay. Just off thinking. Ah, things are a bit complicated."

"I see. I'm Derek, by the way."

"Bryn."

As he seemed much more approachable than the last two times she'd seen him, she blundered ahead.

"Hey, I'm sorry about that tip. It's that I'm kind of broke these days. That's no excuse."

He shrugged. "Don't worry about it. I was having a bad night."

"No, it's…" She sighed and stared at the credit card slip as if deciphering hieroglyphics. "That's not all true," she mumbled. "The real reason I did that is because you were paying attention to my friend and not to me. I was being vindictive."

After a few heavily-awkward seconds, she peeped up at him. He had a slightly stunned expression on his face. People didn't generally admit to such embarrassments.

"I apologize," she said. This time, her voice was clear, no mumbling.

"Really, it's fine. I just hope you find her."

"I do, too."

They both said nothing for several more seconds, digesting her confession. But there was a part of her that was relieved. The admission had opened a door in her psyche—one that was ancient, creaky, and mold-infested —and let in some much-needed rays of purifying light.

"Is she from England?" Derek asked. "Britain?"

"No. Her husband is French. But she's American."

He looked a little confused, then glanced up as a couple entered the cafe. He waved at them, smiling affably, and indicated they should take any table they wanted.

"Why do you ask?" Bryn said.

"Oh, I don't know. Just the way she said, 'loo' instead of bathroom. I almost sent her to the kitchen, because our dishwasher's name is Lou."

"What? When did this happen?" Bryn sat up straight.

"When she came inside asking to use the bathroom. While you were both in the garden."

Bryn furrowed her brows, digging into her memory of their time in the garden.

I'm going to ask for the check, Jules had said after they'd finished eating and determined they had little time to waste or they'd miss the train.

Bryn had nodded, not paying much attention as she scrolled through emails on her phone. But when Jules had returned several minutes later, she'd said she couldn't pay the bill as her phone had died, with her credit card app inside of it. Bryn had picked up the check, leaving her revenge tip.

"She asked for the bathroom?" Bryn said. "Did she go into it?"

"I believe so, yeah," Derek said, grinning. "I know you think I was watching her every move, but I wasn't."

"Thanks, Derek," Bryn said, scrawling her signature. Without saying anything more to him, she hurried in the direction of the cafe's bathroom.

Inside, it was clean, with Mediterranean-inflected tiles on the walls, a sparkling mirror and toilet, and a full dispenser of liquid soap on the sink, a well-known natural brand. A floral scent hung in the air.

Surely, if Jules wanted to use a bathroom, she would have used this one, and not waited until they reached the train station. Could there have been someone already inside when Jules got to the door, someone who took too long? Not wanting to miss the train, she'd left.

Bryn locked the door and hung her backpack on a peg. The room was clearly scoured every day. Bryn hoped whoever had bathroom duties was a little lazy. She opened the lid of the small metal container by the toilet. The inside was jam-packed with feminine detritus.

Bingo.

Chapter Twenty-Two

*D*elon was not in the room. But she noticed his phone charging on the bedside table. He'd been using the same charger she'd bought at the general store. Without thinking, Bryn dashed over and examined the dark screen. She picked up the phone, swiping it awake.

It asked for a passcode.

The room's door opened and she whirled around so violently that the phone yanked out of the charger.

Delon's expression was blank. Then his face registered irritation as he crossed to Bryn where she stood with his phone in her hand. She returned his phone to the table, hand slightly trembling.

"It dinged," she said. "I thought it might be Jules."

He picked up his phone, tapped in the passcode, and stared. "Nothing," he said.

He knew she'd been snooping. Bryn could tell he knew. But he said no more about it. Her stomach was sour with nerves and she couldn't look him in the eyes.

She went to her new hoodie hanging on the back of the room's one chair, picked it up, and pretended to search it for lint.

"Reception told me there's a car service a few blocks away," Delon said. "Only one in town, so I went there."

"Anything?" She blew on an invisible piece of lint, then pulled the hoodie down over her head and wriggled tightly into it. It was one size too small.

"I gave her name and description to the dispatcher. He said he'd ask the drivers."

"She could have used an app."

"Yes, but there's no way to find that out."

He shook off his coat, tossed it onto the spot where Bryn's hoodie had been, and went to the bathroom with his little toiletry bag. He began arranging his items on the shelf mounted on the wall next to the sink.

Bryn hovered near the doorway, watching him.

"I'm sorry for what I said about Jules, how no one would remember me if I went missing. While it's true, this is no time for my issues. I need to put on my big girl pants and get over it. If I can't get over it, then I need to stay away from Jules if we find her. *When* we find her."

He didn't respond.

"Anyway, I wanted to apologize."

"No need to apologize." He finished arranging his toiletries and brushed past her into the room. The way he did so without looking at her indicated he was still mildly annoyed with her. Whether because of their earlier tiff, or because she'd been trying to get into his phone, she couldn't tell. Probably both.

"Oh, and there's some news," she said. "Jacqueline called me."

That got his attention.

"I told her Jules was busy preparing for the Y event and that's why she hasn't returned her calls. But that isn't going to hold her for long. She might call you too, so you need to say the same thing."

"She won't call me," he said, sinking onto the bed.

"Why not?"

He shook his head, slouching over his knees. "Because Jules' parents haven't spoken to me in about a year."

"What?" Bryn sat next to him on the bed. "I didn't know this."

"They never spoke to me much to begin with, so it wasn't a huge deal. But last Christmas, I left their house early. You know how they feel about *that* day."

Bryn knew exactly what he meant. Christmas was sacred in the Aston house. Jacqueline hired a company to decorate both the interior and exterior of the Colonial, spending thousands on decor and electric bills.

"It's always such an ordeal," Delon sighed. "I get through it somehow."

Bryn sympathized. She'd stopped going to Christmas at the Astons several years ago. Once her mother had announced that she would no longer be attending, that she preferred low-key evenings at home or with friends, Bryn jumped at the chance to avoid it as well.

There was an elaborate Christmas Eve dinner followed by an even more elaborate and wasteful morning gift exchange session, followed by another extravagant meal on Christmas Day. None of it was low key in the slightest.

Jacqueline would act like Bryn had never been to the celebration before, and force her on a guided tour of the house and grounds, stopping to show off every last glittery elf and gaudy reindeer. She hired help in the kitchen. It made Bryn uncomfortable to watch as her aunt ordered around the helpers, all of whom were recent immigrants.

Rich would bellow a greeting to Bryn, then ignore her for the rest of the holiday, sometimes squinting at her as if he wasn't quite sure who she was.

"I can't believe you left early," Bryn said, in awe of Delon's act of courage.

"The final straw was that moronic movie Rich wants everyone to watch after the second gastronomic orgy," he said. "Every year, it's the same outrageously stupid one. We have to eat popcorn and laugh like we've never seen it before. It wasn't even amusing the first time I saw it."

Bryn didn't know what movie he meant. She and her mother had always left shortly after the Christmas Day feast, sparing them whatever followed it.

"One of those dumb Christmas movies?" she asked. "*Santa Claus Goes to Town* or whatever?"

"Worse. Something with a dog who makes sarcastic comments in its mind. The movie was made for eight-year-olds. Rich insists everyone watch it. I said I'd be happy to suffer through another viewing so long as we all enjoy a Truffaut film afterward. Perhaps a little

Bergman." He laughed sourly. "That wasn't appreciated. It was even less appreciated when I told Jules I was
returning to the city and she could accompany me or
not. She didn't. You'd think I'd decapitated their cat
instead of skipping out on a profanely horrible movie
about a talking dog."

There was a very long and surreal gap between what
Bryn heard and what she understood. Inside that gap
was her life splitting in two—the before and after. As if
she had been slammed by a car and in that precious
second before she hit the pavement, she understood with
stunning clarity how profoundly her life was about to
change.

He took me to that drive-in.

Right before it shut down.

*I don't remember the name of the movie but it was something
about a dog who talked.*

"Bryn?"

She heard Delon's voice but it was as if it was
coming down a long tunnel.

"Are you okay?" He gripped her leg. "What's
wrong?"

"Delon," she whispered. She placed her hand over
his. "I need your help."

* * *

SHE WAS TREMBLING SO BADLY that when she was able to
unlock her phone, she handed it to Delon so she
wouldn't drop it.

"On the second screen is an app called My Family Tree," she said. "Open it."

Several months ago, Bryn had sent in a sample of her saliva to a company that tested DNA. She hadn't had the nerve to look at the results, knowing there was a good chance she'd be matched with someone on her biological father's side. Or perhaps even with him.

She kept waiting for the perfect time to look at the results. A time when she was brave enough. A time when work wasn't so stressful. A time when she wasn't consumed with her affair with Delon. A time…

Then she'd decided she may never be ready. And that was okay. What was the point, anyway? She wasn't going to call up this stranger who'd forced himself on her mother at a drive-in.

She wouldn't want a relationship with him. She wouldn't want a thing from him. Nor was there any point in telling him what she thought about him. No doubt he didn't consider what had happened to be rape. He got to cast it in his mind, and he would cast it in whatever way allowed him to sleep well at night.

Once, Bryn had suddenly asked, "Mom, did you ever go to the police? After what happened?"

Her mother had stared at her and said, "Police? Bryn, I was seventeen, high as a kite, and wearing a short skirt. What exactly do you think they would have done for me? You don't understand. You just don't understand."

Tell me then, she'd wanted to say, but couldn't say it. Because the truth was, she didn't want to know. It was too painful to know.

"Okay, it's open," Delon said solemnly. "I see some matches here."

Oh my god, oh my god.

"Are there—any big ones? Like a fifty percent DNA match?"

"Mmm. Doesn't appear so. There's a 24 percent one." He looked at her. "Bryn, how much do you want to know?"

Nothing.

I don't want to know anything.

But she owed it to her mother. Not to herself. To her mother. To the mother she never really had. The mother so weighed down by *something* that she remained in a perpetual state of near-adolescence. The mother who numbed herself with alcohol, with bad relationships.

Bryn felt she owed it to her mother to have an idea of what her mom had been carrying. So now, right now, she had to be courageous. She had to finally say the thing she had never been able to say to her mom.

"Tell me," she said. "I want to know."

Delon looked back at the phone. Then he reached over with his other hand and tightly grasped her knee.

"Bryn, you're matched with Rosemary Aston. Rich's sister. She's your aunt. Your biological aunt."

Chapter Twenty-Three

*D*elon walked her to the little park with the statue. She didn't remember leaving the room. She'd heard what he'd said about Rosemary Aston, then they were on the sidewalk. He held her arm tightly and guided her to the bench.

"I don't remember leaving," she said monotonously. "The room. I don't remember leaving."

"Bryn, you… we had to leave," he said.

He held her hand, his face turned to her. He kept trying to catch her eye but she wouldn't look at him. She couldn't bear anyone seeing whatever was going on behind her eyes.

"What can I do?" he asked.

She didn't know what he could do. She didn't know what anyone could do.

I've done everything I can for you, haven't I? Tell me one thing I haven't done for you. I told you I'd take care of things but you—

I told you I'd take care of things.

Take care of things.

"This is why Jacqueline never liked me," Bryn said, staring at the statue. A pigeon was bobbing its way around its base. She had not seen many pigeons in Hudson Hollow. She pictured this pigeon flying in from the city, lost from its family.

"I could tell she didn't like me," she said. "The one time I brought it up, Jules acted like I was crazy."

On the surface, Jacqueline was kind. She would sometimes invite Bryn to go shopping with her and Jules, and even pay for whatever outfit Bryn picked out. But, underneath, it was disturbingly obvious that Jacqueline seemed to resent Bryn's existence.

There were many indications, but one stood out for some reason. During her senior year of college, Bryn had asked Jacqueline if she could stay in Jules' bedroom for a few nights. Jules was living in Europe so her room was empty.

The guest house had been discovered to have black mold in the walls and no one could treat it until after the holidays. Bryn's mom didn't seem to mind sleeping around black mold, but Bryn was always prone to allergies and getting sick. Her doctor had ordered her to keep away from the mold.

Jacqueline and Rich were in Bali. They spent half the year mindlessly traveling from one guided tour to another, smearing their massive carbon footprint all over the globe and never coming into any meaningful contact with the natives.

Bryn wanted to be home for Christmas break, and she couldn't think of a single reason why she wouldn't be granted permission to stay in the main house, given no one else was in it.

But Jacqueline had replied by email, "Sorry, Bryn, we want to leave Jules' room open in case she decides to return home for the holidays."

Bryn had sat staring at the email, stunned at the cold and somewhat cruel dismissal. Jacqueline knew of the black mold in the guest house and Bryn's allergies.

The idea that Jules might suddenly come home and need her room was absurd. She was off having the time of her life and planning New Year's Eve in Paris with her new French boyfriend—guess who. And that's the way it always was.

Bryn should sleep in black mold because there was an astoundingly slim chance that Jules might come home for the holiday and need the entire house to herself.

In asking to stay in the main house without her cousin as custodian, Bryn had unwittingly broken caste. She'd forgotten her place.

"Fuck Jacqueline," Delon said. "Fuck her if she knew."

What did Rich's sister know? Rosemary and Bryn were DNA-matched right there inside the site.

Rosemary Aston was much older than Rich. Probably in her early seventies by now. She and Rich were the only siblings. Bryn remembered Jules remarking last year that Rosemary had dementia and was being moved to a care facility. This would explain why, when Rosemary's DNA matched with Bryn's, the woman didn't bring it up with anyone. She likely hadn't been inside the ancestry website for quite some time.

How much more sense could it make that Rich was Bryn's biological father? It made so much sense that she had a crushing sense of shame that she hadn't put it together before.

Why Bryn and her mother were allowed to live in the guest house, yet were treated like guests who'd stayed too long.

Those strange, heated, low-volume exchanges she'd picked up between her mother and Jacqueline. Jacqueline's voice was always rushed and insistent. Jess would usually end up crying. Bryn had vaguely wondered what the discussions were about but figured Jacqueline was lecturing her younger sister for not being able to hold down a job.

Then the sadness that hung over her mother. The unnamed, undiagnosed *something* that Jess suffered with.

The old framed pictures of Rich around the Colonial. The blonde curls of his youth. Bryn wasn't blonde but she had curls. No one else in the family did. Just Rich and Bryn.

I only remember his first name. John.

Could her mother have chosen any more generic, untraceable name for the imaginary man who'd impregnated her, then skipped town?

Now she understood why Jacqueline felt the need to keep reminding Bryn that Rich was *Jules' father.* This was her way of saying *and he's not yours.*

"One time," Bryn quietly said to Delon. "He read Jules' diary. Rich did. When she was a teen. She was so humiliated and came crying to me. All I could think was, 'Jules, you have a father who cares enough to want to read your diary.'"

There were times Bryn tried to engage Rich in conversation, only to have him turn his head away if anything even fleetingly distracted him. The *I'm not interested in you* vibe he gave off was palpable.

He'd made a deliberate and calculated decision to reject one child in favor of another. He'd made a choice to allow Bryn to grow up feeling insecure and unwanted until, as an adult, those feelings created an inability to engage in healthy, mature relationships, or to have a general sense of wellness and ease. With all of his resources, Rich could have easily offered Bryn a bit of an emotional and financial safety net, a sense that life wouldn't swallow her if she fell a little behind.

When people told her, as a compliment, how responsible she was, she'd want to say, *I never had an option. I never had a fucking option to be anything else.*

"I'm sorry," Delon said, squeezing her tighter.

A jangle pierced the air, Delon's phone. As usual, her heart scrambled alert, thinking it might be Jules. Jules, finally! She'd say she was taking a break from everyone. Or she hated Bryn and Delon for their affair. Or that she was in a basement somewhere, bound and blindfolded, with people who wanted money from her father.

And there was a tiny sliver of *something…*

That if Rich's princess was gone, gone forever, then he might finally feel pain. Pain on the level that Bryn had felt her entire life.

"Jacqueline," Delon said, showing Bryn the screen

with "MIL" on it. He looked a little frightened—and repulsed, as if he smelled something decaying.

Jacqueline was so anxious to hear from Jules that she'd called the son-in-law she hadn't spoken to since last Christmas when Delon escaped from the cartoonish movie that Rich, perversely, wanted to watch despite (or perhaps because of) it being the same one playing when he'd sexually assaulted his teenage sister-in-law.

Bryn had no doubt it had happened as her mother had briefly described it. Her certainty was primal, the hurt and anger trembling in her mother's voice, etched into her face, had been too raw and heartbreaking not to be definitive. Now she understood those strange, low-volume, intense exchanges between her mother and aunt.

I told you I'd take care of things but you—

And she understood the peculiar vibrations between her mother and "uncle" Rich. How they never seemed to look each other in the eyes. Before Bryn could stop herself, she took Delon's phone and tapped the green "accept" button.

"Hi, Jackie," she said.

"Oh, Bryn? Is that you?"

"Yes, it is. May I speak to Rich, please, if he's there?"

Despite Rich being her so-called uncle, Bryn did not have him in her contacts list. The pair didn't have that kind of relationship.

"Of course," Jacqueline said. "But I was hoping Delon could get Jules on the phone for me?"

"No problem. I only need to quickly speak to Jules'

father about the parking situation. I'm the one who did all the research, so she won't be able to help him."

Bryn was careful to use "Jules' father" with Jacqueline rather than "my uncle," understanding all too well the possessive language her aunt preferred when it came to Rich. And she knew parking intelligence would get him on the phone. After thirty seconds or so, she heard, "Well, hello there, Bryn!"

It was his standard delivery: jovial but distant. He always acted like Bryn was a long-lost relative who'd returned after many years abroad. Someone he'd treat politely, but only because he was required to, as she was family—sort of. Unlike Jacqueline, Rich didn't dislike her. He didn't begrudge her existence.

He was barely aware of it.

"So, what's the parking situation up there on the east side?" he asked. "Is there a garage that won't cost me an arm and a leg?"

"You know what *didn't* cost you an arm and a leg?" Bryn said in a low, even tone. "*Me*. In fact, I cost you nothing but use of your guest house. While you and your rape-apologist wife were traveling the world, my mother and I were living on top of each other, feeling guilty about being in your backyard, and being treated like squatters who snuck in and refused to leave.

While you were raising one daughter in your mansion, I was out back wondering who the fuck my father was, and watching my mother drink herself into a stupor because she *did* know.

All those years you were making yourself and your family rich, because you weren't in prison like you should have been. I'm also sure you didn't pay a fucking *dime* in child support. Oh, that bullshit over Christmas? Ah, such a devout Christian. By the way, I have it on good authority that you're going to hell.

So, here's what you can do. Find your own parking, you goddamned rapist."

Pin-drop silence on the other end of the line. She wondered if he'd hung up at some point. Then she heard him breathing.

"Goodbye," she said calmly.

She hung up and began trembling. Remembering that Delon was next to her, she turned to him. His face was paler than she'd ever seen it. He did not move for several seconds. Then he stood and crouched before her on the cold, leaf-littered ground. Wrapping his strong hands around her knees, he said, "I'm proud of you."

She put her hands over his and after a few moments of weighty silence said, "Father's Day will be very awkward this year."

Chapter Twenty-Four

"*S*he's my sister," Bryn said as they walked back to the inn. Delon was still holding her, as if without him, she might fall. And she might.

"Half-sister," he replied.

"Half-sister-cousin. That makes this thing much worse."

This thing.

She pulled on his coat sleeve and he stopped to look at her. The abnormally clear and bright daylight magnified every line around his eyes and the black stubble on his jaw.

Right then, she realized she loved him. But she didn't know if it was *love* love or *friendship* love. And, whatever this feeling was, it hadn't truly come to existence until about ten minutes ago, when he'd kneeled on the leafy ground and wrapped his strong, comforting hands around her knees. When he'd *been there* for her in a way that no one else ever had.

She could not think of another person who could

have supported her better through that dramatic reveal. Jules would have been so shocked that she would have been no help—Bryn would have even felt like she needed to comfort Jules rather than vice versa. *I'm sorry*, she would have felt compelled to say to her cousin. *I'm sorry my very existence has shown you that the father you worship is a shit.*

Amika, out of awkwardness, would have made a series of bad jokes. They would have lightened the atmosphere for a few minutes but not given Bryn what she needed, which was support. Real emotional support.

But Delon. He'd been firm, strong, sympathetic. Everything she could have asked anyone to be. So how could she still—

She clutched his arm tighter and blinked several times, dispersing the vision of a red Peugeot speeding past the deli's camera.

"We need to go to the police," she said. "No more stalling. She's my sister."

He looked off behind her for several moments, then brought his gaze back to her. "Yes. We should go."

He actually grinned. There was something oddly joyous about making up their minds, of breaking free of their torturous indecision.

His phone rang again. This time, Bryn's heart didn't leap. She didn't imagine that it was Jules calling. A small part of herself was beginning to accept that Jules was gone.

"Hello?" Delon furrowed his brows at his phone, confused. Then he shrugged and put it back in his pocket.

"Wrong number, I guess," he said.

They walked into the lobby of the inn.

* * *

"Delon, I have such a headache," she told him once they'd reached the room. "Would you do me a huge favor and go buy me some aspirin?"

She had about five minutes to get him out of the room. She'd watched him unlock his phone to answer it when Amika had called him at the prearranged time. What Bryn hadn't counted on was the news about her paternity that would drive her outside in a stupor before the scheduled call.

Now she'd already lost approximately five minutes as they returned to the room. If he had his phone set to lock after ten minutes of no use, that didn't give her much time to get him to leave.

She also had to hope he'd leave his phone behind. He usually did. He cared less about having his phone on him than anyone she knew. She'd once asked him why this was. He'd said he didn't get a cell phone until his early twenties—a consequence of being French and not American—and had learned to live without it.

However, with Jules being missing, he carried his phone much more than usual, in case she got in touch. Not to mention he'd had it with him in the park. However, as soon as he'd entered the room, he'd dropped his phone on the little desk with the electrical strip and coffee maker.

If he didn't leave his phone behind, there wasn't much Bryn could do. Amika couldn't continue to call him. Her friend had pressed *67 before dialing, a trick the pair had learned long ago to avoid certain sources getting their private phone numbers. Delon would soon catch on that something suspicious was happening if he kept getting "wrong numbers."

They were headed to the police anyway. Presumably, whatever was in Delon's phone would come to light.

"Sure," he said, then stared at her for a long moment. He walked over and placed his hands on her arms.

"Are you really okay?" he asked.

"I'm okay," she said weakly, trying to smile at him.

He kissed her on the cheek, grabbed his coat, and walked out of the room.

He didn't take his phone.

She could not believe her luck. It seemed impossible that he'd left it there. But he had.

She waited about a minute, giving him enough time to reach the street. Then she hurried over and picked up the phone. She slid the screen upward. All of his apps appeared. The phone didn't want a passcode! Her heart jammed jaggedly into her throat. She was so eaten up with nerves that she could barely breathe.

She flipped to the next screen, her eyes darting up and down, looking for an app that would contain his toll records. She didn't know what it would be called but looked for anything with the words "EZ Fare."

Not being much of a phone man, Delon only had two screens worth of apps, maybe a dozen. She quickly came to the end of them, and still had no idea which one she should look inside. Her heart was pounding so hard her vision went blurry and she had to close eyes and rapidly shake her head.

Where was it? Where was it?

She wanted to give the phone enough time of not being used to relock before he returned. But app after app—Weather, Podcasts, Settings, Voice Memos, Messages, Clock, Maps, Calendar, Reminders, Notes—none of it looked like it would contain his toll information.

She flipped back and forth several times, from one screen to the next, and her heart began to sink despondently. She would never know.

Then she looked again.

Wallet.

She had only ever used her Wallet one time. She'd bought a concert ticket on her phone, and a message had informed her that the ticket had been deposited into her Wallet.

She hit the app with her thumb and it opened. Inside was a gray bar that said, "Passes."

Her heart flipped. This had to be it. The recorded toll information went directly into his Wallet. She tapped the gray bar with her thumb and a long list of various passes, tickets, and reservations popped onto the screen.

She quickly scrolled down and saw "EZ Fare Passes." She slid that to the side, where she saw another list. This one had each time the EZ Fare was activated, with date and time stamps.

But horrifically her mind went blank on which date she'd arrived in Hudson Hollow with Jules. She knew the day—Sunday—but not the date. Things had been so insane since Jules disappeared that she'd stopped keeping track of dates.

She glanced at the corner of his phone but it only showed the time, not the date. Shit! She'd have to leave the app to see today's date. She was so nervous that she heard herself whine, like a dog backed into a corner.

She slid the screen up and the Wallet app closed. Seeing the date, she mentally counted back to Sunday, but her mind was so chaotic with near-panic that she could barely count backwards. She tapped each one of her fingers on the phone until she reached Sunday.

Then she opened the app again. She went through what felt like the agonizingly slow process of finding the EZ Fare passes, and clicked on the gray bar.

She was scrolling down the recorded dates when the door opened. The sound was so terrifying that her hand gave one giant spasmodic jerk and released the phone. It went banging to the floor.

She stood paralyzed and breathing heavily as Delon calmly shut the door behind him.

"Can I help you with whatever you're looking for, Bryn?" he asked.

She closed her eyes, unable to say a thing.

"I remembered there's a packet of meds in the bathroom. But I presume you don't really want them."

"Um," she whispered, then pressed her hands up against her mouth.

"You want to know when I passed through that toll on Sunday."

He walked over and retrieved his phone from the floor. He tapped on it several times, then turned the screen to her.

"It's got me coming through the toll at 4:05 p.m.," he said. "That's before you called me about Jules being missing. I couldn't figure out how to delete it. But there's no real point in deleting it anyway. The MTA or Port Authority will have a record of it."

"Oh my god," she said, her entire body shaking. "You killed her."

"For god's sake, I didn't kill her!"

He shoved his phone into his coat pocket and stalked to the window.

"I came up here to catch her with whomever she's been sleeping with, so I could ask for a divorce."

Bryn stared at him, her hands smushed up against her mouth, her eyes big and unblinking.

"I can't have children, alright, Bryn?" he said. "I had cancer as a kid. Only six years old. Testicular cancer. Something like a one in two hundred thousand chance. The chemo burned away all my sperm stem cells. That's why she didn't get pregnant for almost a decade. If she's pregnant now, then the baby's not mine. I didn't think she was coming here with you, but to come meet whoever he is."

Bryn shook her head slightly. She had no idea whether anything he was saying was the truth.

"After she told me that morning, then left, I emailed my urologist," he said. "I'm rechecked every year to

231

make sure there's no relapse. I asked her if there was any way I could get my wife pregnant though I'd already asked various doctors about this dozens of times. She was kind enough to respond on a weekend and said the odds were astronomically tiny. I'd have a better chance of getting hit by lightning. There's a better chance of Rich Aston growing a conscience. I'm happy to show you the emails. You can call her if you want."

Bryn knew a doctor wouldn't give personal health information about a patient to anyone except him. And he could have faked the emails. But she stammered, "Why—why didn't you just tell me this?"

"Tell *you*? I haven't even told Jules. I kept hoping that there was something I could do about it. For a while, I went to a nutcase in Chinatown who gave me 'miracle cure' concoctions." He laughed bitterly, then shrugged. "I get my stem cells checked. Nothing ever changes. Do you have any idea what it's like not being able to give the person you love that one thing she wants? It eats at you, every day, all the time."

He turned from the window, went to the bed, and sank into it. He shoved his face into his open palms.

"I didn't want a divorce because of an affair," he said. "That would be rather hypocritical, considering what I was doing myself. I wanted to give her the life she wanted. She could be with him, be a mother like she always planned."

He pried his face from his hands and wearily regarded her. "Bryn, I've spent the past several years trying to work up the courage to tell her. I took a young, naive, infatuated girl and married her without giving her

232

vital information. I held on to a crazy hope there would be a scientific breakthrough."

He sighed, stretched his arms in front of him, then slouched over his knees. "To be honest, I wasn't sure I loved her anymore. How could I love her and be with you as much as I was? So, it seemed like a divorce was in order."

He stood and slowly wandered back to the window, staring down at the street.

"I came up here and drove around. Went in and out of stores. I thought if I caught her with another man, I could ask for a divorce and she couldn't put all the blame on me. She could get on with her life and I with mine. We could separate the brownstone and whatever else equitably and fairly. But I couldn't find her."

Bryn realized that she and Jules had been inside of the cafe's back garden when he was driving around, so he'd missed them. But he'd stayed long enough to pass Jules on Main Street, just as it was growing dark.

"You drove right by her," Bryn said. "I saw your car on the deli surveillance video. That's why I kept wondering…"

"I didn't see her," he insisted. "I didn't see her at all."

He turned, his face etched with sadness and anguish.

"The toll time-stamp. That video, if it still exists. Every other damn thing I told you about our finances. You and me. It all looks like I came up here to kill my cheating wife in a jealous rage so I could be with my mistress."

She didn't know whether to believe everything he'd

told her, but made a spontaneous decision to continue along as if it was the unequivocal truth. Not to mention it was possible this *was* the truth. She couldn't imagine Delon fabricating a story about being infertile, even if the story would redirect her suspicions. He'd have too much old-fashioned masculine pride for a story like that.

She remembered him once asking her if she was on birth control—something he should have asked her weeks prior, if he'd truly been bothered.

"Of course I am," she'd sniped, irritated with the idea that she was solely responsible for it.

She'd never forget how he'd suddenly let out a short, harsh laugh, like a bark. At the time, she couldn't fathom why he'd done that. But now she understood why.

"This gives us a suspect," she said. "A real suspect."

He glanced sideways. "Who?"

"Whoever she's having an affair with, of course. She did the math and realized the baby wasn't yours but wanted you to think so. Then she came with me to Hudson Hollow. While I'm at the museum, she buys a pregnancy test at the pharmacy. Before we leave the cafe, she takes the test in the bathroom."

At his surprised look, she continued, "I have it. The test. I found it in the bathroom's garbage. I mean, the strip isn't monogrammed. I can't be a hundred percent sure it's hers. But it's in my backpack."

He squeezed his eyes shut, then opened them wide as if trying to see this new information. "Is it positive?"

"Yes. You can barely see the line, but it's there. Once

she confirmed the pregnancy, she probably called the other guy to let him know."

Bryn began pacing, two thumbs on her front teeth, biting their nails. Everything that had happened that day began clicking into place.

"Then her phone dies. She tells me this while I'm in the garden. She and I head to the station but she starts to feel sick. She leaves the station, sees Andy Kroll following her, and tells him off. She gets to the cafe, uses the bathroom to be sick, then charges her phone. She makes another phone call—probably to the other guy again, confirming that he'd arrived. She walks two blocks and gets into a car. It had to be his car. He must live on the upper west side or closer. Riverdale. Or even Hudson Valley."

She clasped her hands together, almost excited. "He's our new prime suspect. He's our only suspect."

"Why would he hurt her?"

"Delon, don't you watch the ID channel?" she asked incredulously.

"I'm afraid I don't. But I feel like I'm living in it."

"Because he's married. And probably has young kids and major assets and a high profile. While here, Jules shakes off the idea of fooling you and tells the other guy the truth. Depending on his reaction, she may have even threatened to inform his wife."

Delon straightened, pressing his shoulders back, seeming less defeated. Bryn had apparently given him hope that someone else would end up in prison.

"I know Jules," Bryn continued. "She wouldn't get casually pregnant by some rando, even if she suspected you and me. She believes too much in the ideals of marriage. He has to be someone she already knew. Someone she saw enough to give her a chance to fall in love."

She covered her mouth. "Oh, I shouldn't have said that."

"I have bigger things on my mind than whether she's fallen for someone else, Bryn," Delon said.

"Then we need to figure out what married guy is in her circle, someone she comes into contact with regularly. He'd have to have a lot to lose—a *lot* to lose—if he got another woman pregnant. So much to lose that he'd—"

They said nothing for a long beat, then, at the same moment, they locked eyes.

"Holy shit," Bryn said. "You don't think... "

"I do," he said, quietly. "I do think."

Chapter Twenty-Five

*T*hey sat in Delon's car on Sutton Square. It was only a 45-minute drive from here to Hudson Hollow if you took the I-87 North. And that was with traffic. On a Sunday, driving extra fast, it would have been a half an hour spin from the east side, then along the Hudson River.

More than enough time for a man to get to Hudson Hollow between when Jules would have called him with news of a pregnancy, and her coming out of the cafe after charging her phone.

"Exclusive" didn't begin to describe Sutton Square. It consisted of only a dozen townhomes on a quiet *cul-de-sac* overlooking a private acre of garden. The East River was so close you could step into it. Boats slipped past and the tram swung along the bridge into Roosevelt Island. The homes cost about $25 million each.

Fashion designer Thom King lived in one of the townhomes, the best one, on a corner lot. Bryn knew exactly where the designer lived because she'd been to his home several times with Jules for an annual party that he'd host the night before the Met Gala.

Bryn didn't find the parties particularly interesting, but there was lobster and shrimp and caviar and champagne and the view would stun you into awed silence. Bryn was counting on the fact that it was too cold for Thom to be in the Hamptons, and Jules had always said the designer was a homebody and workaholic who was scared to fly, so there was a decent chance he'd be around.

"You're sure you want to do this?" Delon asked.

"I don't see any other way. I'll call if I need help. If you can't get inside, then I guess you need to try 911."

"I don't like this," he said, peering out of the windshield. It was getting dark, and the lights on Roosevelt Island Bridge began to glow. They could see the postcard scene through a gap in buildings. Delon was, of course, double parked.

"He may not even be here," she said. "We've got to try."

"We? I feel like I'm not doing anything."

"You're watching the car. And if I need help, someone needs to be outside. Remember, if I dial you, then I need help, even if I don't say anything."

"*Je n'aime vraiment pas ça*," he murmured.

Bryn quickly leaned over and kissed his stubbled cheek. "I'll be back in twenty," she said. "If you don't hear from me at all, come ring the gate."

"*Pas bon*," he sighed.

* * *

Outside the townhome was a small gate on a side entrance. This was the door she and Jules always used. She pressed the call-button, but it made no noise, so she had no clue if it was working. Eventually, a female voice crackled through the little sound system.

"Yes?"

"Hi, I'm so sorry to bother you. I'm Bryn Bastid. Jules Aston-Callais is my cousin. Thom knows me. I need to speak with him. It's about Jules, and it's urgent."

"Hold on, please."

There was a rather long wait in which Bryn began to wonder if anyone would appear. Then the door opened to reveal an extremely pretty, almost shockingly thin woman in her thirties. Bryn easily recognized her as Christy, Thom King's wife.

"You're Jules' cousin?" the woman asked.

"Yes, you probably don't remember me, but I come to Thom's Met Gala parties with her."

"Oh." Christy looked perplexed but like she was trying to be polite. "You can open the gate now," she said.

Bryn pushed the gate and walked down a small set of steps. Christy stood in the doorway. She was brunette, quite tall, and had been one of Thom King's regular models and still looked like one. She was wearing a stylish pajama set, her hair pulled back to reveal high cheekbones that earned her a very good living, and naturally full lips that other women needed fillers to accomplish.

Bryn knew the couple had two children. Rather famously had them. They were fraternal twins, a boy and girl, about six years old. They often appeared in the press and on Christy's social media.

Christy and Thom had one of those "perfect" marriages. They were photographed at events—movie premieres, fashion shows, restaurant openings—usually with their ringleted, matching-outfitted children in tow.

The children—Exeter and Echo—were Thom King models from infancy. Bryn recalled seeing their wrinkled newborn faces on social media, both wearing cloth headbands that said "ExEc"—Thom's new children's line. The babies were out of the womb for a few minutes —if that—before becoming ambassadors of his global brand.

Thom impregnating another woman, a married one to boot, could easily rupture this family fairytale that sold millions of dollars' worth of clothing, furniture, and home decor every year.

The designer had always taken a particular interest in Jules, from the time she'd been right out of college and was selected as an intern.

Her astonishingly rapid rise to his head publicist had fueled a lot of gossip. Bryn had always felt that he was attracted to Jules—he stared intently at her when he thought no one was watching, not just looking at her but *studying* her. But given that most men stared at Jules, Bryn couldn't get a handle on whether that meant anything. Nor did Jules ever mention that the designer acted inappropriately with her.

Of course, there were plenty of rumors that Thom King was gay, and his wife was a cover. Which never made sense to Bryn. Many famous male designers were gay and didn't try to hide it. Thom King happened to be one of the few who wasn't.

Jules had quit her job about a year and a half ago, when *The Suburban Aristocrats* began climbing the charts. She did not have enough time for a busy job, book marketing duties, and writing a new novel. So she'd said, anyway.

But now that Bryn suspected Gilda was the author of Jules' sophomore book, she wondered if Jules had quit her job for another reason. Perhaps an attempt to sever an affair with Thom.

Either way, the pair still seemed fairly close. Thom came to occasional book events. Several times, when Bryn and Jules had been out, she'd witnessed calls come in from Thom. Jules would have a short, banal discussion with him, then promise to call back later.

Bryn felt more comfortable that Christy was home, which meant Thom was unlikely to try to murder her. But she also knew this pushed her plan to get him to admit to an affair with Jules further away.

"Is Thom home?" she asked.

"Well, yes, but he's working. Is there something I can do for you?"

"I really need to speak with him privately. It's about Jules. It won't take long at all."

Christy raised her thick, luxurious eyebrows. She

clearly thought Bryn was audacious to come to Thom King's house and demand a private audience with the world-famous designer. Bryn scrutinized Christy's haughty beauty, wondering if she could have been the one to send Jules a series of threatening letters, telling her to leave town.

Christy backed away and held her long, painfully thin arm out. Bryn entered into a roomy foyer laid with black and white checkered marble tile.

"If you could wait in there, I'll see if he's available," Christy said. She indicated a room off to the side.

"Thank you so much, I won't take up much of his time, I promise."

Bryn entered a long sitting room cum library, with lots of dark walnut and crimson velvet furniture, and hundreds of books shelved to the twelve-foot-high ceilings.

Bryn was too anxious to sit, so she paced, staring at the artwork, mostly abstract paintings. She hoped Delon wouldn't panic and buzz the gate, and debated texting him a message that she was okay. But she decided to stick to their agreement of no phone communication.

Within about five minutes, Thom King entered. He was dressed in black slacks, a crisp white t-shirt, and a tan vest. Even at home, he looked like he could step right into a magazine photoshoot. His silver-flecked hair was slicked straight up in front, and he was wearing eyeglasses with round, grayish-tinted frames. Despite it being almost December, his face was flushed pink, as if he'd walked off a beach. She realized he'd likely had his skin sandblasted with microdermabrasion.

"Bryn," he said, warmly, as if he not only knew her perfectly well but had been expecting her arrival. He closed the door behind him, then shook her hand. His palm was soft as a marshmallow. "Nice to see you again."

"You too. I'm sorry to disturb you."

"No worries, just putting the finishing touches on the spring collection."

He indicated she should sit on the Victorian-style sofa, then he took a seat in a matching chair, legs crossed, torso folded forward, an expression of slight concern on his face, wondering why Jules' cousin would appear at his door with no warning.

"Christy said it was something about Jules. Can I help with anything?" he asked.

Bryn had lost all the bravado she'd had when she first entered this rarefied atmosphere. Jules was comfortable around people like Thom King and his model wife. Rich was an entertainment attorney and it wasn't unusual for his clients to visit the Colonial. Jules would sometimes excitedly tell Bryn about meeting a well-known musician or actor.

But Bryn was not comfortable in this crowd. With the famous fashion designer sitting across from her, her instinct was to roll over and subserviently show him her belly. She had to remind herself that this man may have murdered Jules to preserve his fashion empire.

"Jules told me everything," she said, surprised and thankful her voice didn't tremble. "All about the two of you."

She figured that asking him if he was having an

affair with Jules would go nowhere, so she'd earlier decided to act like she knew about it—and to sound utterly nonjudgmental.

"Oh?" he said, his tone and expression revealing absolutely nothing.

"Yes, I know everything. I was with her in Hudson Hollow on Sunday."

He smiled a little, seeming bemused. "I'm not following."

"Thom, I know. She told me."

He took off his glasses, looked at them as if he didn't know how they got on his face, then replaced them on his surgically-sculpted nose.

"I'm afraid there's been a mix-up. I have no idea what you're referring to."

"She's pregnant."

His brows flew up for a moment, then a genuine smile slid across his pinkish face. "That's wonderful. I know she's wanted that for a long time. I'll have to send her a gift."

Bryn started to feel sick with the conviction that the designer really didn't know what she was talking about. But she had to make one more big push, as she wouldn't get another chance. If she left here not knowing whether or not Thom King had killed Jules, she and Delon were back to being prime suspects.

"Thom," she said, leaning toward him and lowering her voice. "I know you're the father. It's okay. Her husband is parked outside. He knows too. If I don't return within ten minutes, he's calling the police. All we want to know is where she went."

His expression ran the gamut from shocked to mystified, and finally landed on insulted. "Is this a joke?" he asked.

Bryn pushed forward though her heart-rate had quadrupled. Thom might dress like a fop and have hands soft as a baby's ass but the gun-metal in his voice and eyes made clear that you didn't want to get on his bad side. And Bryn had shifted to his bad side.

"Not at all," she said. "Thom, she *told* me. We don't care about that part. We only want to know her whereabouts."

"I have no idea what she told you," he said, standing. He was much taller than Bryn, and her skin prickled all over with chilly fear. She had the strong urge to apologize profusely and get out of his house as quickly as possible. "But I'm most certainly not the father of Jules' child. Did you say her husband is outside? Why doesn't he come in and we can talk? There's obviously been a miscommunication. It will be nice to see him again. Devon, isn't it?"

Bryn ignored the mangling of Delon's name and plowed on despite every fiber in her yelling at her to leave.

"All I know is she told me you two were having an affair and she's pregnant. Then she went missing." She stood and maneuvered to the door side of him so she could run out of the room if needed.

"Missing? Is this some kind of prank?" He looked around as if he might see a camera.

"I wish it was."

He chuckled uneasily, crossed to a fireplace, and

tapped the white marble mantle several times, then turned.

"I don't believe she told you this," he said. "It doesn't sound like her at all. Besides, she knows perfectly well about Christy and me."

"Can you elaborate?"

"My partner, Mateo, is upstairs. He's lived here for five years. Nothing against Christy. She's the most beautiful woman in the world and the mother of my precious children. But sometimes it's nice to have a little meat on the bones, you understand?"

He paused as if expecting Bryn to agree. She didn't.

"Jules knows Christy and I don't have the typical bougie marriage. I mean... *everyone* knows." His eyes flicked pointedly at her from behind his spectacles. "Everyone who matters, anyway."

He shrugged, a little apologetically, and relaxed his posture. He now seemed more curious than affronted.

"I'm not interested in Jules that way," he said, calmly. "Every other way, *yes*. Other than Christy, she's my best muse. Everything looks good on her. Sadly, even other designers. But I can't imagine why she'd tell you we're sleeping together."

"I—I don't know either," Bryn stammered. She had the distinct impression he was telling the truth.

"Hmm," he said, mulling something over. "Could she have had a bad reaction to... well, the addies?"

"Excuse me?"

"Oh, dear. You didn't know? Jules has a bit of a—I wouldn't call it a problem, exactly..."

He definitely meant a problem.

"Perhaps the stress of the second book coming out. That talk is coming up. Isn't that soon? She could have taken too much." He stared at her as if to say, *What can one do?*

If this had been any other time, Bryn would have argued with him. Fiercely. She had never seen her cousin take drugs or even talk about taking drugs.

But… she didn't know her cousin as well as she'd always thought, not if Jules was pregnant with her lover's baby. It also hit her how much energy Jules always seemed to have. Her cousin often bragged about awakening at the crack of dawn even if she'd been out until late the night before. Bryn had always chalked this up to another of Jules' superpowers. But perhaps this particular superpower had pharmacological assistance.

Besides, Thom was giving Bryn the "out" she needed to excuse barging in here and accusing him of an affair. It was best that she go along with anything he said.

"It's possible. Her behavior has been strange lately."

"I know a tremendous counselor," he said. "He's superb. You might consider an intervention. You don't have any idea where she is?"

"No. She told me she was pregnant with your baby, then took off somewhere."

"Oh, dear," he fretted, slipping his phone from his pocket. "Sounds like this little habit has gotten worse. She's having an episode. There's no reasoning with a person when they get like this. Believe me, I know."

He tapped his phone and stood with his hand on his hip and an expectant look on his face. Bryn half-wondered if Jules would actually pick up, given it was Thom calling. For a brief moment, Bryn imagined her cousin answering the phone, and Thom glancing over as if to say, *Why did you think she was missing, you little crazy person?* Bryn took another step toward the library door.

"Hi, Julesy," he purred into her voice mail. "Would you mind returning my call, love? Your cousin is here and we're concerned about you. No judgement. There's no shame in asking for help. Give us a ring, doll."

He hung up, then looked at Bryn as if he'd done everything possible. "She'll be in touch," he said, confidently.

"Yeah, maybe. Thank you."

Suffering a reaction from drugs or not, Jules would never ignore a phone call from Thom King. She'd be even more likely to pick up a call from the designer than from her own mother.

Jules was absolutely gone. *Gone, gone, gone.* This time, Bryn's stomach didn't twist and lurch. Instead, it settled numbly into her new reality of Jules being... *not here.*

She had no idea what to do next. But Thom King suffered no confusion and began rather forcefully herding her toward the door.

"This is very concerning," he said, as they reached the checkered hallway. "I'll have my assistant get in touch with Darren, the counselor. You can set something up. I may not be there myself, as I'm very tied up these days. But I'll be there in spirit. Poor Julesy. Do I have your number, Bryn?"

She told him her phone number and he tapped it into his phone. "Sorry I made such a—such an accusation," she said, not sure she was really sorry. But as Thom hadn't confessed to an affair, she didn't mind pretending she was.

"It's got to be a bad reaction." He eyed the marble staircase that curved to the upper floors, then lowered his voice. "Similar happened to Mateo last year. Went overboard on Percs, insisted I had poisoned his coffee, and disappeared for three days. Why I stick with cannabis. God's relaxant. Doesn't make you lose your mind."

He smiled benevolently. "I'm sure she'll come down and be there for the talk. She wouldn't disappoint her fans."

He ushered Bryn toward the open door, something he managed solely with his forceful but mannered *please leave* body language.

"Be sure to keep me apprised," he said. "If I don't respond, it's because I'm very preoccupied with the collection. She'll understand. Tell her to look out for a bundle from the new ExEc collection. Not even on the shelves yet."

He grinned dreamily, probably imagining Jules' offspring decked out in his children's line. "A baby," he said. "How fantastic. I hope she gets off those addies, especially now. Nasty stuff."

He paused, leaning down toward her ear, as if imparting great wisdom. "Do you know what makes Jules so special?" he asked.

Halfway out the door, Bryn crossed her arms. "Why don't you tell me?"

"It's not that she's attractive, blonde, thin, and tall,"

he mused. "I have hundreds of models like that. None of them have what she has."

His eyes narrowed as if he was inspecting something, scrutinizing it for the barest of flaws. "It's that she's not perfect. If you catch her in the right lighting, at the right angle, she's almost… unattractive. *That's* what makes her perfect. Because real perfection is just a bore."

Chapter Twenty-Six

*D*elon stood at the end of the *cul-de-sac*. As soon as he saw Bryn approaching, he hurried over and grabbed her, hugging her tightly.

"I was about to buzz the gate," he said.

His concern over Bryn's safety touched her deeply. She had not grown up with anyone much concerned about her safety. Besides Jules and Amika, she couldn't come up with anyone much concerned about it now. To hear his anxious voice and feel his arms locked around her gave her a warm, tugging sensation in the heart.

"Come on," she said. "I don't want anyone to see us."

They hurried back to the double-parked car and sat inside, staring back at the short, cobblestoned street of Sutton Square and the gorgeous, glowing bridge at the end of it.

"I don't think it's him," she said. "He's got a male partner and his wife upstairs. I doubt he'd have the time for Jules, too."

She turned to Delon. It was now completely dark, and difficult to read his expression. "Do you know anything about her using prescription medication? Maybe even abusing it?"

"No. No, I don't. Why?"

"According to Thom King, she has a habit. With something he called 'addies.' I don't know what that is exactly. Adderall?"

"He's full of shit," Delon said, glaring out of the passenger window, as if he might storm into the townhome and confront Thom over such louche gossip. "I think I'd know if she was on drugs."

"Delon," Bryn sighed. "If she's having an affair, then how much do we know about her at all?"

"What's that got to do with where she is?"

"Jules seemed jittery and a little odd right before she left the station. And she implied she was sick. Maybe she was going into withdrawal."

"Not my Jules," he said, adamantly.

"Delon, *your* Jules was sleeping with another man, according to you. Did you know about that until the moment she said she was pregnant?"

He didn't respond, face hard set and jaw immobile.

"We need to consider all possibilities. She could have called a dealer, and that's the person whose car she got into."

"A dealer," he snorted. "Sounds absurd."

Annoyance raked her gut. He was clinging to a vision of Jules as the golden girl with no secrets, even though that vision went in direct opposition to what he knew about her—or what he claimed to know about her.

And he was stubbornly adhering to this vision rather than following a clue that might lead to her whereabouts.

"Fine. It's absurd. But on the off-chance it's not, we need to go to the brownstone and look around."

"Dealer," he grumbled, starting the car.

Chapter Twenty-Seven

*a*t the brownstone, Bryn went directly to the primary bedroom, and into the *en suite* bathroom. She opened the mirrored cabinet over the sink, scanning the shelves for a prescription bottle.

Delon stood in the doorway. "You're not going to find anything," he said. "I'd know if my wife was an addict."

"I'm not going over this again," she replied. But indeed she found nothing, and closed the cabinet.

"This is too obvious," she said, scanning the bathroom, trying to decide whether to tackle the hutch that contained what looked to be at least a dozen fluffy white towels.

Jules had created a gallery of black and white framed photos around the powder blue wainscoting, all the photos of her and Delon in various states of marital bliss. Bryn did not wish to be in the direct line of vision of these snapshots of a marriage that looked like one thing when she knew it to be another.

"She'd either hide them in the house somewhere or she'd carry them with her. If she's getting them off the street, then she wouldn't have a prescription, anyway. They could be in any kind of little container. If we look around, maybe we can find out who she's getting them from."

"You think the dealer left behind a business card?" Delon snorted, retreating to the bedroom.

"Maybe," she said, following. "*You* hand out a business card."

"Really, Bryn, you're comparing me to a drug dealer?"

Before she could respond, he thrust one palm up in a *let's not argue* gesture, then shook off his coat and tossed it to a chair. The idea of Jules doing drugs seemed to bother him more than the idea of her having a lover. Another cultural difference, Bryn imagined. While Americans thought nothing of stuffing themselves and their children with every conceivable prescription medication, the French were more lackadaisical about sexual fidelity. At least, this is what she intuited from Delon's behavior and her viewing of the occasional French New Wave film.

"Delon, think about it for a minute," she said. "That job with Thom King was extremely intensive. She'd work a full day, then go to a runway show and not get home until midnight. There were all kinds of parties and events. She was hardly home for years. How did she keep up that pace?"

"Trying to keep up that pace is a big reason she quit," he said.

He began yanking off his sweater. Bryn knew the t-shirt underneath was next. Then he'd be shirtless, muscles rippling below his perfect, silky skin, and she'd be unable to do anything but want to make love to him.

"Can you please not strip and listen to me?" she said.

He halted, the sweater wound around his arms, the t-shirt riding up his abdominals.

"Well, continue," she said. "But leave the t-shirt on, okay?"

He smirked, then flung the sweater to the floor. So, he did that at home too and not only at her place. Who raised this man?

"She might have needed some help getting through those kinds of working hours," she went on. "Before she knows it, she's addicted. She keeps trying to get off them but goes into withdrawal and needs more. That could have happened upstate."

He sat on the bed and untied his shoes, brown leather sneakers that managed to look comfortable and fashionable at the same time. Bryn walked over to the French double doors that led to a tiny balcony over-looking the park. It was so tiny there was only one chair on it and the chair butted up against the balcony's stone railing. She stared at the black antique lamp-posts casting a muted glow on the sidewalk ringing the dark-ened park.

"Maybe she owed the dealer money," Bryn contin-ued. "You did say you two were broke. The plan could have been to hold her until you or her parents or Thom King or whoever paid up, but something went wrong."

He shoved his shoes to the side with his foot, removed his socks, and lay on the bed, his hands drumming his flat stomach.

"I suppose it's all possible," he murmured. "Anything is possible. But if it's true, then I know nothing, absolutely nothing, about Jules. The woman I've been living with for a decade."

"She'd say the same about us."

He heaved a sigh, and stopped thumping on himself. "I guess you're right. But what do we do now?"

Bryn closed the balcony door and sat on the end of the bed. She turned to stare at him. "The same thing we've been saying for days that we're going to do, then talk ourselves out of."

"The police."

"The only way to get a handle on where she went is to know the last person she called. If you can't get into her cell records, the only ones who can are cops. They can subpoena them."

She reached over and pressed her hand on his thigh.

"Delon, we've got to trust that they'll do their jobs. They'll realize it wasn't us. It might take them a while, and we might spend some time in jail. We might go bankrupt on lawyers, and we might end up all over the news. Okay, forget *might*. All of that will happen. But the police will eventually figure out it wasn't us. Because it wasn't."

He reached down and held her hand. "It won't look good that we waited so long," he said.

"No, but if they do even the slightest bit of investigating, they'll see that we've been all over searching for her. Would we do that if we were guilty?"

"We would if we didn't want to *look* guilty."

She lay down next to him, pulling her body tight against him, her free hand clasping his bare shoulder.

"We've got no choice," she said. "The Y event is tomorrow night. If she doesn't show up, Gilda or her parents will call the police, anyway. We might as well beat them to it."

"What about you? And the NYPD? How do we know you'll be safe with them?"

"Let's report her missing in Hudson Hollow. At least then someone besides the NYPD knows I walked into a police station."

He wrapped his arms completely around her and kissed her temple. "I'm still hoping she's out there having a good laugh at us," he said. "Speaking of which, what did that person who keeps emailing you have to say? Your 'pal'?"

"Oh, right!" Bryn jolted out of Delon's embrace and sat up. "I completely forgot about that."

She scrambled off the bed and found her phone inside of her backpack. She went into her email, her eyes scrolling quickly down the messages.

She had a new one from yourpal12345.

With a shaky finger, she tapped on it.

Strange game you're playing, Bryn. I did you a huge favor, didn't I? I did it at my own risk. Why no thank you?

Your pal

I promise you I'm not playing a game. Can you please be more specific as to what you did for me? Because I'm lost.

It seems it's time for us to speak. Obviously, wires are crossing. The only way to move forward is in person.

How about Prospect Park, the abandoned music pagoda near Nethermead. Nine p.m. Tonight.

I'll say 'It's your pal' so you know it's me.

Come alone, Bryn. I'll know if you don't, and I'll disappear for good.

You wouldn't want that, would you?

And don't bring your phone. I'll be checking.

Your pal

"They wrote back!" she cried. "The person wants to meet up. Tonight! Alone."

She raced to show Delon her phone. He read, a crease between his brows deepening.

"Bryn, no," he said, lowly. "You can't go meet this person by yourself. What if it's the same one who threatened your boss?"

"I'll be fine. There are people in the park."

"At the pagoda at night? This late in the year, there'll be no one around."

He was right. The abandoned pagoda was basically inside of the woods. She doubted there were any lamps nearby, and it was fairly far from the nearest pathway. It might have once hosted bands but, these days, it was nothing but a deserted shelter for those with no homes or those caught in the park during rainstorms.

"This could be her," Bryn insisted. "The person is familiar enough with the park to know about the pagoda and how secluded it is. Jules and I have biked past there many times."

He looked so deeply concerned that her heart swelled with emotion.

If this ordeal had taught her anything, it was that Delon truly seemed to care about her as a human being, and wasn't only using her for sex. She wondered when his feelings had changed. Before all of this started or only recently, when they became bonded by trouble?

"Notice how the person wants to meet up one night before the Y talk," she said. "If it's Jules, that way, she can still make the event. She'll come out of the shadows, say 'Tah-dah, you bitch!' and read me the riot act. I don't blame her. Not at all. I'll apologize and mean it. But if she's pregnant with another man's baby, then... it's kind of even, isn't it?"

She realized this was her hope—that Jules had been having her own affair all along, and therefore Bryn's behavior was excused. She would no longer need to feel guilt or shame.

But the hope only lasted for a few moments before the poisonous sense of shame trickled back in. Jules could have started her own affair in retaliation after finding out about the one between her husband and cousin.

Even if that wasn't what had happened—even if Jules *had* started her affair first—this didn't excuse what

Bryn had done and continued to do. Jules was her sister. Her cousin. Her friend. Her protector.

And Bryn had willfully betrayed her.

Bryn was genuinely attracted to Delon, more than she could control. But the truth was, sleeping with Jules' husband had been her way of saying *fuck you*. Fuck you to the world that always told Jules she would get everything positive that it had to give, and told Bryn she would get none of it.

But sleeping with Delon had not been the answer. In fact, it had only complicated things to the point where Bryn could no longer separate past and present trauma.

It was time to grow up and stop saying *fuck you*. It was time for Bryn to take what was coming to her, to apologize and make amends to Jules if she could.

Bryn had spent so much of the one life given to her obsessing on her cousin, on what she had that Bryn didn't have. She could never get that time back. But it wasn't too late to save a lot of future time.

"What if it isn't her?" Delon asked. "What if it's a dangerous person? I should come with you."

She tucked into his side, staring at the little glowing cell screen still in his hand.

"No," she said. "I need to do this myself."

Chapter Twenty-Eight

*B*ryn stood in front of the full-length mirror inside Jules' walk-in closet. She pulled the hood of Jules' waterproof jacket over her head and continued to stare at her reflection.

Delon came up behind her. He didn't need to say anything, the look on his face said it all. He did not want her going into the park by herself to meet the emailer.

"I see him," she said. She reluctantly pointed to the end of her nose. "Here, on the tip. The way it kind of bulbs out a little at the end. He's got that, too."

The pair stood quietly, looking into the mirror.

"I hate seeing him," she said.

Is this why she'd never enjoyed a mirror? Why she would give her reflection a perfunctory glance, making certain her clothes fit or her mascara wasn't smeared, but otherwise did not, like most young women she knew, linger on her image?

Had she, on a subconscious level, always seen him?

Delon turned her from the mirror and bent so he was eye level with her.

"I don't think you should go alone," he said. "Especially without your phone. I can come and hide. In the trees."

"Don't be ridiculous." She pushed him back a little. "The person said they'll disappear if I don't go alone."

"I'd rather have the person disappear than have something happen to you," he said, pulling her back.

She snapped the flap under the jacket's hood. The temperature had dropped precipitously, and there was a light dusting of rain spritzing down. She left the closet and went to Jules' sturdy French provincial dresser, where there was a small Lumen flashlight sitting in a decorative bowl. She tucked it into one zippered pocket. As instructed, she wouldn't take her phone, but she needed to illuminate her way into the black night of the park.

"Here," Delon said, lifting her hand. He placed a small metal tube into her palm. "Take this."

She looked at the tube, which was black and pink. It took her several moments to realize she was looking at a tube of pepper spray.

"What the hell is this?" she asked, even though she knew what it was.

"Jules used to carry it around sometimes. Unfortunately, she didn't have it with her upstate."

Bryn stared at the tube. She'd never known Jules to carry pepper spray. Of course, her cousin didn't share every tiny detail of her life with Bryn. Obviously. But Bryn felt she would have known if Jules carried pepper spray. She would have at least seen it at some point. Wouldn't she?

"I can't bring this," she said. "The person said they'll check me for a phone. I don't think they'll like seeing pepper spray."

"Bryn," he said, practically snarling. "You can't go off and meet some lunatic in the park."

"I'm not taking this." She plunked the tube on the dresser and grabbed a pair of thin latex gloves in the top drawer.

"What am I supposed to do here?" Delon asked, trailing her down the staircase to the first floor. "Stand around wondering if you're dead or alive?"

"You don't need to wonder *anything*. I'll be back in an hour. With Jules or without her."

"And if you're not?"

At the bottom of the stairs, she turned and grasped his arms. She went up on tip-toe and kissed his cheek.

"I'll be fine. This nightmare is going to be over soon. I can feel it."

She rushed out the door and took the brownstone steps before he could stop her.

SHE KEPT on the lighted pathways for as long as she could but approximately ten minutes into her walk, she had no choice but to veer onto a wooded, unlighted path that would bring her to the pagoda. The path crossed over a planked bridge with a still creek below it.

It was cold, damp, and blindingly dark. Without the flashlight, she wouldn't have been able to navigate anything. Even with the light, she only knew where she was going because she'd biked or jogged on these trails many times before.

Who else but Jules would know that Bryn was so familiar with this part of the park? It had to be Jules sending the emails. It *had* to be.

Bryn wondered what exactly her cousin would say to her. And what Bryn should say back. How could she explain to her cousin everything that had gone on in her mind for the past thirty years—how much resentment and envy she'd had bottled up inside of her. How that resentment had proliferated within until it had eventually manifested in wanting to take Jules' husband away in some fashion? That there was nothing else Bryn could take from Jules—not her looks, her career, or her parents' love.

But Delon. *Him*, she had a chance of taking. There was no way to excuse or apologize for her actions. Bryn accepted that Jules might hate her forever and never want to see or speak with her again. She could live with that. What would be difficult to live with was this acidic sense of shame eating through her veins. Would that ever go away?

To her left, Bryn saw the hulking dark mass of the pagoda through the thicket of forest. Her heart began to thud hard and erratically, the chill of fear glazing her skin.

What if the person wasn't Jules? Then what?

She took a succession of deep breaths, trying to slow

her heartbeat. It wasn't that late. Though she saw no people—especially not in this freezing drizzle—she trusted there would be at least a couple of intrepid types in the park. If she screamed, someone would hear her. Someone would come to help.

She clung to this rather infantile idea so she could summon enough courage to keep pushing through the pitch-dark towards the pagoda, following a dirt path foot-stamped into the earth. The pagoda stood at least ten feet high on an exposed stone foundation. Rickety wooden steps led up to the large concrete platform. White columns supported the flared verdigris copper roof, its underbelly rowed with recessed lights that no longer worked.

She didn't see anyone on the platform, but it was difficult to tell from the ground. She swept the small flashlight's beam to the steps and reluctantly made her way to their bottom.

Her "pal" hadn't made it clear whether to meet inside or outside of the pagoda. She definitely preferred outside. If the person wasn't Jules, and perhaps was a threat, Bryn could run away, so long as she wasn't on the platform.

She could dash over the bridge, along a pathway with a few scattered lamp-posts, and keep running until she hit the lake and the bike path, and from there, could make her way out of the park. Inside of the pagoda, she would be trapped.

Bryn didn't know exactly what time it was as she didn't have her phone. She'd estimated it would take her fifteen minutes to reach the pagoda from the brownstone, and had given herself ten minutes leeway. She should be early. But she didn't know for certain.

She swept the flashlight beam away from the steps. On all sides stood dark woods, thickest and blackest behind the pagoda. She occasionally heard loudish crashes that made her heart spasm, but the sounds belonged to small creatures rustling about in the layers of brush.

It had gotten cold enough that she could see her breath curling in foggy wisps out of her mouth. Turning the light to the steps, she decided she better head up them in case the person was waiting for her. She was already regretting that she hadn't taken the pepper spray that Delon had tried to force on her.

Up she went, up, up, up, her feet heavy with caution and fear, her heart pushing thickly against her chest, *bump, bump, bump.* At the top of the steps, she swept the beam from side to side around the platform, half expecting to see a homeless person camped there. But the freezing drizzle had deterred even the homeless from the park.

Her breath came quickly, spasmodically through her lips. And her heartbeat sped up again after she'd managed to calm it slightly with the idea that a scream would bring someone to help her. The truth was, no one was going to help her. She was alone, and had nothing and no one to assist her. The most she could think to do would be to try to use the small flashlight to bonk someone on the head if needed.

Suddenly, a loud, jolting metallic clanging shuddered along the floor—she realized her foot had kicked a large can that someone had left behind. She just began to recover from that shock to her senses when she heard, "Hello, Bryn."

She jumped and flung around toward the voice, nearly dropping the flashlight.

"I'm your pal," the voice said.

A silhouette emerged from a corner of the pagoda. She could only see the shadow because of the cast-off glow of the flashlight, its beam gone astray toward the pagoda roof. Bryn instantly knew the person opposite her was not Jules. The voice was male.

She was too frightened to say anything.

"Put the flashlight down," the man said.

Bryn did as she was told, pointing the beam at the ground, though she didn't turn it off.

The man came closer. He was wearing all black that blended seamlessly with the night.

"Turn off the light," the man said.

Now she detected a borough accent. It was fairly thick. The man had grown up in the city, that was clear. Given that he knew where the music pagoda was, he'd very likely grown up in Brooklyn. Bryn was so nervous that she couldn't find the power button but she finally managed to hit the right spot on the flashlight's handle. The pagoda was plunged into utter darkness. All she heard was her rapid, heavy breathing.

Crash.

Animals in the brush.

"Turn around," the man said. "I'm not going to hurt you."

Vibrating with fear, Bryn turned, trying to tighten

her hold on the flashlight so her trembling hand wouldn't drop it. Through the trees, she could see a pathway that gleamed with a lone lamp-post about fifty feet from the pagoda.

I can run, she kept telling herself. *I can run down the steps and out of the park. I can run, run, run.*

"Hold out your arms," the man said. "I need to pat you down for a phone or weapon."

She held her breath and did as she was told. The man's hands were firm and no-nonsense. He expertly patted her down, running his palms along her sides, then to the outside and inside of her legs, grabbing her ankles, and running his hands back up her legs, along her back, then patting her front, including her breasts. This didn't feel any more invasive than when a gynecologist inserted gloved fingers into her uterus. The pat down was strictly business.

I can run, she thought. *I can run if I need to.*

When his hands left her body, she heard nothing for a few moments, then he said, "You can turn around now." His voice had moved farther away.

She turned and couldn't see him at all in the black dark. A silver sliver of moon peeked around the swollen rain clouds but it wasn't enough to illuminate much of anything.

"Who are you?" Her voice barely projected, coming out a hoarse whisper, her throat muscles coiled tight with fear. She cleared her throat and tried again. "Who are you?"

"Don't worry about that."

Other than the New York accent, there was nothing

in his voice that offered her any kind of identification. The voice was deep but not too deep. He didn't sound young or old, but rather as if he was somewhere in the vast stretch of years between teen and nursing home patient.

"I sent a video to your personal email," he said. "Are you telling me you didn't get it?"

"I didn't get any video. I swear I didn't."

A huffing sound came from him, like a heavy sigh. "I'm guessing it was too large," he said. "Too many gigabytes for your provider. I couldn't risk putting it in cloud storage."

She had the terrible, despairing idea that the video was of Jules. Jules, bound and blindfolded, begging Bryn and Delon to do whatever her captor wanted.

And Bryn had never received the message. Her cousin had been out there all of this time, somewhere terrified and suffering, and she still was. Now the man would tell her what he wanted in exchange for returning Jules. Bryn presumed it would be money but how would she get that? Delon said he didn't have any, and Bryn certainly didn't.

She'd have to ask Rich, the man she'd called a rapist not long ago. Still, he'd want his daughter back. His other daughter. If Bryn had been kidnapped, she'd be finished. Rich wouldn't give up five dollars for her. But Jules would get all the money he had. He would even interrupt one of his trips for Jules. He'd call his travel agent and say, "Get me on the next plane to New York! I don't care how much it costs!"

Yes, she'd have to call Rich and Jacqueline. They'd

do whatever they needed to do for Jules. They'd even quickly get over what Bryn had said to Rich that morning. None of it would matter with their daughter needing help.

"I don't have any money," she said. "I can get you some though, I promise. You just have to give me a little time."

Why had the man decided to get ransom from Bryn and not Jules' wealthy parents? Did he think journalists made a ton of money or something? Or had he simply thought that sending the video to the parents was too risky and they would immediately call the police while he—rightly as it turned out—figured Bryn wouldn't?

Silence. Then another crash. A squirrel or chipmunk hopping about in the brush.

"I don't want money," the man said tersely. He even sounded insulted.

"I—then, then I don't—" Bryn shook her head and could say no more. She was too baffled with whatever was happening.

A feeble glow appeared at the opposite end of the pagoda. She could barely make out the man's knuckles and the shape of his head. He was looking into his phone. Then he swiftly walked towards her, the screen pointed away from him, so he remained in black shadow. The screen moved in an eerily disembodied way towards her, as if floating through the air.

It stopped about a foot from her. She stared at the phone, then looked up to his face—or what should have been a face. He hadn't told her not to look at him but as soon as she did, she was nauseated with the notion that he'd kill her since she'd looked directly at him.

Only, there was nothing there. Where a visage should have been was a smooth void absent of discernible features. She squinted, realizing he had something covering his face—a thin, translucent mask. It made him look inhuman.

He turned his featureless face to his phone again, then held it toward her. On the screen, images were moving. She refocused from his strangely expressionless face to the phone. She leaned forward, concentrating on what she was seeing.

On the screen was a man. Then a girl appeared in the frame, and then another girl, and behind the man, came yet another girl. Two blondes and a brunette. All pretty. Bryn's eyes and brain finally coordinated, sending messages to each other.

The scene began to take on a narrative.

The man looked familiar. He had black cropped hair with a smear of silver on each sideburn. He was smiling with all of his big, fleshy cheeks. He said something, but what, Bryn couldn't tell. The girls giggled and crowded closer around him.

Then the man's face turned in such a way that Bryn noted a black soul patch on his chin. One of the girls—a blonde—flung her arms around him and kissed him on the cheek. Now Bryn realized that the girls were all wearing lingerie tops. Their arms were pale and very thin. Their faces all had something about the features that Bryn intuited as foreign—defined cheekbones, almond-shaped eyes, and pointed chins.

She felt her mouth falling open as she stared at the screen, pulling the scene fully into her awareness, giving it meaning.

The man in the video was the police commissioner. And he was with three barely-dressed young women.

But these weren't young women. They were girls.

"How old are they?" she asked quietly.

"Not old enough," the man said.

"Where is this?"

"Moscow."

Bryn stood catatonic, staring at the screen. The girls tumbled over the police commissioner, giggling with high-pitched, girlish shrieks. The police commissioner— Tony Melani—had his mouth open in a half-laugh. He spoke again, then snuggled his jowls into the thin neck of one of the girls. Then all four of them toppled out of the frame.

The man in the flesh mask pulled the phone away and the pagoda plunged back into darkness.

"They're underage?" Bryn asked. "Underage for the States?"

"Two are fourteen, one fifteen."

She paused, the information sinking grotesquely into her mind. She very well remembered being fourteen. It was the year that she became starkly aware that her cousin was what boys wanted, and she was not.

That summer, she'd highlighted her hair and spent untold hours struggling to tame her kinky curls in an effort to look more like Jules. Her breasts had started to bulge out from her shirts, drawing stares from complete strangers, including men much older than herself, men walking with their wives and children. The year her gym teacher—female—pulled her aside and suggested she needed a better bra, one more up to the task.

But her mind wasn't nearly as developed. It was mushy and scattered. She'd felt inferior, insecure, and also indestructible. Sex was everywhere and nowhere at the same time. She wouldn't lose her virginity for several more years. Looking back, she realized how fortunate that was—as if she'd escaped a minefield, where all around her, young girls were blowing up.

"How do you know their ages?" she asked the man.

"I know."

She turned her eyes away from the screen, choking down her revulsion. The police commissioner was middle-aged. In his forties or fifties. And married. She also knew that he had children. How many, she didn't remember exactly. Even if these girls weren't underage, the video would ruin him.

"Do you have proof of their ages?" she asked.

"Of course." He sounded irritated.

"How can I get the video?"

"I'll reconfigure it and send it again."

"I'll need some kind of proof that it isn't deep faked," she said. "I'll have to send it to experts."

"Do what you need to do." There was a long pause before he said, "So now do I get a thank you?"

"Thank you… I guess."

"You guess? I could send this to anyone. *The New York Times* would kill to have it." He stepped closer to her. He wasn't tall, only a few inches taller than herself. She instinctively felt that he was bulky and muscular—she could feel his physicality in his hyper-masculine energy.

"I'm no snitch. A little side nook is one thing. But I got a daughter this age."

"Yes," she said, not wanting to risk saying anything that could be the wrong thing.

"I chose you," he said. "Out of all the hacks in the city, you're the one I chose to run with this."

"I understand," she said, cautiously. "I appreciate it."

He still had possession of the video and could decide not to resend it. She had to be extremely careful how she treated him.

"You know why I chose you?"

"I don't."

"Because you're the best-looking one," he said, chuckling a little. "The hottest reporter. I had to choose someone. I suppose I'm that shallow."

Bryn's mind flipped through her work colleagues: Amika and the third reporter on the police commissioner tip beat, Molly.

Out of the three of them, Bryn would have guessed most men would say Molly was the most attractive. She had wavy, dark-brown hair, doe-brown eyes, and the cherubic features that were generally considered pleasing. Something about humans being drawn to faces that resemble babies.

And Amika, with her bolder, less symmetrical, features, was striking in a more unique way.

But herself? Plain. She knew it. *Plain.*

It was against the odds that the man would choose

her, but hadn't Delon, as well? Delon, who could have any woman? Who, in fact, already had a stunning wife? And how goddamn ridiculous that women spent so much of their lives in some kind of beauty contest they'd never asked to be in.

"Well, thank you," she said, really wanting to tell the man to shove it.

"Do me a favor, Bryn," he said. "Take that hood off for a minute. Let me see you."

Her heart began to thud and her fingers grew tingly inside her gloves. She didn't want to anger the man and have him change his mind about sending her the video. But nor did she want to conduct a mini beauty pageant for him.

"Just for a minute," he cajoled. "I'm putting my life at risk for you."

The thought of those young girls in the video made her quickly unsnap the hood's flap and snatch it down from her head. She heard nothing for several long beats and then a beam of light sliced through her eyes before she could squeeze them shut.

"Who are you?" the man demanded.

She flung a hand in front of her face, trying to block the penetrating beam of light. "I'm Bryn. Bryn Bastid."

"Bullshit," he said, angrily. "Bryn is blonde. She's beautiful."

Bryn turned her face away from the bright white beam. She weighed running down the steps and out of the park. She could run pretty fast. If she went right now, she could get away from him.

But she still wanted that video.

"I swear to you I'm Bryn. Why do you think I'm blonde?"

"Because I have your picture."

The beam dropped away from her face and she fluttered her eyes open. The man wasn't far from her. He again held out his phone. There was another image on the screen. This time, it was a still image.

She quickly blinked her eyes, unable to see much of anything. The fluorescent beam had temporarily blinded her. He moved the phone closer and she kept blinking until the shadowy shapes clouding her vision cleared. She stared at the screen.

Jules was on it.

Smiling with that white, slightly protuberant smile. Her crystalline-pale, blue-green eyes. Her long, tousled, buttery blonde hair. There were people on either side of Jules, but Bryn could only see their sides as they were cropped out.

"That—that isn't me," she stammered. "That's my cousin. Jules."

The man took the phone back, looking into it. His fingers traced the screen.

"It says it right here. 'One of our own, CD reporter Bryn Bastid…'"

"Please!" Bryn said, voice rising. She thrust out her hand for the phone. "Please, can I see it?"

To her surprise, the man handed her his phone. She slid her fingers together on the screen, trying to retract the photo back to its complete image. But the screen didn't respond to her touch. She had to take off the glove and shove it inside of her pocket, then try again.

It was the photo of Jules at her bookstore event the summer before last. On her right was Gilda. On her left was Thom King. And, slightly in front of Thom, was Bryn.

Bryn's eyes roved down to the caption. It had mixed up Jules and Bryn, misidentifying them. Anyone looking at the picture who didn't know them would think that Bryn was Jules and vice versa.

"The caption is wrong," she said. "The blonde is my cousin, the author. I'm Bryn, the girl here." She placed a finger over her image on the screen.

The man had his hand out so she returned his phone. He kept his head down examining the screen, then looked up at her. His featureless, horror-movie face gave her the chills.

"Well, that's very unfortunate," he said. "I'm not the only one who thinks she's you."

"What do you mean?"

"This is the picture that got shared in the hangout."

"What's the hangout?"

"What it sounds like. Where a bunch of us hang out. Anonymously. Where we can talk and complain about things we can't otherwise. It's where the video circulated. Where you—or this lady—circulated."

"You're a cop, aren't you?"

"Well, give her a prize."

Your investigation skills need some improvement, she thought but didn't dare say.

"So, a bunch of cops think she's me."

"Like I say, this is the picture that got sent around.

Someone noticed a girl on the investigation team was pretty smoking, and it got shared."

"Does anyone else know you sent me that video?"

"You better hope not. You might not be standing here otherwise."

There was a pulverizing silence as the harrowing certainty of what had happened, the obscene repercussion of this photo and its caption took shape in Bryn's mind. A small wave of hysteria gathered in her chest, gaining force as it rushed up her throat and out of her mouth.

"Oh my god," she gasped. "Someone took Jules when they meant to take me."

Chapter Twenty-Nine

"*D*elon!"

She jogged past the staircase and into the kitchen, where she imagined he would be. He wasn't.

"Delon!"

Louder now. Shouting.

She jogged into the dining room that merged into the living room, which overlooked the street. Not there.

She turned and raced up the stairs, picturing him coming out to the second-floor landing. But she still didn't see him.

"Delon!" Even louder now. Could he be in the bathroom?

She bounded up to the third floor and ran down the hallway to the primary bedroom.

"Delon! Where are you?"

The door to the *en suite* bathroom was open. He wasn't there.

She couldn't remember where she'd left her phone.

She went around the primary bedroom, calling for it. Its computerized British male voice answered, "I'm right here," and she found her cell sitting on top of Jules' dresser, next to the ceramic bowl from where she'd taken the small flashlight.

She unlocked her phone and was about to hit Delon's number when she recalled they'd agreed not to contact each other by phone. But why? She couldn't remember exactly.

"Fuck it," she said, pressing his number.

To her surprise, she heard his cell's familiar melody. She ran out of the bedroom, and down two flights of stairs, the phone going to voicemail just as she located it on the kitchen island.

"Delon, where are you?" she asked, despite staring at his phone. It made no sense to leave him a voicemail, but rational thought had fled.

Why wouldn't he be here? Her mind zapped to Delon being taken. The same people who'd taken Jules had now taken him.

It was the NYPD. One crooked cop or many crooked cops.

Someone figured out the cop in the flesh mask had sent her video of the police commissioner with three underage girls. That person, or persons, had taken Jules, believing they were taking Bryn, in an attempt to prevent Bryn from giving the incriminating video to her newspaper.

At some point, that person, or persons, had likely realized they'd made a mistake. Now they'd be coming for the real Bryn. This person may have reached the brownstone while Bryn was meeting with the whistle-blower in the park. Not finding her, they'd taken Delon instead.

"Jesus!" she cried breathlessly, voice bouncing off the white kitchen walls.

She had no idea where Delon had put his car keys. She ran to the front door and turned the lock, then hurried up the stairs, and back to the primary bedroom. She frantically cast around various surfaces, looking for his keys.

She was shaking so badly she didn't know if she would be able to drive. But it seemed safer to be inside of a car than on the subway. Not seeing the keys, she decided to try the kitchen again before accepting that Delon must have the keys on him, and getting out of the brownstone. The subway was two blocks away. She'd get on the train and head to a PATH station.

She'd do what the whistleblower cop had told her to do: Get out of the city. Go anywhere. Just don't be where the NYPD can grab you and do whatever they want with you.

But she worried about being on the subway. What was to stop an officer from simply walking up to her and handcuffing her and dragging her away? No one would get in the middle of that. But she didn't dare stand on the street waiting for a car service. Who knew who'd pick her up.

She was fleeing down the stairs when she heard the lock on the front door click, and saw the door knob turn. Stunned with fear, she could think of nothing to do but run back upstairs. Taking the stairs as fast as she could, she heard, "Bryn?"

She turned. Delon was in the doorway, staring up at her.

"Delon!" she shrieked. Her eyes shot over his shoulder, expecting to see a man behind him—one of the dirty cops who'd taken him. But no one was there. He shut the door and gaped at her.

"What the hell happened?" he asked.

She ran down the stairs and threw herself at him. "You're here," she gasped. "I thought you'd been taken, too."

He pushed her back by her arms and stared into her face. "Was it Jules or not?" he demanded.

"No, no..." She stood trembling, trying to catch her breath. "It—it wasn't Jules. We have to get out of here. Out of the city."

"Who was it? Who did you meet?"

"I'll tell you later, let's get in the car. Now!"

He patted the pockets of his coat. "Okay, I've got everything. I guess. Where are we going?"

"Come on, we don't have time for this. They could be coming."

"Who's coming?"

She ripped away from him and jettisoned down the stoop to the sidewalk. She felt safer outside. This way, she at least stood a chance. She could run away or scream for help. Anyone who grabbed her would at least be caught on someone's home surveillance.

Delon turned and locked the door, then came down

the stoop, moving slower than she wanted him to move. They picked up their pace on the sidewalk, walked a block to his Peugeot. Every second, Bryn anticipated someone suddenly appearing in front of her, gun in hand.

"Bryn, where are we going?" he asked, once they were safe inside the car.

"New Jersey."

"What?" He turned and stared wide-eyed at her. "Where?"

"Newark."

"What the hell for?"

"Just go!" she ordered, pointing down Prospect Park West.

They drove until they hit a red light at Grand Army Plaza. Bryn peered over her shoulder through the rear windshield, looking for... she didn't know what exactly.

"Bryn, what is going on?"

"It wasn't her," she said. "I met with a cop. I don't know anything about him. He had a mask on and I'll never be able to identify him. He'd sent me a video of Tony Melani—the police commissioner—with three underage girls. But I didn't receive the video. The file was too big or something."

The light turned and the car took a left, heading toward Manhattan. She gestured at Delon's phone, which he'd snapped into a holder on the dashboard.

"Put in 11 Centre Plaza, Newark."

"Why, Bryn?" he asked, insistently. "Why?"

"Because that's an FBI bureau. Cops or even the commissioner himself took Jules. They thought she was me. We need to report everything outside of the city. That's the nearest FBI building."

At the next light, Delon began tapping into his phone. "There's no such place."

"FBI headquarters! Just put it in!"

"Okay, okay. I got it. 11 Centre Place, not Plaza."

The car moved again but they hit traffic and slowed to a near-stop. Bryn anxiously peered out the back window. "Tell me how this happened," he said.

"There was a picture of Jules and me at a book event. The caption got us mixed up. Someone must have looked at my social media and saw where I was. He drove up but had a picture of Jules for identification, not me."

Besides the wrong picture circulating in the cop "hangout," Bryn had months ago deleted all social media photos with herself in them, in a fit of pique over how heavy her face looked. The person could have easily figured out where Bryn was but, because of her lack of personal photos, did not have his idea of what Bryn looked like corrected.

"Then he saw Jules and talked her into his car," she said. "He probably flashed a badge, and made up a story. She would trust a cop. Or maybe he just pointed a gun at her."

Bryn grabbed the dashboard, then pulled on the handle of her door to make certain it was locked. "Your door is locked, right? They're all locked?" she asked breathlessly.

"Yes, they're locked."

The car began moving again. Delon kept flicking his

eyes to his phone, a maps app open. "It's bringing us to the Holland Tunnel," he said.

She didn't like the sound of his voice. "So? What's wrong with that?"

"Cops will be sitting right there. They probably know my license plate already."

"Can we get around them?"

He looked intensely out of the window for several moments, then said, "Let's turn back and take the Verrazano."

Chapter Thirty

They'd been driving for half an hour, and had just crossed the Verrazano Bridge into Staten Island. Every five minutes or so, she turned and stared out the back window. There were always headlights behind them, and their bright shine made it impossible to know if they belonged to the same vehicle, if the pair were being followed.

"Where were you?" she asked. "Back at the brownstone. Where did you go?"

It was something she'd been wondering about since the second he came through the door but the question had gotten buried under the more urgent task of getting the hell out of the city.

"Went to the deli," he said. "I couldn't stand waiting for you a minute longer. I was going insane."

Bryn stared at his inscrutable profile but said nothing.

A deli is where you went to get potato chips or beer or batteries or cigarettes. It wasn't where you went when you were waiting to see if your missing wife or the woman you were sleeping with, or both of them, came back from the park alive.

"I don't know, Bryn," he said, apparently sensing her skepticism. "I could hardly think. I went for a walk and ended up at the deli."

"You didn't follow me?" she asked, sounding more accusatory than she'd intended.

"No. I didn't follow you."

He gripped the steering wheel and leaned into it but it was too dark to get a good read on his expression. They stayed silent for a long time. Outside the windows, it got darker and emptier. At some point, Bryn realized they were passing by a forest. Miles and miles of forest.

"Delon, where the hell are we?"

"New Jersey."

"Yes, I know that but…"

She angled toward the phone screen. The blue dot of the car was headed south in the vast expanse of New Jersey. She wasn't very familiar with the state but felt that the city of Newark was a lot closer to New York City than where they currently were.

"Are we lost?" she asked, really meaning are *you* lost?

"No, Bryn, we're not lost. It's just that it kept me on 95 and there hasn't been anywhere to turn around." He kept continually flicking his eyes up to his rearview mirror. "And I haven't wanted to frighten you."

"Why?" she asked, trying to swallow down the hysteria that immediately snapped to attention, rising up her throat like coppery acid. "Frighten me about what?"

Her voice was slightly shrill. She hated how instantly terrified she sounded.

"I'm pretty sure that car has been behind us since the Beltway," Delon said. "But it's really hard to tell."

She whirled in her seat, staring out the back window. The headlights that stared back at her looked like any other headlights.

"I've been going slower to see if it'll pass me, and it won't," he said.

"Oh god."

"Just stay calm."

She turned back to the front windows. All around were endless masses of dark trees. She hadn't seen a highway sign or light in a while. Tilting the phone holder in her direction, she peered at the map on the screen. It was entirely green, indicating they were in the midst of a huge rural area.

"Are we in the Pine Barrens?" she asked. For the moment, her voice was more awed than anxious. She'd heard about the Pine Barrens. Over a million acres of pure wilderness. Lakes, swamps, mountains, and forests.

"I'm trying to find a place to turn back north, okay?" he said. "Please don't panic."

"How did we get this far south?" she practically shrieked.

"I told you! It took me on I-95! And I was distracted with this guy behind me." He looked again into the rearview mirror. "We'll turn at the next exit."

"Jesus! We've got to get out of here."

Beyond the limitless forest, the vast sky was blacker

than she'd seen it in a very long time, billions of stars burning white-bright.

The only other car she saw was the one right on their tail.

"We should get gas, too," he said.

"What?!" This time, it was a full-on shriek.

"It's not like I knew we'd be taking a long trip! I didn't have a full tank."

She clenched and unclenched her fists, trying to slow her galloping heart, staring at the unfathomably endless pine forest on all sides of the car. Boundless amounts of trees and darkness and spooks and ghosts and legends.

She had to not go off the deep end. The doors were locked and even if they ran out of gas, the person following them couldn't get inside.

But… if the person was a cop, he'd have a gun. He could shoot right through the windows, then say that he'd felt threatened or thought he saw one of them reach for a weapon or…

A cop could say anything and be believed. Everyone knew that.

"Are you sure it's the same car behind us? All the way from Brooklyn?" she asked, almost ashamed at the raw, childlike terror in her voice.

"No, I'm not certain. Bryn, please." Delon smacked the steering wheel with the ball of his palm. "I've got to concentrate. Just stay calm. Nothing is going to happen."

"We might as well go to Philadelphia at this point!"

"Will you let me handle this? Please?"

Bryn bit down hard on her thumb knuckle so she'd

stop screeching at him. She'd never seen such a massive expanse of woods. How many crazy stories were out there about the Pine Barrens? How many videos were online, each titled some variation of "My Terrifying Night in the Pine Barrens!"

And *this* is where they end up?

Several more minutes passed with nothing but dark columns of trees outside and no exit anywhere. She leaned toward his phone on the dashboard. Green was all over the map but the blue dot of their car was gone.

"We're not getting a signal right now," he said. "I didn't want to scare you. It will come back."

Bryn groaned and sank her head into her hand. She felt like her insides were going to gush out of her ass. How many more things could go wrong? They were running out of gas, they were in the middle of the goddamn Pine Barrens, and there was someone following them. They would have been better off walking into a Brooklyn precinct.

"I can't believe this," she moaned. "This can't be happening."

"I'm telling you everything is fine," he said. "We'll find an exit soon enough."

"How much gas do you have?"

"Just let me worry about it, Bryn."

Her heartbeat jerked into her throat, beating erratically on her windpipe. That meant not much. She didn't dare look at the fuel gauge. If she saw it in the red, she would start crying.

"Listen," he said. "I've got to try to lose this asshole. I'm going to head into one of these little roads."

"What little roads?"

"Every once in a while, we pass a little road. I have no idea where they lead. Maybe people live out here."

"What if we called 911? Wouldn't New Jersey cops show up?"

"Check your phone for a signal," he said.

She looked at her phone screen. The four tiny bars at the top were grayed out. She went into her contacts and hit Delon's number. Her screen said "Calling…" and nothing happened.

"Jesus Christ," she said, her voice whiny with fear. "This is a fucking horror movie."

"Hold on tight," he said, and suddenly veered the car off the main road, turning so sharply that Bryn was thrown into the driver's seat. She grabbed the armrest on her door, and pushed her feet into the floor, bracing herself.

The car sped down a completely black one-lane road, the only illumination coming from the headlights. She whipped around and looked behind them. No headlights.

The Peugeot zoomed along the narrow road, bumping over broken asphalt. They were headed deep into the pine forest.

"Slow down," she pleaded. "If you hit a deer or something, we're doomed."

"He's gone," Delon said, staring into the rearview mirror. "Now we have to wait to see if he turns around."

"What if he does?"

"Then we know for sure what we're dealing with. It's

a one-way road back there. He's not going to turn around on it unless he means business."

Delon drew the car to a stop. He began to back up. The car dipped deeply in the back, as if they'd gone off the shoulder. Startled, Bryn grasped the seat.

"Fuck," he said.

"Jesus Christ, now what?"

"Bryn, please calm down!"

He shook off his coat. "We're stuck in something. Let me check it out."

"No!" she cried, digging into his shirt sleeve with her nails. "Don't go out there."

"It's fine. I just need to push in the back. I've done it before. It's nothing to worry about. It's a small car, okay?"

He maneuvered his phone out of the holder, sliding his finger along the screen until a bright funnel of light emerged.

Just before he opened the door, he turned to her and grinned. "It's okay, Bryn," he said. "We'll be fine. I promise."

Chapter Thirty-One

*B*ryn sat rocking in her seat, her gaze sweeping along the dark, hulking mass of woods all around to the small, empty road, expecting at any moment to see the white, stabbing headlights of the car that had been following them.

Delon had left his door open. Repeatedly, she felt the car jolt a little, as if he was trying to move it. Each time that the car bucked, bile sloshed around in her stomach. If she hadn't been so frightened, she would have gone outside and tried to vomit.

Suddenly, Delon popped his head back through the open door. She nearly had a heart attack.

"I need to find a big branch," he said. "To jam it under the wheel."

She stared disbelievingly at him, mouth agape.

"We're in the woods," he said. "Won't take long to find a thick stick."

"I thought you said it was no big deal and you could push the car!"

"I was wrong. I'm going to close the door enough so there's no light. But it looks like that car wasn't following us, anyway. We're being paranoid." He grinned impishly. "We'll be out of here in no time. Trust me?"

"Just hurry up, please!"

"Do you trust me?"

She said nothing.

The door was almost closed when he yanked it back halfway, sticking his handsome face through the opening. "Bryn, I won't let anything happen to you," he said. "I promise I won't."

Then he shut the door.

This was too surreal. Too perfectly fucked up. It made no sense how perfectly fucked up it was. When he got them out of whatever the car was stuck in, no doubt it would sputter out of gas. Then whoever had been following them would reappear at the end of the road. Bryn realized she'd have no choice but to flee into the wild, dense acres of pine forest. It was so dark she would crash into one tree after another.

She traced her hand along the door until she felt the little knob, and she flicked it back, but the door stayed shut. It was locked. She thought of her mother. Raped because Jess had no way to open a car door. Bryn's existence due to a locked door.

Her mind rewound to Delon entering into the brownstone after she'd returned from the park. Something about the look on his face hadn't been right. And nothing seemed to make sense about him going for a walk and ending up at the deli. He apparently hadn't bought anything. Or had he?

None of it seemed right. None of the entire night. Nothing seemed right this minute either. It all seemed too something.

Too planned.

Her eyes roved to the steering wheel. She reached over and felt for the keys in the dash but they weren't there. He'd taken them with him.

He followed me, she thought. *He followed me into the park.*

It hadn't been small animals she'd heard crackling about in the brush, but Delon's feet kicking aside leaves as he spied on her interaction with the mystery emailer. She remembered the pepper spray he'd pressed into her hand, claiming it belonged to his wife. Jules would have mentioned carrying pepper spray. In one of their conversations, she would have mentioned it, wouldn't she?

A monstrous vision sprang upon Bryn, assaulting her imagination.

Delon pepper spraying Jules in his car. Grabbing her by the back of the head and jamming the tube into her mouth.

Bryn shook her head to disperse the awful, too-clear vision. Her eyes roamed to Delon's coat squished on the seat. His long, black, wool coat, with its classic, fitted silhouette. He looked beyond handsome in it. The moon shone down, casting enough light that she could distinguish the black of the coat from the dark vinyl of the seat.

Why had he returned back to the brownstone so late? Once Bryn left the masked cop at the pagoda, she'd jogged out of the park, wanting to get to the brownstone as quickly as possible. Delon was a runner, as well. There was no way he wouldn't have beaten her back. Yet, it had been at least ten minutes that Bryn was alone, searching for him, before he'd opened the front door.

Even if he'd wanted to avoid seeing Bryn, there were several alternative pathways in the park that he could have taken back to the brownstone. The only explanation for the amount of time it had taken for him to return home was that he hadn't *run* back.

He'd walked.

Something stopped him, she thought. *Something stopped him from running.*

She dug her fingers past the flap of his coat pocket, and lowered them down into the aperture. Their tips brushed something hard, smooth, and metallic.

The pepper spray tube?

She traced one finger along the object's nail-hard surface. It dipped into circular ridges. Panicked, she yanked her hand out of his pocket. Heart thumping madly, she reached over in slow motion and directed her hand back into his pocket, as tense as if reaching into the mouth of a live shark.

With her other hand, she lifted the flap up completely, and inch by inch slid the object upward.

It was a gun.

Chapter Thirty-Two

She found Delon about fifty feet away from the car. It was so blind-dark that at first she couldn't see him, but as her vision adjusted to the night, she rooted out his silhouette from the surrounding black canvas. He was crouched low on the ground, jerking something back and forth.

The only illumination came from the sharp-edged waning crescent of enamel-white moon peeking out from behind thin, ragged rain clouds. She could hear loud crackling sounds, as if he was scrounging in the brush. Was he really looking for a large branch to free the car?

Or was he digging a shallow ditch for Bryn—one next to her cousin?

Her hand was violently shaking, so she reached over with her other hand and clapped her wrist, stilling its trembles.

Then she raised the gun.

"Where's Jules?"

Her throat muscles had gripped her larynx with fear and adrenaline, so her voice came out weak, strained, and warbling. She'd never before pointed a gun at another human being. But she'd held one. Last year, she researched a story on the long process that it took to legally obtain a gun in New York City and had taken a shooting lesson at a gun range. She knew how to hold a gun, and she'd even fired one.

But that had been under controlled circumstances. She'd been wearing ear muffs and had an instructor who'd told her every little thing to do. This was an entirely different animal. Not only did her hand continue to tremble, it was blind dark out. She was pretty sure if she fired, she would hit nothing but one of the thousands of trees all around them.

"What did you do with Jules?" she demanded. This time, her voice was more like a scream, a desperate scream. The sound startled her, propelling through the deep forest.

"Jesus fucking Christ, Bryn," Delon said. "I never put the safety catch back on. Please. Put the gun down. Point it away."

"Is she here? In these woods? Is this where you buried her?"

When she raised her voice, it was tougher to keep a steady grip on the gun, so she resolved to keep her voice lower, more in control.

"Bryn," Delon said, with a slow and regulated tone. He methodically raised one arm, holding it out toward her defensively. "I did not do anything to Jules. I swear on my life I didn't. Rich gave me that gun over Christmas."

"Yes, let's hear the latest lie."

"After that guy tried to push his way into the house when she was alone, she swore me to secrecy, worried about her mother's reaction. But then she went and told her father. The next thing I knew, Rich was handing me a gun. It was the real reason I left over Christmas. He and I got into a thing about it. I didn't want a gun in the house. But he told me I had to protect Jules. I somehow was talked into taking it back with me."

"Funny how you never mentioned that when you told me the story about leaving. You blamed it on a dog movie!"

"What was I supposed to say? That I had a gun? You already thought I killed my wife!"

"You've got a story for everything. It's really impressive! You had more than enough time to pick her up in Hudson Hollow, kill her, bury her here, and drive back."

"Then I'd have three toll passes on my record. I had one. Will you please think for a moment what you're saying?"

"First of all, you interrupted me and I never saw the records. Secondly, you realized your mistake when you drove up the first time, then took the back roads for the next two trips."

"Bryn…" He raised his other hand in the same cautious, measured way. "You don't know what you're talking about. Can we please, *please* talk without a gun in my face?"

"You've talked enough, asshole. You've talked yourself out of this more times than I can count. I assume you drove out here to kill me, too. I want to know one thing before you give me those keys and I leave you here. Why? Why'd you kill her? Was it because of us? You got her pregnant and thought I'd leave you for good? Testicular cancer! Oh, that was good. How'd you come up with that one?"

"Every single thing I told you is the goddamn truth!"

"Or did it have nothing to do with us? You just wanted to sell the brownstone and collect on the insurance? Huh? Was that it?"

Her shoulder started to ache. She'd only had the gun pointed at him for a minute or so, but she remembered how difficult it was to keep an arm elevated for a long stretch. She knew that soon, her shoulder muscle would fail her, her arm would droop, and she wouldn't be able to hold the gun on him any longer. People didn't understand the arm strength it took to hold a gun.

She heard the crackle of snapping brush and realized he was inching toward her.

"Stop!" she shouted into the dark, vast silence. "Delon, I swear I will do this. I will shoot you! Don't come closer!"

"Bryn, please!" he begged. "You can call Rich and ask him about the gun."

"Oh, right. To a guy who I just called a rapist this morning. I'm sure he'd love to chit-chat. Did you forget there's no signal out here, shithead? And who cares if he gave you the gun you used to kill Jules? Why are you carrying it around? Let me guess. To kill me, then bury me and the gun out here in this damn endless forest next to Jules."

"I have it because I followed you to the park, of course. Did you think I was going to let you go meet some stranger? You were convinced it was Jules, but I wasn't."

"Delon, every single thing leads to you. Every single thing! Just tell me why you did it. I need to know. Was it because of me? Tell me!"

"I'm not going to tell you our marriage was perfect. It wasn't. You should know that more than anyone. Between the affairs, the financial problems, and the baby crap, we hardly had a marriage at all. I should have been a man and asked for a divorce years ago. But, Bryn, I swear to you, I swear on my mother's life, I did not kill her!"

Suddenly, a wide beam of light streaked through the trees. Startled, Bryn jerked around. Then, remembering she needed to keep the gun on Delon, she whipped back in his direction.

His dark silhouette was closer to her.

"Stop!" she shrieked.

"Bryn, they've followed us," he said, his voice vibrating with barely-controlled panic. "It's that car. We need to go."

"Don't move!"

She tried to look behind her and keep her eyes and the gun on Delon at the same time. A vehicle was rolling down the one-way road toward them. She couldn't determine anything about the car—its color, its make, its size, nothing. All she could see were its bright white headlights.

"Bryn, please!" he begged. "We need to go now!"

She watched the car continue down the lane, closer and closer. She was utterly paralyzed. There was danger on one side of her, danger on the other. And she didn't know which danger to prioritize.

"Just trust me, Bryn!" he pleaded. "I wouldn't hurt you. I love you!"

She turned back toward him, mouth hanging open. Despite the high drama of the circumstances, what he'd said was so shocking that it momentarily took precedence over everything else.

"I don't know why," he said. "I guess because we're both kind of messed up. We get each other, don't we?"

He'll say anything, she thought. *Anything at all.*

"Please, Bryn," he said. "Please trust me. Put down the gun."

Now the car was close enough that she heard its engine. Within a few moments, it would be so close that she'd have no choice but to escape into the forest. But how could she run into those terrifyingly deep-black woods? She could see nothing in them, absolutely nothing. Delon would follow her. How could she shoot him if she couldn't even see him?

Frozen with indecision, she turned back to Delon. It seemed as if he was even nearer to her.

"Get into the car, Bryn," he said. "I've got the keys. I think I can move it. We've got to get in before it's too late."

She got into the car of a man she trusted.

Couldn't fend him off.

"No," she cried, a knot in her throat. "No, I—I can't—"

The blindingly-bright headlights were almost next to them, so close that the forest was lit up like a stage.

"Bryn," Delon said, continuing his slow, methodical walk toward her. "We're not going to get away. It's too late. But I'm a pretty good shot. I used to skeet shoot."

Bryn was shaking so badly that she was certain she wouldn't be able to hold the gun much longer, let alone shoot straight. Let alone get into a shootout with a trained police officer.

She realized something else. Her holding a gun was the perfect excuse the dirty cop driving toward them would need to kill them both. And if she handed over the gun to Delon, he would start shooting, and give the cop even more of an excuse.

"Give me the gun, please," he said, holding one arm toward her. His hand seemed so near that if she reached out, she'd graze his fingertips. "Just trust me, Bryn. Give it to me."

At this point, she was so terrified and confused that her teeth began to chatter, the top row clanking onto the bottom. She turned back and for a moment didn't see Delon. He must have taken those few seconds she was looking behind her to run off into the dark endless forest. Of course, he'd left her here to fend for herself—left her alone to get shot by a dirty cop.

But then he loomed out of the neon white of the headlights behind them. He was directly in front of her, reaching for her. He was a moment away from grabbing the gun.

An immense and extremely loud pop cracked like a small explosion. Her body jolted backwards so forcefully that she was thrown to the ground. When she hit the hard earth, she heard another loud pop, and the gun jerked as if it was alive. Then the hard metal was gone from her hand.

Something strong and acrid singed the air around her. She recognized the stench as the burn of gunpowder. She remembered the peculiar smell from the day she'd spent target shooting for her article. She couldn't take a breath for what seemed a long time. All the air had been punched out of her lungs. Everything around her was white and blurry, and she had no idea what was happening.

"This is an LPI. 10-53, 10-54," she heard. "Country Road 539. We got a little no-name dirt road here just past Bryant Road, headed south. Approximately quarter of a mile in. Request EMS."

A radio squelched and an unintelligible staccato voice crackled through the forest.

"Delon?" she struggled to say. Then louder, more desperately: "Delon?"

She pushed off the sodden, leaf-littered ground, spine drooped forward. Something had happened. Something terrible, life-changingly horrific had happened. Her brain kept pushing the thing away, refusing, for her own protection, to fully reveal the thing to her. But she sensed it all around her, crouching behind the innumerable trees, waiting to pounce.

"Not breathing," she heard. "No pulse. Starting CPR."

"Delon!" she cried. The sound ripped through her windpipe as if it was an object, a ragged-edged knife. She managed to stand, her body swaying as if it was fighting a strong wind. She staggered toward the voice. It belonged to a man. A familiar male voice. Where had she heard that voice before?

The crisp scoop of moon widened its silver glow. On the ground she saw two figures in shadow, at the edge of the spotlight of the headlights. She stumbled toward them, trying not to fall over. She watched as one figure hunched over the other, the second figure unmoving on the ground.

"What's going on?" she called.

She stared at the scene on the ground. Dimly, some-where in the unfathomable depths of her consciousness, she realized the unmoving man on the ground was Delon.

"Oh my god," she moaned. "Oh my god."

"Bryn, what happened?" the man said. "He's been shot."

"Oh my god."

"Bryn! Tell me what happened."

"He—he—" She was shivering all over, as if she was having a seizure. Maybe she was. She was going into some kind of shock. Any moment, she would fall to the ground and be unable to speak or function. She had to say it all now. Someone had to hear it.

"He killed her. Jules. He killed her!"

The figure's dark silhouette bent forward. He placed

his mouth on Delon's mouth, one hand over his nose, the other around his face. Then the man straightened and pushed up and down in quick, short, hard thrusts on Delon's chest. He did this over and over until he stopped and said, breathlessly, "Jules? Bryn, he didn't kill her."

These words went round and round in her mind, circled her in the darkness, meaning nothing. Meaning everything.

"What—what are you…? What do you…?" Finally, she screamed, "What are you talking about? Who are you?"

The man went back to forcefully pressing up and down on Delon's chest. Then he grunted, "Andy Kroll, Bryn. It's Andy Kroll."

She covered her mouth, unable to say anything.

"Jules Callais is in Montenegro with Max Hortense, Gilda's husband."

He bent over, placing his mouth on Delon's mouth, then he straightened and pushed up, down, up, down on Delon's chest. "Max Hortense has been embezzling from the agency and took off about a month ago. I've been tailing Mrs. Callais ever since. We didn't know where he went at first. When she gave me the slip to join him, I turned my attention to you, hoping you'd lead me to her. But earlier today, I finally got confirmation of their location. I was following you to give you the news. Where's the gun?"

"The what?"

"The gun, Bryn. Where's the gun? Are you holding it?"

"No. No! I—I dropped it. I have no idea where it is!"

"Well, don't walk around too much, you might step on it."

"Can you bring him back?" she cried, desperately.

"I'm trying," he huffed. "I'm fucking trying."

He placed his mouth back over Delon's, pushing air into his lungs. Ignoring the directive to not walk around, Bryn staggered to the pair and dropped down next to them.

"Did you call for help?" she screeched.

"Yes, an ambulance is coming. Hopefully, it can find us. I'll radio again if they can't. Bryn, I'm armed. Do not pick up that gun. If you do, I'll have to shoot. Do you understand me?"

She groped over Delon's body until she found one of his hands and pulled it to her. "Please don't go. Please stay with me! Please don't go! I'm begging you!"

But she knew he was gone. She felt no spirit in him. He'd flown off somewhere.

She would never see him again. Never make love to him again. Never feel the muscles of his arms. Never taste his skin. Never see that look on his face that seemed to say, *Bryn, you're a pain in my ass but, god help me, I can't stay away from you.*

She would never get to tell him she loved him, too.

"Why would you shoot him?" Andy asked, sitting on his heels. He seemed exhausted, and as if he'd given up.

"I didn't mean to!" she screamed, clutching Delon's hand to her lips. His flesh was growing colder and colder and colder. His spirit was gone and his body was following.

"He—he said he loved me," she choked.

Salty tears ran down her face, pooling in her open mouth. She barely heard the far-off, atonal wail of an ambulance.

"I could see that," Andy said. "I could definitely see that. Couldn't *you* see that?"

No, she couldn't see that. Because she wouldn't have known what to look for. Not that kind of love—the romantic kind. Her mother loved her but in a confused, obligatory way. Jules loved her, but in an easygoing, familial way that had likely corroded once she began to suspect Bryn's betrayal.

But the kind of soul-consuming, painful, thrilling love that is romantic love—the kind of love that makes you lie, cheat, and steal—that love she'd never felt before from anyone. So how could she have recognized it?

"I didn't see it," she said, pressing Delon's cool, lifeless hand to her cheek. "I didn't see it."

"Shame," Andy said. "Real shame. People never see what's right in front of them."

He sighed, then levered onto one knee and pushed himself up to stand.

"Bryn," he said, hovering directly over her as she held Delon's smooth, cold hand to her face. "Listen to me and remain calm. There's probable cause that a crime has been committed. Therefore, I'll be placing you under citizen's arrest."

Chapter Thirty-Three

*I*t was a rainy Tuesday when Bryn was called out of her cell and a correctional officer escorted her to the visitor's "lounge" (they actually called it that).

Visitors always arrived first. Staff didn't want inmates sitting there waiting for someone who'd been delayed or might not show.

So, the visitor was sitting by herself at one of the window tables. She always knew how to get the best table, even though the window overlooked a side yard surrounded by multiple layers of chain link fencing coated with razor wire and leered at by cameras.

The first thing Bryn noticed was how radiant Jules looked. The second thing was how heavily pregnant.

She was about six months along but looked like she might give birth any minute. The detention center dress code had a long list of do's and don'ts—but true to form, Jules still appeared stylish in her tan maternity skirt and plain, long-sleeved black blouse, and her knee-high, flat black boots, with her hair swept back in a low bun, face makeup-free but luminescent.

Bryn had never seen her cousin look so natural and breathtaking, yet rather than envy squeezing her heart, Bryn felt a buzzy, warm feeling, knowing Jules finally had what she'd always wanted. A baby.

Bryn sat down, and Jules, who had stood when Bryn entered, did the same. For a while, they only stared at the plain white plastic table between them, saying nothing. Then Bryn's eyes roved to the one piece of decor in the room. A painted mural that said, *If you don't overcome your past, your past can overcome you.*

Bryn's eyes had landed on the mural during all of her visits. It seemed a rather taunting message, and one given much too late for everyone in here. She'd once complained about it anonymously in the little suggestion box that the correctional officers had in the day room. Naturally, her complaint had been ignored.

Jules ventured, quietly, "Do they record conversations in here?"

"No. Not that I'm aware of."

She nodded slightly, keeping her body turned outward, as if her stomach was too big to tuck under the table.

"Congratulations," Bryn finally said.

"Thank you." Her cousin attempted to smile but it was a feeble one. "I'm glad to see you."

Jules' pale eyes flicked over Bryn, taking in her bright orange jumpsuit. Bryn knew the attire was shocking. Her mother, upon first seeing her, had burst into tears and could barely carry on a conversation through her entire visit. Bryn asked her mother not to return until she could keep control of her emotions as, these days, Bryn was not up to the task of mothering her mother.

When Amika visited, she'd kept up a relentlessly positive and somewhat deranged pep-talk. *This is only a pit stop, Bryn. You'll get out of it, I know it. Didn't that crazy bitch who killed her kid in Florida? And that chick in Italy? And O.J.? Are you writing? Take notes. This will be a bestseller.*

Bryn and Jules mutually stared out the window for a while at the thin, gray drizzle. Finally, Bryn decided to ask the main thing that was on her mind.

"Why'd you come back?"

Jules grimaced and kept her pale eyes on the grime-coated windows. She'd placed herself in such a way that she wouldn't have to see the other people in the room.

"Because I feel like I got you into this mess," she said. "If I'd only told you what I was going to do…. But I'm not going to lie. I figured if you both spent a couple of nights worried about me, it would serve you right."

For a moment, her pale eyes narrowed. It was a look Bryn had never seen on Jules before—vindication. Bryn didn't ask how Jules had known of her affair with Delon. It hardly mattered now.

"But once I got to Montenegro, Max told me I couldn't contact anyone. For our own safety. Not even my parents." She sighed and glanced down at her swollen abdomen. "We had a few disagreements about it but…"

She looked up at Bryn, her translucent eyes shimmering.

"I figured, if I was out of the picture, you and Delon

would continue on," she said. "At some point, I'd be able to tell everyone I was okay. It wasn't very well thought out."

Bryn listened to the low humming wall of chatter surrounding them. She'd learned that most of the women in the detention center were sad cases—uneducated, mentally ill, addicted to one thing or another, with horrifically difficult childhoods that had set them up for failure. Bryn had thought she'd had a rough childhood until she'd heard what some of the women had gone through. Many also had young children, even babies. Bryn wondered why the country didn't come up with a better plan for dealing with women like this, but it hadn't.

"Why that morning did you tell him you thought you were pregnant?" Bryn asked. "You knew the baby wasn't his."

It was one of the few things Bryn still had some curiosity about. Even if Jules didn't know about her husband's infertility, she'd obviously been able to time the conception, given that she'd run off to be with Max Hortense.

"Because… to be honest, I guess I still loved him." Jules said this apologetically, as if bewildered by her feelings. "At the time, I didn't know about—" She shook her head a little. "I didn't know about his issue. I knew we couldn't seem to conceive, but I didn't know why. Every time I tried to get us to a clinic, he'd come up with some reason why we couldn't just then. I didn't find out until I spoke to his mom after what happened." Bryn noted that Jules, like herself, Jules was euphemistic in her language regarding Delon, avoiding words like *death, dead, kill, murder.*

Jules paused, struggling. Then she said, "I thought, whether or not he suspected the baby wasn't his, that he might go along with it. Maybe a child would make him…"

Faithful.

Bryn had no doubt this was the unspoken word.

"I had no real intention at that point of joining Max, living life on the run in some foreign country," Jules continued. "I could handle Europe. But a tiny non-extradition country in the Balkans?"

She shuddered, looked down the life growing inside of her, then out the windows again.

"But the second I told Delon, I could tell by the look in his eyes that wasn't going to happen," she said. "He would want a divorce. I could see who he wanted to be with."

Bryn's body spasmed on her hard plastic chair. There it was again. It wasn't only Andy Kroll, with his heightened observational abilities. Even Jules had seen it. All those times Bryn couldn't believe Jules how blind her cousin was, and yet Jules had known—and in a deeper way than even Bryn had known.

It was Bryn who'd been blind, not Jules.

And yet Jules had said nothing about what she knew. Instead, she'd quietly gone about weighing her options and doing what was best for Jules. In this case, to become impregnated by Max Hortense, a guy who might have had a short, squat build and a hairless head, who may have been married himself, but who also had a love of books, working sperm, and career success— though not enough for his own standards, thus why he began stealing from his own agency.

"I couldn't bear everything that was going to happen," Jules said. "And maybe it was wrong to keep a baby from its real father." She reverently rubbed her protruding stomach. "I grabbed my passport when he was in another room. It was so spontaneous. I could hardly think. I forgot my charger. After I took the test at the cafe, I emailed Max to buy me a plane ticket and then my phone died. I knew I'd have to call a car service, have access to my credit card. So I needed to get away from you and find a charger. I couldn't think how to do it. Finally, on the platform, I knew it was real. I had to go. So I came up with an excuse and took the plunge. My biggest fear was you were going to follow me."

"What about Andy Kroll?" Bryn asked. "You saw him?"

Jules nodded slightly, casting her gaze down.

"As I was coming out of the station. Gilda had hired him a few weeks before, supposedly because I was getting threats." She made a huffing sound. "I figured the letters were really from her. She wanted to keep an eye on me to see if I'd follow Max abroad. She knew about us. That became painfully clear when I read the plot she wrote." She sighed, rolling her crystalline blue eyes toward the stained drop ceiling. "I yelled at him and he seemed to go away. Then I charged my phone in the cafe and ordered a car to the airport."

They fell quiet. Bryn focused on the murmurs of

visits all around them, wondering what personal drama everyone else was discussing. A young child shrieked, the piercing sound ricocheting off the granite walls.

"I didn't mean to," Bryn said, basically whispering. "Delon. It was an accident."

Jules, as if grateful the talk had taken a turn from her behavior to someone else's, unexpectedly reached across the table and held Bryn's hand.

"I know that," she said. "I *know* that."

"Did Rich really give him a gun?"

Bryn already knew from her attorney that the gun had been registered to Richard Aston of 11 Hollis Hill, Seaside, CT. But she didn't know if Delon had stolen it.

"Yes. Dad gave it to him. After a guy tried to break in while I was alone in the house."

"I guess he—*your father*—wanted to protect you," Bryn said.

Jules meekly withdrew her hand and they sank into silence again. Bryn did not want to get into her paternity, or Rich, or her mother. There was enough going on. All of that would have to be a conversation for another time. Or not. Her relationship with Jules always depended more on what they didn't say to each other than what they did.

And that was one conversation that they would never see eye-to-eye on. Pointless sounds would carom round, leading nowhere positive. With Delon, they might reach common ground, for they had both loved him, though in different ways.

But not with Rich. With him, there could never be an inch of common ground. Trying to find any would be painful, destructive, and ultimately, futile. As far as Bryn was concerned, her primal inability to trust Delon in that crucial moment—and to get into a car with him—stemmed from Rich.

The way Jules had withdrawn her hand and stared down forlornly at the plastic table made Bryn fairly certain that Jules knew something. Her parents must have told her, though Bryn knew Rich and Jacqueline would have sold their daughter a sanitized version of events, one they probably even believed themselves.

"I'm not going to leave you to deal with this on your own," Jules said, glancing back up. "I negotiated my return with Gilda. I'll give her all the information I can about Max but she has to keep me out of any lawsuit or prosecution."

A few months ago, Bryn had been called out of her cell to meet with a man who introduced himself as her new attorney. Before that, she'd had a court-appointed one. It quickly became clear the man, who'd spent a decade working in the Southern New Jersey prosecutor's office, was her best chance of not spending the rest of her life in prison.

As it turns out, taking a gun from a lover's pocket, tracking him into the woods, holding the gun on him, and then *accidentally* shooting him wasn't much of a defense.

At first, a small, depraved part of herself had imagined her bio-father, Rich, had hired the new attorney. He was the only person she could think of with that kind of money. But the attorney had revealed Bryn's patron: Gilda Hortense.

While the agent's husband had taken off with two million dollars of company funds, *A Woman Stands Alone* was a bestseller, and Gilda was raking it in. The night of the Y event, Gilda came out on stage and announced that *she* was the book's real author. She'd also announced that the book's fake author, Jules Aston-Callais, had run off to Montenegro with Gilda's embezzling husband.

The announcement was a sensation. Combined with the next jaw dropper—that "Gwen" had killed "Fabian" —and the story was in the press for weeks. The book blasted up all the bestseller lists.

Gilda told Bryn (through the jail's email system) that she felt she owed Bryn a lawyer. Bryn's alleged crime had given Gilda a bestseller, after all. And that bestseller saved her agency from bankruptcy. As this was not the time to look a gift lawyer in the mouth, Bryn accepted.

"Are you sure they don't record conversations in here?" Jules asked, lowering her voice to where it was difficult to hear her over the room's thicket of murmuring.

"What is it?" Bryn said, leaning forward. "Tell me."

"I've got something that might help you." Awkwardly, Jules leaned sideways so she could be heard over the echoing conversations.

Her pale blue eyes roamed several times around the room, then held Bryn's gaze.

"I told Gilda I wanted to write the follow-up book without her help. But she said there was too much at stake. That I wasn't good enough."

She shot a cautious glance over Bryn's shoulder, then continued.

"She said my dialogue was terrible. Stiff and unnatural. That if I wanted to get better, I needed to record real conversations. Study them. Listen to how people spoke."

She widened her pale eyes, as if asking if Bryn knew what "record real conversations" entailed. Bryn only silently communicated with a barely-perceptible nod that she understood. She didn't, but she needed Jules to keep speaking.

"I asked Delon to practice with me," Jules said.

Bryn leaned in even closer, so their heads were almost touching.

"I had him play Fabian, and me Claire," she said under her breath. "I had Claire tell Fabian she was seeing another man. I was talking more and more to Max, and maybe that was on my mind. Anyway…" She stared at Bryn, blinking rapidly. "At first, he kept saying things like, 'Well, Claire, I want you to be happy.' I finally yelled at him that he had to make the dialogue exciting. And to stop using the name Claire because in real life people don't use each other's names. To talk real. So, in the next session, he came out with, 'I'll fucking kill you, you disgusting, filthy little whore.'"

She widened her eyes, as if she'd heard the words all over again. "He sounded so convincing," she said. "But when I turned off the recording app, we had a laugh."

She cradled her stomach protectively, and again her gaze flicked around nervously before refocusing on Bryn.

"I erased all the recordings but that one. There's no way you can tell it's not real," she said, a little breathlessly. "I couldn't bring in my phone so you can't hear it, but I can give it to your lawyer. I'm willing to say that I was recording him because I'd begun to feel threatened. If you had good reason to think he'd killed me, this would speak to your state of mind at the time. It would be a mitigating circumstance. You thought you were next."

"My lawyer already knows that," Bryn said. "Because that's exactly what happened."

"Yes, but with that recording, you'll have proof. Delon's own words in his own voice. The prosecutor won't want that played in court. This makes a better chance of a plea down. You only have to say that I'd told you about the conversation. You could even say you heard the recording yourself. That's why, when I disappeared, you became convinced he'd killed me. Then you found the gun in his jacket… "

She trailed off and leaned back on her bolted plastic stool with a small grunt. Not the most comfortable seating for a heavily pregnant woman.

"It's worth a try, don't you think?" she asked.

Bryn breathed deeply, then regretted it. The visitors lounge had a strong medicinal smell from whatever disinfectant was used to clean it. At least it smelled better than the day room, where the toilet bowls were always filled with stuff you don't want to hear about.

"I can't have everyone thinking he's the murdering type," she said. "He's not."

"Jesus, Bryn," Jules hissed, clawing her hand on the table. Bryn noticed her cousin's nails, normally pristinely manicured in neutral colors, were bare, with uneven lengths. "He'd want you to do this."

Maybe. Maybe he would. She could hear him.

Bryn, I'm dead and you're not. It's a little late to worry about my reputation. If you can get out of this Caged Heat scenario, then do it.

Bryn often had conversations with him. At first, she hadn't wanted to even think about him. At all. The brain is a wondrous thing. Her gray matter had so successfully pushed Delon out of its jellied folds that there were long periods, ten or even fifteen minutes at a stretch, when she forgot that he was dead, let alone that she'd been the one to make him that way.

Then, little by little, he began coming to her. First, in dreams. Awake, he began whispering to her. He'd tell her a joke or remind her of something they'd done together. Like the time they'd ordered Chinese from the takeout place downstairs. They'd devoured so much that they felt sick afterwards.

Remember how stupefied we felt from all that greasy food, Bryn? I didn't eat Chinese again for months. But I'd kill for some now. I mean, not KILL. There's been enough killing. Too soon?

It was comforting that they could still speak. It wasn't the same, of course. In some ways, it was better. They certainly didn't argue like they used to. What was left to argue about, anyway?

We did so much to avoid prison, she said to him one night. *And that's the exact thing that got me here. They should teach us in school. 'Hey, kids. If only they'd gone to the police, they'd be fine right now!' This is what we call irony.*

Little risqué for kids, don't you think, Bryn?

321

"I have to think about it," she said to her cousin.

Jules leaned back. For the first time, she seemed more relaxed, even happy. A brief glimpse of how she would have normally looked if none of this was happening.

"It's a girl," she said.

Bryn smiled. Just what Jules had always wanted—for the first child to be a girl.

"Still going to name her Autumn?" she asked.

"Wow. You remember that."

Bryn laughed a little and nodded. She wiped her nose with her hand. Her nose was constantly runny thanks to whatever fungus was growing in the detention center's walls.

"I'm going to name her Jacqueline Bryn," Jules said.

Bryn didn't want to be anywhere near her aunt, not even in a baby's name. But she didn't say this. Instead, she said, "I'm honored."

Chapter Thirty-Four

*R*ight before the turnstile by the security checkpoint, Jules and Bryn hugged. With Jules' big, rotund belly, it was an awkward, half-side hug.

"There's something else," Jules said. "The brownstone sold two days after being listed. Six million. Goodbye to the Burgundy estate, too. It was in Delon's name, so I inherited it. I'm not a monster, so I bought his parents a cottage. They needed to downsize, anyway."

"Huh. Delon told me he couldn't sell the estate."

"He was never Mr. Financial Wizard, was he?" Jules raised one of her brows. They were still well arched despite the fact that it appeared she was no longer having them professionally shaped. Being pregnant had turned her into one of those crunchy granola types. Bryn could even see thin threads of silver-gray ribboned in the roots of her natural dark-blonde hair. If Thom King was correct and Jules ever did have an issue with "addies," Bryn had absolutely no doubt she didn't now.

Jules would probably want to give birth at home in a warm bath with a sitar playing on a CD.

"I lowered the estate by a few million and off it went," she said.

Now Bryn understood. Jules hadn't returned from abroad to help her. She'd returned because of the massive amount of money she needed to collect on.

"I know Gilda got you a great lawyer, but I won't let you rot here," Jules said. "I'm hiring a prison consultant for you."

"No need, babe," Bryn replied. "I've been here five months. Know my way around the joint pretty good."

Jules stared at Bryn for a long moment with her dazzlingly pale blue eyes, her lips open. "How strange," she said. "You sounded just like a prisoner right then."

"I'm not a prisoner, I'm a detainee."

"Right, of course."

Awkwardly folding her hands on her round belly, Jules looked around the room, for the first time truly taking in the scene. She seemed appalled and more than a little frightened. Bryn could not recall ever seeing her cousin frightened before. It gave Bryn a small rush of triumph, knowing Jules wouldn't last a day in here.

"Well, then I'll send money to your commissary account," Jules said quietly.

Bryn didn't respond. She didn't volunteer that, because of her fame—or rather her infamy—she had plenty of money on her books. Strangers sent her money. All the time.

Once Bryn's story hit the news, outsiders began wiring money to her commissary account. They also wrote to her. Mostly women. They conflated Delon and Fabian, and told her that they were glad that Bryn had killed the cheating bastard.

Every week, Bryn ordered a bunch of things from the commissary, then resold them out of her cell. She didn't get goods in return. She got favors.

The first thing she did was have the pod boss, Mellie, moved to her cell's bottom bunk. The officers didn't care if you switched cells, so long as you didn't cause problems about it. With the pod boss on the bottom bunk, no one could get to Bryn and her large stash of goods, because Mellie, who made excellent shanks from bedpost parts, would have killed anyone who tried.

In exchange, Bryn kept Mellie in e-cigarettes, candy bars, peanut butter, and honey buns. Mellie also spread goods out to her crew—inmates willing to do whatever she wanted, whether it was punch a girl in the mouth or pee in a cup for one who needed a clean drug test.

Bryn also had a couple of girls who scrubbed her cell and toilet, because she wanted it done right, and the trustees were lazy as hell about it. Pretty soon, Bryn's cell was the only one that didn't smell disgusting or have roaches.

She also got Mellie's girlfriend, Razor, put in the cell next door to keep Mellie happy. Bryn didn't allow the pair to smoke clones in her cell. They could do that nasty shit somewhere else.

Packages from the outside weren't allowed, so Bryn had a trustee on her books who had an outside girl who smuggled things in for her. Bryn had an e-reader, waterproof shoes for the shower, scrunchies that could hold her thick hair, good soap (not the medicinal liquid crap they sold in commissary), ear plugs (good luck sleeping if you didn't have them because the younger girls stayed up all night smoking clones and shrieking), and curl conditioner for her frizz.

To keep the C.O.'s from confiscating her contraband, she gave them things, as well. Everyone wanted something. Jail wasn't so bad, once you made it so no one fucked with you. Then, it was kind of like a high school summer camp. Bryn had been a good reporter. She'd been good at being broke. She'd been good at having an affair.

But she was, to her dismay, *great* at being an inmate in a federal correctional facility.

"Don't think too long about what we talked about, okay, babe?" Jules asked, keeping her voice low, as if anyone cared what she had to say.

"I won't."

"Bryn," Jules said, reaching out to touch her hand. "I hope you won't take this the wrong way, but... you look *good*, you know?" She appeared befuddled and smiled a little. "I'll see you soon, okay?"

Bryn watched her beautiful cousin and half-sister retreat through the locked door that would lead to security, and then to the free, wide-open world. She watched and watched, until Jules could no longer be seen. Then, she turned, making her way back through the visitor's lounge.

"How was your visit, Lo?" asked an inmate named Penny as Bryn approached her table.

"Lo" was short for Lois Lane. One of the old timers

had given her that nickname, after the reporter in the Superman universe.

"Fine. She won't be back before the holiday, though." Bryn enunciated clearly, shaking her head back and forth, back and forth, so she wouldn't be misunderstood. "Definitely won't be back before the holiday."

"Are you sure?" Penny said.

"Absolutely sure."

"Maybe next time."

Bryn shrugged and headed to the security door that would bring her back to the day room. She nodded at several of the girls having visits who greeted her as she passed. She never nodded at them first, but as long as they showed her respect, she showed it right back.

Out of the corner of her eye, she watched as Penny headed to the bank of pay phones and punched her PIN number into a phone. Penny was calling her girlfriend, who was in the parking lot, waiting for the signal that would determine whether Jules lived or died.

Bryn knew Penny and her girlfriend would be disappointed with the order not to kill Jules. No reunion for them. Seeing her cousin's swollen belly nearly bursting with growing, innocent life, Bryn couldn't do it. Besides, she might decide to tell Jules to hand over that recording. She knew Jules wasn't lying about it, for as soon as her cousin mentioned it, a memory had surged forth: Delon, sitting at his kitchen table, commiserating with Bryn after her meltdown in the walk-in closet.

At one point, she pulled me into some kind of dialogue improvement exercise.

Bryn would have to talk to him about it.

She lifted her arms while the officer gave her a half-hearted pat down and waved a metal detecting wand through the security door. Because Bryn had given the officer a bunch of commissary sausage the week before, she could have easily smuggled in any contraband that she desired. But she hadn't asked Jules to bring her anything.

After all, there was nothing her cousin had that Bryn wanted.

Not anymore.

Also by C.G. Twiles

About C.G. Twiles' psychological thriller, *The Perfect Face:*

"An out of this world thriller." —Liz Alterman, author of *The Perfect Neighborhood and You Shouldn't Have Done That*

Looks can be deceiving

Reporter Maddie is ecstatic to be on a picturesque Greek island for her summer holiday. But then she meets a beautiful 12-year-old girl, Ruby, traveling with a woman claiming to be her mother.

Soon, Maddie suspects the girl is being trafficked to a nearby private island, one owned by the brilliant and reclusive billionaire Dexter Hunt. To help the girl, she joins forces with a local man and a rival reporter.

Maddie may have checked into the billionaire's notorious island—but can she ever leave?

Other psychological thrillers by C.G. Twiles:

The Little Girl in the Window: A Psychological Thriller

At 14, Romy accidentally killed the town's beloved prom queen, Misty. Years later, when a crisis forces her to return to the scene of the crime, a little girl with eerily blue eyes begins appearing in her window, taunting her. Who is she? And how does she seem to know Romy's darkest secret?

The Little Girl with a Secret: A Psychological Thriller

After finding her best friend and fiancé in bed together, Sara flees to Amish country to heal. Soon she finds herself embroiled in the locals' many secrets. One of them is so explosive her life will never be the same.

The Trauma Child: A Thriller

After witnessing a violent crime, 10-year-old Arial begins acting very differently. Single mom Neely will do whatever it takes to get her daughter back. And you won't believe what it takes…

The Neighbors in Apartment 3D: A Domestic Suspense Novel

Cintra's compulsive lying has torn her family apart. But when she notices a chilling sign taped to her neighbors' door — "I'm being held" written in childish handwriting — she's determined to help the kidnapped boy, regardless of who believes her… —BookBub

The Last Star Standing: A Psychological Thriller

A forgotten talent show winner has a second chance at success. But first, she'll have to kill the runner-up.

How far will Piper go to save her family and reclaim her former glory?

Brooklyn Gothic: A Modern Gothic Romantic Thriller

A young, idealistic reporter working in a Brooklyn Gothic mansion begins to suspect that her new boss—and lover—is keeping dark secrets. For fans of the Brontes, Daphne du Maurier, Darcy Coates, and Ruth Ware.

The Ghost Wife: A short tale of suspense

Tabitha wants one thing for the holidays: For her family to face reality. And the reality is… she's dead.

So why are they acting like she's still alive?

Neighbors and Other Dangers: A Psychological Thriller Box Set

Three heart-pounding, up-all-night psychological thrillers in one economical box set: *The Neighbors in Apartment 3D, The Last Star Standing,* and *The Little Girl in the Window.*

The Perfect Psychological Thriller Box Set

Three nile-biting suspense tales with jaw-dropping twists in one economical box set: *The Perfect Face, Brooklyn Gothic,* and *The Ghost Wife.*

About the Author

C.G. Twiles is the pseudonym for a longtime writer and reporter who has written for some of the world's largest magazines and newspapers.

She enjoys traveling, animals, old houses, ancient history, and cemeteries. She lives in Brooklyn.

Please find her on social media, she'd love to connect!

facebook.com/cgtwiles

instagram.com/cgtwiles

goodreads.com/cgtwiles

bookbub.com/profile/c-g-twiles

Acknowledgments

Thank you once again to my regular readers, you're the ones who consistently read, engage, share, and review, and you're the reason I'm still writing.

Writing and publishing has never been easy, but it's more difficult than it has ever been, thanks to AI—which was created by stealing the copyrighted works of writers who took years honing their craft, and poured their hearts into their stories.

To my writers's group: Sasha, Kanika, and Tony. Your input is invaluable. Once again, thank you to my astute beta reader: Megan Easley-Walsh.

Gratitude to my writer friends who understand the struggle: Finola and Christina.

Mom, you are no longer with us, but I think you would have really enjoyed this one. It ends just the way you like it!